Gift OF LOVE

*Gifts are given in love
in these four modern
romance stories*

Carol Cox
Pamela Griffin
Veda Boyd Jones
Darlene Mindrup

Practically Christmas ©2000 by Carol Cox.
A Most Unwelcome Gift ©2000 by Pamela Griffin.
The Best Christmas Gift ©2000 by Veda Boyd Jones.
The Gift Shoppe ©2000 by Darlene Mindrup.

Illustrations by Gary Maria.

ISBN 1-57748-810-5

Published by Barbour Publishing, Inc., P.O. Box 719, Uhrichsville, Ohio 44683 http://www.barbourbooks.com

Member of the
Evangelical Christian
Publishers Association

Printed in the United States of America.

Gift
OF LOVE

Practically Christmas

by Carol Cox

Dedication

To Dave, who made this possible

INTRODUCTION

Practically Christmas by Carol Cox
Practical—that is how Sara Jennings always approached life's decisions. But this Christmas season Sara has been called to small-town Missouri to help her great-aunt with a most peculiar problem. Who could not love Sara's aunt for her holiday cheer and her loving gospel message? How can the man Sara meets on the train stir such a practical gal into making some quick decisions about the course of her future?

A Most Unwelcome Gift by Pamela Griffin
Fragile—Jared and Tessa Baker's four-year marriage seems to be hanging on by a thread. Jared's job has become his mistress, and Tessa sits at home feeling useless and unappreciated. A simple dinner visit finds them stranded during Christmas week in a rural cabin. Will they discover a quick way back to town and life's demands? Or will they relax and confront the problems threatening to tear them apart?

The Best Christmas Gift by Veda Boyd Jones
Stranded—Elaine Montana has put her van into a ditch while on an icy mountain road and is responsible for the welfare of seven junior high girls. Clay Stevenson comes like an angel out of the dark to help them to a rustic cabin. The storm is lingering; will they make it home for Christmas? And will Clay find the peace he was seeking in his isolated retreat?

The Gift Shoppe by Darlene Mindrup
Confused—Every time Michael Compton comes near shy Amy Latimer she gets flustered. But he seems to have a secret lady friend for whom he enters Amy's gift shop each month to buy a special present. Can Amy quench the desires of her heart and be satisfied with the friendship Michael offers? Or will Amy succumb to the depression of love beyond her reach?

Chapter 1

"Excuse me. This is the last vacant seat."

Sara Jennings looked up from her notes and stared bleakly at the man standing in the aisle. He gestured at the book bag she had placed on the seat next to hers in hopes of discouraging fellow travelers.

"It's the only seat left," he repeated apologetically.

Sara grimaced, moved the bag, and turned back to her notebook. The four-hour train trip to Aunt Esther's would give her plenty of time to think and plan. If she was left alone.

The throbbing vibration increased, and the train pulled away from the platform. Sara caught sight of a waving hand and gave a perfunctory wiggle of her fingers. Geoffrey had stayed right up until departure time, although she'd hoped that, being studiously ignored ever since she boarded, he would have taken the hint and gone home.

"Your husband?" her seatmate asked.

Sara shook her head, keeping her gaze fixed determinedly out the window. "No." Maybe he'd be easier to discourage than Geoffrey.

"Are you going far?" Then again, maybe he wouldn't.

"Just to Minton." Eventually he might get the idea.

"Really? Me, too." His voice held such pleasure that Sara turned to take a good look at him for the first time. She decided he couldn't be much more than thirty, with a slender frame that spoke of a naturally athletic build rather than a physique developed in a gym. He still breathed quickly from his hurry to board at the last minute. His sandy hair was tousled, loose strands hanging across his forehead above deep green eyes that regarded her with approval.

Sara allowed herself a moment's smugness at having arrived earlier than the recommended thirty minutes prior to departure time. No panicked dash at the last minute for her. If people made plans and followed them sensibly, life ran so much more smoothly. And if he'd just settle back in his seat and leave her alone, she could go on according to *her* plans.

"Do you live in Minton?"

Sara sighed and closed her notebook, admitting defeat. "No, my great-aunt invited me to visit her over the holidays." What a welcome invitation it had been. Even Aunt Esther's indication that she needed help with a little problem didn't faze Sara. Handling some minor difficulty for her great-aunt would provide a welcome respite from the pressure-cooker pace of life in St. Louis. Not to mention Geoffrey's insistence on resurrecting their broken engagement.

A tiny frown marred her forehead. Geoffrey had seemed to accept the return of his ring with good grace, even insisting they remain friends. But his overly attentive behavior of late roused Sara's suspicions that he wanted to renew their former relationship. Still, it was nice of him to offer her a ride to the depot. . . .

She realized her seatmate was talking again. "What did you say?" she asked automatically, then bit her tongue. No point in encouraging him.

"I said my name's Zack. Zack Taylor."

Sara lifted one eyebrow. "Zack, as in 'Zachary'? As in 'Zachary Taylor'?"

Her unwanted companion shrugged and grinned. "My dad was a U.S. history buff. I guess the temptation to name his son after a president was too much for him. I've always been grateful our last name wasn't Fillmore. I don't know if I could have gone through life as Millard."

Sara laughed in spite of herself. "And do you have political aspirations?"

"Worse. You're about to hear my deepest, darkest secret," he said, looking around as if checking for eavesdroppers. "I'm a lawyer," he confided in a stage whisper.

"No!" Sara pressed her hand to her throat in mock horror. "I never would have guessed."

"Thank you," Zack said gravely. "I take that as a compliment. And do you have a respectable job, or do you do something equally reprehensible?"

"Nothing so exciting, I'm afraid. You're looking at the founder, proprietor, and sole employee of Just-Write Editorial Services."

"You're self-employed? I'm impressed."

"I didn't start out that way. I worked for Seton

Electronics—editing their newsletter, writing brochures and catalog copy, that kind of thing—until they decided to downsize."

Zack made a sympathetic face. "Ouch."

Sara nodded rueful agreement. "There went my job. The work still needed to be done, though, so I went back and asked if they'd consider hiring me to do the same job, only on a freelance basis. They were happy to do it, gave me referrals that helped me build up a client base, and the rest, as they say, is history."

"Now I'm really impressed," Zack said, applauding softly. "Resilience, initiative, bouncing back from adversity. . .quite a success story."

At one time Sara would have agreed, but lately she'd begun to wonder. Should success make her feel increasingly harried, more anxious with every passing day? She closed her eyes, wishing she were at Aunt Esther's already. Thankfully she'd caught up on her work, making it possible to leave the weekend after Thanksgiving and stay through Christmas. Minton had been a peaceful haven during childhood visits. She hoped it hadn't changed.

"Do you ride the train often?" Zack's voice brought her back to the present with a jolt. "Sorry," he said with a penitent smile. "When you ask questions for a living, it's hard to break the habit."

"It's all right," Sara answered, surprised to find she meant it. Her opportunity for solitude and quiet reflection had evaporated the moment Zack appeared in the aisle, but suddenly it didn't matter. Slipping the notebook into her book bag, Sara settled back and prepared to enjoy the trip. . .and Zack's company.

Don't get interested in him, her ever-practical mind warned. *You'll never see him again.* Granted. But what harm could there be in a casual conversation with someone who had such an obvious zest for life?

❦

Sara deposited her bags next to a bench outside the Minton depot and strolled along the porch, enjoying the evening quiet. Aunt Esther was late, but Sara didn't mind. How long had it been since she noticed the night sky? And the stars! She'd forgotten how much brighter they were away from the city and how many more she could see. The crisp, clean air had a bite to it, and Sara snuggled deeper into her down-filled jacket.

She settled onto the bench and leaned back, stretching her legs out in front of her, wondering when she'd last felt so relaxed. The train ride down had helped. So had Zack. His exuberance made her open up in turn, reviving a spark and vitality she thought she had lost.

"Not bad for the first few hours away from home," she murmured. Zack had grabbed his bags as soon as they were available and headed out the door with a cheery "Nice to have met you," obviously feeling, as she did, that their meeting was a pleasant interlude, nothing more.

Sara turned her thoughts to Aunt Esther and whatever her "little problem" might be. Her great-aunt led such a joyful existence, it seemed impossible to imagine anything major going wrong. Most likely, she needed some minor repairs on her house. Aunt Esther was getting up in years, after all, and it must be hard for her to deal with repairmen, especially during the holidays. No problem. Sara was young and capable; she'd take care of everything.

With that issue settled in her mind, Sara glanced toward the street and saw Aunt Esther waving from the rear window of an approaching taxi. She enveloped Sara in a warm hug as soon as she stepped onto the curb. "It's so good to see you, dear."

Sara's mind bounced back and forth between the past, where Aunt Esther was an energetic, vivacious figure, and the present, which included a great-aunt much more frail than Sara remembered. "I'm glad I could come," she said, all her protective instincts springing to the fore. Whatever Aunt Esther needed, Sara would handle it.

During the ride home, Aunt Esther pointed out features Sara might recognize, as well as newer additions to the town. Sara drank in Minton's quiet calm, feeling the healing peace seep into her troubled soul. To her relief, Aunt Esther's mind seemed as sharp as ever, her ebullient love of life undimmed by the passing of years. Sara chided herself for not coming sooner. With her parents spending their retirement years involved in short-term mission projects overseas, she missed having family around. Spending more time with Aunt Esther would be good for both of them.

"What's the problem you needed help with?" she asked, eager to jump into her new role as protector. Aunt Esther stopped her happy chatter and drew herself up with a disdainful sniff.

"A neighbor of mine, an older gentleman, has been

causing trouble. I'm afraid he doesn't like my Christmas decorations. He says they're a nuisance." Her voice quavered. "He. . .he's even threatened legal action if I don't take them down."

Sara's thoughts flew to the simple manger scene she remembered from her childhood. Setting up the half-sized figures of Mary and Joseph keeping watch over the little manger on her lawn had been one of Aunt Esther's chief delights. What kind of Scrooge could take offense at that?

She was still fuming when the taxi turned onto Aunt Esther's street and immediately slowed to a crawl, keeping pace with numerous other cars creeping ahead. Sara frowned. She never remembered a traffic back-up in Minton, and certainly not on a quiet residential street, but then, she hadn't been there in years. She craned her neck to see if she could spot the obstruction ahead.

She couldn't see a thing except the long line of cars inching its way along. Aunt Esther didn't seem to notice anything amiss. Sara looked again and did a double take. Didn't the sky seem much lighter a couple of blocks ahead? The cab inched its way along the packed street, and Sara tensed. That glow in the sky, the slow-moving traffic. It all added up to one thing— a fire.

She cast furtive glances at her great-aunt, who seemed oblivious to the situation. Should she worry her, perhaps unnecessarily? Better to wait and find out for sure, she decided. Who knew what that kind of shock might do to an elderly woman?

The taxi moved along at a snail's pace, with Sara looking anxiously from the bright glow to Aunt Esther, then back again. The road curved to the right up ahead, blocking her view, but surely the source of the light came from the block where her great-aunt lived. The thought of trying to explain to Aunt Esther that her home had been destroyed made Sara's stomach knot up, and she took several slow, calming breaths.

They rounded the curve at last, and Sara blinked in disbelief when she discovered the cause of both the glow and the traffic jam. Life-sized figures representing Mary and Joseph knelt by a manger. A meticulously painted backdrop behind them showed the stable's animal residents peering curiously from their stalls.

On the other side of the lawn, a group of shepherds accompanied by at least a dozen sheep approached, apparently just coming in from the hills where a choir of luminous angels hovered in the sky. Above the stable hung a large star, spreading radiant beams made up of thousands of tiny white lights. More strings of the miniature bulbs wound around every branch of every tree and shrub in the brightly lit yard.

A yard that looked terribly familiar.

Chapter 2

Open-mouthed, Sara turned to her great-aunt. "That. . .that's not. . .*your* house?" she croaked. The taxi pulled to a stop, confirming her fears, while Aunt Esther nodded complacently. Standing on the sidewalk, with her luggage at her feet, Sara floundered for something—*anything*—appropriate to say. But what could possibly be appropriate for something like this?

"You can see I got larger figures and added a few things."

Sara nodded dumbly, acknowledging the understatement of the decade.

Aunt Esther touched Sara's arm. "Bring your bags, dear, and let's go inside. You don't want to take a chill." They made their way up the walk, passing onlookers who had ventured into the yard for a closer view. Aunt Esther had a word for each one, her eyes sparkling like the myriad white lights.

"Isn't it wonderful?" she asked in the warmth of her front hall. "The newspaper runs an article on it every year. It draws visitors from all over northern Missouri for weeks. Weeks! Such a marvelous opportunity for them to reflect on the true symbols of Christmas." She steered Sara upstairs. "Usually I offer them cocoa or hot apple cider, but I made an exception tonight, since I wanted to meet you at the station."

Tossing her bags at the foot of the bed in the room she'd used as a child, Sara sank onto the welcoming mattress. She tried to focus. "You serve hot drinks to all those people?" She hadn't meant for it to come out in a squeak.

Aunt Esther didn't seem to notice. "Only the ones who come into the yard. I couldn't possibly run back and forth to all those cars." She gurgled with laughter at the thought. "They like to visit, and it gives me the opportunity to share one of my little tracts with them."

"Tracts?" This was getting stranger by the minute.

A faint blush tinted the older woman's softly wrinkled cheeks. She took a small sheet of paper from the top of the bureau and laid it on the nightstand. "I've left one here for you to look at later tonight. That's what this is all about, you know." She waved a hand toward the window.

From Sara's room, the upper part of the lavish display was plainly visible. "It's a way to attract people, to remind them of what Christmas really means, and show them how Christ can be part of their lives all year long." Her face clouded and her shoulders slumped. "It's a shame Marcus is so set against it."

"He's the one who's been giving you problems?" At Aunt Esther's dejected nod, Sara felt a twinge of sympathy for the complaining neighbor. This spectacle must disrupt the neighborhood for weeks on end.

"What exactly has he been doing?"

Aunt Esther twisted her hands together, and her voice shook when she spoke. "It wasn't so bad at first," she explained. "He'd call and fuss about the lights disturbing him. He just sounded like a grouchy old man who needed something to complain about. Then it started getting worse." She paced the room with quick, nervous steps. "He's become quite aggressive, coming over nearly every night and shouting at me in the most belligerent manner. Yesterday," she continued with a haunted look that tore at Sara's heart, "he informed me that if I didn't remove everything immediately, he'd take me to court."

Sara's momentary sympathy for the neighbor vanished in a heartbeat. She studied her great-aunt, obviously struggling to regain her usual attitude of peace and goodwill. Sara noted the trembling hands and quivering chin. *All right, Buster,* she fumed, *you wanted a fight—you've got one.* Just wait until he found out he was up against a feisty young woman instead of a fragile older lady!

They talked over mugs of steaming cocoa until nearly midnight, long after Aunt Esther had unplugged her outdoor lights and plunged her yard into darkness. A sudden pounding at the kitchen door made Sara jump, and her cocoa splashed across the table. "What on earth. . .?"

Aunt Esther drew herself up as much as her diminutive stature would allow. "That must be Marcus."

"Do you want me to deal with him?" Sara shoved her sleeves up, ready for battle, but her great-aunt was already opening the door. "Just remember, I'm right behind you," Sara whispered.

Aunt Esther stepped out onto the stoop. Sara noted her aunt's position with approval—it gave her a clear advantage of height over the man who stood at ground level, just inside the circle of light spilling from the doorway. Tufts of white hair protruded from under a gray fedora, matched by bushy white eyebrows that drew together over a hawk-like nose. The black overcoat added to the effect, making him look like the lead character in a production of Dickens's *A Christmas Carol*. "Right in character," she muttered.

"What is it, Marcus? It's awfully late for a social call." Aunt Esther's voice was steady, but Sara saw the slight tremor in her hands.

"Don't play innocent with me, Esther Brown!" The gravelly voice grated on Sara's nerves. "You know very well why I'm here. I've brought legal counsel with me. *Now* we'll see what happens."

Sara narrowed her eyes, trying to see him more clearly, and noticed a movement behind him. Someone was standing there, half-hidden in the darkness.

I'd hide, too, Sara thought bitterly. Persecuting a helpless old lady was hardly something to be proud of. She shifted her weight to peer over Marcus's shoulder, but the unseen companion moved farther behind him. *What a coward! I wonder if he does all his harassment late at night.*

"Meet my nephew Zachary," Marcus announced, stepping to one side and pushing a sandy-haired young man into the light.

Sara gasped, then glared furiously, recognizing her former seatmate. He met her gaze for a brief moment, then looked down at his shoes.

It was time for Sara to step in. "It's late, and my aunt is cold." She placed her hands protectively on Aunt Esther's shoulders. "Why don't you. . .*gentlemen* go home and deal with this at a decent hour?" Without waiting for a reply, she guided Aunt Esther back inside and slammed the door.

෮

Sara looked at the red numerals on her bedside clock and sighed. It was 3:00 A.M., and she was wide awake. Aunt Esther had gone to bed hours before, sure she'd go right to sleep after a good session of prayer, but Sara was wound too tight to relax.

Here was her opportunity to make up for the quiet time she'd lost on the train, she thought wryly. The still of the night was a good time to do some serious thinking about Geoffrey. She sat up and wrapped her arms around her knees.

Marriage to Geoffrey Ashton Powell III had seemed a good idea, a practical one, when she'd accepted his proposal. As his wife, she would have security and a fine home. She and any children they had would never want for anything.

It sounded so sensible that Sara found it hard to explain to herself, much less to a baffled Geoffrey, why she couldn't go through with it. Although his personality did lean a bit to the plain-vanilla side, Geoffrey was good looking, polite, and a successful businessman. Life with him would assure her of a smooth road ahead.

Somewhere along the line, however, she had realized with an increasing sense of discomfort that to Geoffrey marriage was more a social partnership than a loving relationship between husband and wife. Sara was well aware romance could flame, then fizzle, but she would have been happier if Geoffrey had shown the teensiest bit of romantic interest in her instead of looking on her as a commodity to enhance his social standing.

Was she being impractical in deciding to look for something—someone—to give her the fulfillment and companionship she longed for? She didn't know, and she was no closer to sleep now than when she'd started trying to sort things out.

Sara flung herself out of bed in disgust and pulled on her cozy velour robe. Maybe a glass of warm milk would help. Passing the window at the end of the hall, she paused to look out into the night. The sky was black velvet, studded with jewel-like stars.

She turned from the window, then glanced out again, her attention caught by movement on the front lawn. Watching intently, she saw it again, by the stable. A man's figure moved stealthily in the shadows. She stiffened in alarm and reached for the telephone on the nearby table. Better to call the police first, then alert Aunt Esther.

She pulled her hand back. Better yet to get a description to give the police in case the miscreant left before they arrived.

Sara pressed her nose to the glass and squinted, trying to make out details. A tallish man, she decided, well muffled in a heavy scarf and coat, wearing what looked like a fedora. Sara sucked in her breath, recognizing Marcus.

What on earth could he be doing? She watched him spread his arms wide and turn in a slow circle. *Is he dancing?* The idea of the old curmudgeon performing some sort of moonlight dance on Aunt Esther's front lawn was so bizarre, Sara leaned against the window sill and stared, fascinated. Lights from a passing car flickered across the yard, silhouetting Marcus and the long, slender strands extending from his hands.

Sara straightened, understanding. He was taking down the lights! He was also trespassing, she thought grimly and reached for the phone again, keeping her eyes focused on the elderly vandal.

She had the receiver in her hand when she noticed his movements had changed, becoming more jerky, and she realized with a jolt of glee that he'd managed to wrap himself tightly in the strings of lights. Then movement stopped altogether except for a few frantic twitches. *That ought to hold him 'til the cops get here,* she told herself, starting to punch in the number.

Wait. Her hand froze in midair. There might be something even more gratifying. Sara opened the Minton phone book, turned on the small table lamp, and ran her finger down the *T*s. If he and Zack shared the same last name. . . There it was: Marcus Taylor.

She counted seven rings before Zack's groggy voice answered. "Mr. Taylor?" she said sweetly. "This is Sara Jennings. You might want to come and retrieve your uncle from my great-aunt's front lawn."

She listened patiently to the sputtering that issued

from the receiver. "He seems to have become entangled in something," she explained. "And be sure to bring a flashlight," she added in honeyed tones. "All *our* lights are turned off."

She replaced the receiver gently, cutting off the squawks from the other end, returned to her bed, and immediately fell asleep.

Chapter 3

Zack swung his legs over the side of the bed and forced himself to sit up. He propped his elbows on his knees and scrubbed his face with his hands, reliving the previous day's events. When Uncle Marcus issued his mysterious summons for Zack to come help with a legal issue, it seemed reasonable to assume the old boy wanted to make another set of changes in his regularly revised will. Not a problem.

Better yet, his uncle's mandate gave Zack sufficient excuse to take a leave of absence from Schuyler, Temple, and Wells until after the first of the year. Once Uncle Marcus's minor crisis had been dealt with, Zack would have some much-needed free time to reassess his direction for the future. He looked forward to a few weeks spent with no outside distractions.

No distractions? Zack rocked his head from side to side and moaned. Even after years of experience with his eccentric uncle, he had been totally unprepared for behavior bordering on lunacy.

The train trip passed pleasantly enough, especially with Sara Jennings to talk to. It had been a long time since Zack met a woman with such quiet command of herself. Unlike most women he knew, she didn't feel the need to fill every moment with meaningless chatter. In fact, he had been the one to keep the conversation going, not wanting it to lapse into silence. He left the station with a renewed sense of well-being, ready to make the desired changes to Uncle Marcus's will and begin his carefree holiday.

Instead, he found an irate uncle fuming over "a public nuisance" and demanding that Zack institute legal proceedings immediately. Zack spent two hours calming his uncle down and another two getting the story out of him. By the time he'd filled half a legal pad with notes on Marcus's grievance and his late-night excursions, Zack could see more grounds for the neighbor bringing charges of harassment against his uncle than for Marcus's complaint.

His recommendation to postpone their visit to the neighbor until the following day fell on deaf ears. Operating on the theory that the squeaky wheel got the grease, Marcus vowed not to let a night go by without voicing his displeasure to Esther Brown. He would go, he said, with Zachary or without him. Zack heaved a resigned sigh and tagged along. Someone had to turn the heat down on this imbroglio before it reached the boiling point.

After Marcus's description of his high-handed neighbor, Zack expected an overbearing ogress instead of the petite older woman who'd answered his uncle's insistent knock. When Sara Jennings appeared behind her, he was flabbergasted. And when that contemptuous gaze bored into his, Zack felt small enough to crawl into a crack in the sidewalk and wished he could do just that.

The few hours of sleep he managed to get hadn't brightened his outlook. Zack cast a bleary-eyed glance at his alarm clock and winced. Nine o'clock. Sleeping in during this visit would have been nice, but he would have preferred doing it by choice. Not because he'd been up until after one trying to calm his uncle, then awakened again barely two hours later by Sara's call to extricate Marcus from his wire cocoon.

Zack shook his head again. *What had possessed him to pull such a stunt?* He wondered, not for the first time, if his uncle's mental stability was all it should be. A performance like that had the potential to escalate this dispute into outright warfare.

Wearily, Zack dug a flannel shirt and jeans out of the suitcase he hadn't yet had time to unpack. The sugar-coated tones he heard on the phone in the wee hours had set warning bells clanging in his brain. Someone needed to defuse this situation, and it looked like he was elected.

Twenty minutes later, freshly showered and shaved, Zack strode down Jefferson Drive. Most of the yards, he saw, sported Christmas decorations, some more lavish than others. But none could compare with Miss Esther Brown's all-out extravaganza. Zack chuckled aloud. She must be something. It was a shame he wouldn't be meeting her on happier terms.

Crossing the street, he spotted Sara replacing the strings of lights. There was no sign of Esther. *Probably just as well.* Zack didn't relish the idea of facing a fluffy elderly lady in distress, especially when he'd been cast in the role of the villain's sidekick in this drama. He smoothed back his hair with both hands and summoned up his most winning smile.

Sara stood on tiptoe, trying to loop a wire around the end of a redbud branch. She wasn't much taller than her aunt. Certainly no more than five-foot three. Funny how she'd seemed so much larger the night before, hurling those scorching looks at him.

"Here, let me help you." Zack lifted the wire and set it in place. Sara murmured a thank you without meeting his gaze and moved to unsnarl a tangle of lights near the stable.

Zack swallowed his disappointment and tried again. He located the end of one section and, attempting to thread it back through the knots in the jumbled mass, tried to understand what was happening. Whether in the courtroom or dealing with clients in his office, Zack was accustomed to commanding attention. Feeling at a total disadvantage was new to him. And he was definitely not used to being ignored. Maybe it was time for a slight change in tactics.

"You've made a lot of progress," he said heartily and got a frosty glare in response. Yesterday, those brown eyes had reminded him of the cinnamon sticks his mother used to flavor her apple cider during the holidays. They held the same color, the same hint of a playful mixture of sweetness and spice. Today, an icicle would look warm in comparison.

"I had help." Sara's tone was as glacial as her

demeanor. "Some of the neighbors came over earlier. *Much* earlier," she emphasized, pulling a yard-long section of wire free. "It may surprise you to learn all of them were upset about this. No one has a problem with Aunt Esther's decorations. In fact, they like them. And these are people whose houses are on either side of Aunt Esther's and directly opposite. Not," she added pointedly, "across the street and four doors down."

Zack felt a flush creep up his neck. Couldn't she see he was trying to help? He wasn't the bad guy. He made an effort to keep the frustration out of his voice. "I wanted to explain why I came here last night."

"I know why you came," she fired back. "I called you, remember?"

"Not then. The first time." Zack felt ridiculous, like a child caught up in a schoolyard argument. He was doing his best to heal the breach; she could at least meet him halfway.

"To bully an elderly woman?"

Zack sighed and redoubled his efforts to unravel the lights. How could Marcus have created such a multitude of knots in so little time? Boy Scouts could take lessons from his uncle.

"I am not in the habit of bullying people of any age." Zack measured his words carefully. "I came because I spent the evening listening to my uncle ranting about your great-aunt. I was concerned about his behavior and wanted to make sure he didn't cross any legal boundaries himself. I didn't want him setting himself up to be sued."

Sara appeared to soften during his explanation but

bristled at his last statement. She drew herself up, planting her fists on her hips. "Aunt Esther isn't that kind of person. She'd never dream of doing such a thing! Not even with the encouragement of some money-hungry shyster," she added, with a dark look at Zack.

He flushed again. The implication that he might be a motivating force behind Marcus's threats was plain, and he resented it. True, some of his colleagues at Schuyler, Temple, and Wells operated exactly that way on a regular basis, but he wasn't about to give Sara the satisfaction of admitting it. He gave her the look that usually made recalcitrant witnesses wilt. Undaunted, she glared right back at him.

How could she be so formidable when the top of her head barely reached his chin? Zack suddenly wondered how it would feel to rub his chin against her short, curly chestnut hair. Even in that pugnacious stance, she looked absolutely adorable. With the determined tilt of her chin and the upturned nose framed by her heart-shaped face. . .

Whoa, Counselor. Zack yanked his wayward thoughts to a halt. This was a delicate bit of negotiation, not the time to dwell on the delightful appearance of the opposition.

He gave her what he hoped was a charming smile. "How about the two of us joining forces to work this out? Something needs to be done, and soon, but I don't think either of our relatives will make a move to break the deadlock. It looks like it's up to you and me. What do you say?"

Sara held his gaze with that disconcertingly direct stare. Zack felt as though she looked right through him, probing to determine his true intentions. "Something you should know right up front," she stated, "is that Aunt Esther isn't likely to back down one iota. This is not merely a light display to her, and it's not just about her rights, either. Although," she added, jabbing her finger at him, "she does have rights, and I intend to see they are protected.

"You have to understand that Aunt Esther sees this as a ministry." Sara narrowed her eyes and waited. When Zack didn't offer any comment, she went on. "It's more than holiday decorations; it's her mission field."

Zack's lips parted. Finally, something in this whole ridiculous affair began to make sense. "You mean this is her way of reaching out with the Christmas message?" He considered the idea, then nodded his approval. "I like it." He was rewarded by an appreciative glow in Sara's eyes, the warm cinnamon look he remembered from the train.

"Then you'll make your uncle see reason?"

Zack hated to squelch the expectant gleam so quickly. "Frankly," he told her, trying to postpone the letdown, "I can't understand why he's so opposed to it. The figures are beautifully done, and the effect must be spectacular at night." The corners of his lips tilted upward. "Okay, maybe 'overwhelming' is a better word, but I don't see anything wrong with it.

"The problem is," he continued, and watched the coldness creep back into Sara's expression like frost forming on a window, "my viewpoint doesn't matter. My uncle is the one who needs a change of heart, and making that happen won't be easy."

"Just what does he have against Christmas, anyway?"

Zack stared at the winter-brown grass and shuffled his feet. "Considering what you've seen of him, it may be hard to believe this, but my uncle is a Christian, too."

He didn't have to look up to confirm Sara's reaction. Her sniff of disbelief told him plenty. "I agree, he isn't acting like one right now." Zack squirmed inwardly. Where was his professional demeanor when he needed it? He had confronted difficult adversaries in the courtroom with aplomb, but he couldn't bring himself to face one pint-sized, chestnut-haired woman who had the most expressive eyes he had ever seen. . . .

Knock it off! He raised his head, determined to stand firm, and found Sara eyeing him speculatively.

"You may be right," she conceded. "Having you help by working on your uncle might be the most logical way to deal with this." She nodded slowly. "Working together instead of against each other. It makes sense. All right, how do we start?" she asked, squaring her shoulders.

Zack smothered a smile. No point in telling her she reminded him of a soldier standing at attention, awaiting orders. He had a feeling the comparison would not be appreciated.

"We need to map out a strategy," he said, moving the conversation to more businesslike terms. "How about discussing the situation over lunch? A working lunch," he added hastily, at Sara's doubtful glance. "Pick you up at noon?"

"All right," she answered crisply. "If you really think it will help solve this mess. Where do you want to go?"

"I could borrow my uncle's car, but I'd have to answer a lot of questions. Let's pick someplace within walking distance."

"Nearly everything in Minton is within walking distance," Sara told him, laughing.

Zack spread his hands in surrender, and the string of lights he was working on unraveled, falling into an orderly pile at his feet. Zack grinned. Things were going to work out fine.

Chapter 4

I t's amazing how little this place has changed." Sara scanned first one side of the street, then the other, surveying familiar sights from her childhood visits. Greer's Market, Minton Hardware, the public library—they were all still there. Mr. Wilson's jewelry store was now a coffee shop and the old TG&Y had found new life as a dollar store, but the overall feel of Minton was still the same.

Zack walked beside her, keeping himself between Sara and the street, and studied the scene without comment. He looked relaxed in the same flannel shirt and jeans he had worn earlier. The lack of power dressing reassured her. She'd been a little afraid he'd show up for lunch in a three-piece suit. Sara smiled inwardly, remembering how much fun he'd been to talk to on the train. He hadn't seemed like a stuffed shirt then, but you couldn't always tell. She never would have guessed he could be related to someone like Marcus, either.

"Do you see that as good or bad?"

Sara started at Zack's question and scrabbled frantically in her mind, trying to remember what she'd said.

"Most people feel progress is necessary for real growth," he added.

Sara shrugged. "At one time, I would have found it incredibly dull." Short-term visits with Aunt Esther were one thing, but for every day, she'd believed a person needed more stimulation than a small town like Minton could provide. "But now," she added, surprising herself, "I like the idea of a place that's steady enough not to change. I see it more as stability than monotony."

Zack studied the peaceful scene. "I see what you mean."

Sara stifled a giggle, imagining Geoffrey's expression if he heard her remark. The frenetic pace of city life acted as balm to Geoffrey's soul. Selling, socializing, and networking were the breath of life to him. A comment like Sara's would make him think she should be committed.

Zack took Sara's elbow and steered her into the Iron Kettle, another Minton institution that had stood the test of time. It was a mark in his favor. If he'd chosen Minton's one upscale restaurant, she would have suspected he was trying to impress, perhaps intimidate, her.

Sara glanced around the homey dining room while she followed the hostess to their table. She didn't recognize any of the patrons, which was just as well. That way they wouldn't be interrupted by friendly chitchat. This time was slated for serious discussion, and Sara intended to get down to business.

After some deliberation, she ordered the breaded

veal cutlets, smothering a grin at Zack's choice of chili. Geoffrey would have selected grilled chicken or possibly the trout. Sara didn't think Geoffrey had ever sat down to a real, down-home bowl of chili in his life.

❦

Zack watched Sara eat, relieved that the food seemed to have mellowed her prickly mood. Since their encounter that morning, he'd felt as though he were tiptoeing around a pool of gasoline with a lighted match in his hand, trying not to do anything to set off another explosion.

He relaxed enough to appreciate his chili. Sara looked like she was enjoying her meal, too. Zack wondered what it would be like to eat a meal together without the specter of Scrooge hovering between them. He could imagine Sara's expressive face turned toward his.

Sara looked up and stared straight into his eyes. "You said you wanted to map out a plan?" she asked briskly. She pushed her plate aside and produced a notebook.

Zack started. "Of course," he said, returning to reality. "I thought I'd let you eat your meal in peace."

"I'm finished now." She held a pen ready, waiting for him to speak.

So much for pleasant daydreams. They were back at the negotiating table. "I think the best solution would be to get the two of them together to discuss things rationally."

Sara raised an eyebrow. "How do we manage that? And is your uncle capable of carrying on a reasonable discussion if we do?"

Zack winced. She had a point. "I'll make sure he behaves himself," he promised, hoping he'd be able to keep his word.

"Mm." If Sara's response was any indication, his statement hadn't inspired confidence.

"I also believe we should meet at your aunt's house." He tried to inject a more positive tone into his voice. "She shouldn't feel as threatened if she's on her home territory."

"And having your uncle away from his will keep him a little off balance." Sara gave him an approving smile.

Zack appreciated the smile but wished she had chosen a different phrase. Given last night's escapade, he was none too sure just how balanced Marcus was.

"So we're agreed on the place," he said, pleased to make progress. The waitress appeared, and they both ordered hot apple pie.

"I have to admit," he said with a chuckle, "last night came as a shock. I never dreamed you'd be there, and your great-aunt was nothing like what I expected from Uncle Marcus's description."

"Oh?" Sara grew very still. "And just what were you expecting?"

Zack shrugged. "The way he talked, I thought she'd be a fire-breathing dragon." He laughed again. "I can't tell you how relieved I felt! She certainly wasn't the dotty old lady he'd led me to believe."

Another chuckle died instantly when Sara dropped her fork onto her dessert plate with a loud clank.

Her spicy brown eyes were going into flame-thrower

mode again, and her mouth was drawn into a thin line.

"He actually called Aunt Esther a dotty old lady?" She wadded her napkin into a ball and slapped it down on the table. "That's it. A difference of opinion between neighbors, I can understand. But to go around casting aspersions on my aunt's character and sanity. . ." She shoved her chair back and stood, grabbing her notebook and pen and jamming them into her purse.

"Wait!" Zack held up a placating hand. "Don't go, please. Our only hope is to work this out together."

Sara glanced around uneasily, seeing the covert but fascinated attention her outburst had drawn from the other diners. She sank slowly back into her seat and smoothed out her napkin.

"Is there anything else?" she asked primly.

Zack let out the breath he'd been holding.

"If we're agreed on the four of us getting together at your aunt's house. . ." He stopped inquiringly, then continued when Sara nodded agreement. "Then all we have to do is decide on a time. Would this evening be agreeable to you?"

Sara considered the idea, then shook her head. "Last night upset her more than she let on. She needs time to recover. Besides, she already missed out on talking to her visitors last night, since she had to pick me up at the depot. I'd hate to disrupt her routine two nights in a row. What about tomorrow, or the day after? Maybe late afternoon, instead of evening? There would probably be less friction if we had our discussion before the lights are turned on."

"Excellent points." Zack beamed. She was talking

now, instead of reacting, and her use of "we" and "our" indicated a sense of partnership in this enterprise.

He leaned back and took a sip of the Iron Kettle's excellent coffee. Things were looking up once more. "I'm optimistic about this. As I told you this morning, Uncle Marcus is a believer, so the Christmas decorations can't be the real issue. If we can get them talking and find out what the root of the problem actually is, we should be able to work out something mutually acceptable."

"Spoken like a true lawyer," Sara murmured but with a spark of mischief in her eyes that took the sting out of the words.

Zack grinned. Playing on the same team was infinitely more enjoyable than being at odds.

"So that much is settled. We'll get them together, and with me watching Uncle Marcus's temper and you making sure your aunt's stubbornness doesn't get in the way, I see no reason—"

"Stubbornness?" Sara bounded to her feet with a vehemence that made him flinch.

"With the browbeating she's taken from that overbearing uncle of yours, you call *her* stubborn?" She pivoted on her heel and stalked out of the restaurant.

❦

Sara regretted her impulsive action even before the glass door swung closed behind her. She hurried down the sidewalk, anxious to put distance between herself and the fallout from her show of temper.

What had gotten into her? Flying off the handle like that was totally out of character for her. Normally, she prided herself on her ability to think through a problem dispassionately, looking at it from all sides before choosing the most practical course of action.

Had her actions a moment ago been based on clear thinking? No. Cool-headed and rational? Hardly. *How about ridiculous and immature?* Sara grimaced, recognizing the truth and feeling its sting.

What did Minton do to her? Or was it Zack who had this effect? Sara didn't know. And, whichever it was, would she call the effect good or bad? She didn't know the answer to that, either.

She heard the quick tap of footsteps behind her, and a moment later Zack appeared at her side. He panted slightly, and his hair tumbled across his forehead, reminding her of the man she'd first met on the train.

"I guess I owe you an apology," he said, trying to catch his breath.

Sara shook her head, blinking away the tears of embarrassment that sprang to her eyes. "I'm the one who should apologize. I acted like a child and embarrassed us both. I'm sorry."

She glanced up at Zack. "I guess Aunt Esther isn't the only stubborn one in the family, is she?"

Zack laughed ruefully. "I'd say there was fault on both sides." He gave Sara a lopsided grin that tugged at her heart.

She stopped in the middle of the sidewalk and extended her hand. "Are we still allies?"

"That we are." Zack took her hand in a strong grip that sent warmth all the way up her arm.

They walked on at a more leisurely pace, savoring the feeling of companionship. After two blocks, Sara broke the silence.

"I'm worried. Can Marcus really take Aunt Esther to court? Could he force her to give this up? We talked a lot last night, and again this morning after I redid the decorations. I'm ashamed I haven't taken the time to get to know her through more than just cards and letters since I've been an adult. This is what she lives for, Zack. It's what keeps her going. She looks forward to this all year. I'm afraid of what will happen if it's taken away from her. What would that do to her spirit, her will to go on? I can't bear to think I might lose her just when I've started getting to know her again."

She ran her fingers through her curly chestnut hair. "As I told you this morning, the other neighbors are uniformly in favor of what she's doing. One of them told me he and his wife came to know the Lord because of Aunt Esther's influence.

"I know your uncle sees her as a dithery old woman." She saw Zack wince. "And I'll grant you she looks soft and fluffy on the surface, but I know her commitment to Christ. It runs deep; it's the center of her being. Please don't let him take this away from her."

Zack took a moment to answer, and when he responded he didn't address her concern directly. "Earlier," he said, "you mentioned the term 'mission field.'"

Sara smiled. "When Aunt Esther was younger, she volunteered for foreign missions. Her dream was to serve the Lord in Greece or Turkey. She poured her whole heart and soul into studying and preparation. It wasn't until she took her physical that she learned she had a heart murmur. It was only a minor problem—you can see it hasn't slowed her down—but in those days it was enough to keep her from being sent to the field."

Zack shook his head sympathetically.

"Some people would have given up, but Aunt Esther said it opened her eyes to the people around her. God showed her He still had souls for her to win, and she didn't have to travel halfway around the globe to do it. She's spent her lifetime spreading the word to her neighbors."

Sara slowed her steps and put her hand on Zack's arm, drawing him to a stop. She looked deep into his eyes, willing him to understand. "The things your uncle sees as proof of her flightiness are the very things that show me her dedication to bringing the gospel message to the people she can reach right here in Minton. Aunt Esther can't go out and preach, but if she can do something to draw people to her. . ."

Zack whistled softly. "She's quite a woman, isn't she?" He tucked Sara's hand in the crook of his arm and began walking again. "Now all we have to do is get Uncle Marcus to see that."

"You said Aunt Esther didn't fit the picture Marcus painted for you," Sara said, a smile playing about her lips. "You're not quite what I would have expected, either. Somehow, you don't fit my idea of the typical corporate attorney."

Zack chuckled. "Just how many attorneys have you known?"

Too many, Sara thought, remembering some of the self-important individuals she'd met with Geoffrey at his endless social functions. She shrugged. "Enough to have the feeling most of them aren't quite as exuberant as you are. They seem to take themselves so very seriously."

"I'm very serious about my work," Zack assured her. "I got into law because I wanted to make a positive difference. But since life is a gift from God, it was meant to be lived with joy, don't you think?"

Sara pondered that concept. In her experience, life was a series of challenges. The best way to get through each one was to meet it head on, assessing it rationally, analyzing the pros and cons, and choosing the most pragmatic solution.

"I don't know," she answered doubtfully. "That sounds like something Pollyanna would say. It seems so. . .impractical."

"And is being practical the answer to everything?"

"Isn't it?" Sara answered, a defensive note in her voice. "It seems to me it's the best way to meet life. You have more idea what to expect. There are fewer surprises, fewer risks."

"Life itself is a risk," Zack countered. "And all surprises aren't bad, are they? I didn't expect to meet you when I boarded the train for Minton, for instance. But believe me, I'm glad I did."

Chapter 5

By the next week, Sara was ready to concede that life presented many surprises, not all of them bad. Marcus made a compromise of sorts, agreeing to stop badgering Aunt Esther. That counted as a pleasant surprise, although Sara suspected its motivation stemmed more from embarrassment at being caught in his nighttime antics than from any sense of goodwill.

However, he balked at getting together to talk, which Sara saw as disappointing, but not surprising at all. Zack reported continued efforts at breaking through his uncle's resistance, but with no success to date.

Aunt Esther resumed her evening ministry with transparent relief, but Sara couldn't shake the feeling of waiting for the proverbial shoe to drop. Given Marcus's penchant for unusual behavior, who knew whether he would abide by the cease-fire agreement or had plans to try another underhanded scheme?

So far, her fears had proven groundless. Marcus made no more late-night forays. No process servers appeared at Aunt Esther's door. *Good*, Sara thought.

That was the kind of surprise they didn't need.

Freed from the worries of Marcus's hounding, Aunt Esther lost her haunted look and drafted Sara into duty as co-hostess. Late afternoons saw them getting organized for the evening visitors. Just before dusk, they filled Crock-Pots with cocoa or apple cider. Sara then set them on a table outside, plugged them into an extension cord, and completed the preparations by carrying out stacks of foam cups, napkins, and Aunt Esther's tracts.

Sara didn't know whether to marvel more at her great-aunt's unsuspected writing talent or her unfailingly gracious treatment of every person who ventured into her yard. Only the night before, a family walked up to the refreshment table. The parents accepted a cup of cocoa for their daughter, but the father waved away the proffered tract with a smile.

"We got one last week, and we wanted to come back and say thank you for. . .all this." He swept his arm in an arc, indicating the brightly lit scene. "There's something about this place that draws us back, and that little paper you handed us last time really gave us something to think about."

He stared at the figures, his gaze lingering on the manger. "There's something more to it than just lights and decorations, isn't there?" he asked, his voice barely above a whisper.

"There is, indeed." Aunt Esther's warm smile took in all three of them. "Can you stay and talk? I'd be happy to tell you more."

The man hesitated, then shook his head. "Not

tonight. Maybe another time." He glanced at his wife, caught her look of longing. "Definitely another time," he stated. "We'll be back."

"You're welcome any time," Aunt Esther told him. "Even after the holidays." She watched them go, then turned a radiant face to Sara. "We'll see them again."

Sara believed her. She, too, had seen the hunger in their eyes. How many people in her own circle of acquaintances had that same hunger? And how many times had she missed seeing it? Maybe Aunt Esther had the right idea.

Not everyone was interested. Sara bent to scoop up another discarded cup at the edge of the yard and stuffed it into a half-full garbage bag. Part of the nightly ritual was gathering the cups and crumpled tracts left scattered across the yard.

Aunt Esther was adamant about the unvarying routine. "Every aspect of our lives is a witness. If I set this up to proclaim the Good News, then leave debris to be blown around my neighbors' yards by morning, which message do you think they'll hear?"

Sara straightened with a weary sigh, easing the kinks from her back. How had Aunt Esther managed to do this on her own? It was enough to keep the two of them busy for hours each evening, but for one elderly lady. . . Sara shook her head in admiration. What kept Aunt Esther going?

A picture of the young family formed in Sara's mind. Their yearning expressions showed an emptiness that could be filled only by inviting the Babe in the manger into their hearts. That was Aunt Esther's motivation.

Sara felt more determined than ever to make sure Marcus didn't interfere.

Ƶ

One day followed another, with Zack calling every morning to report his progress, or lack of it. Marcus's mood fluctuated from near capitulation one moment to adamant refusal the next. Setting a time for working out their differences seemed as distant a prospect now as it had at first.

Sara adopted an attitude of cautious optimism, relaxing enough to spend her mornings taking long walks and getting reacquainted with Minton. Its un-hurried pace began to have an effect on her outlook. She reveled in the release from stress and felt a freedom she hadn't known in years.

On this morning, she strode along, head held high, arms swinging loosely at her sides. What a change from the tightly-wound walk she had when she first arrived. Sara enjoyed the difference but couldn't put her finger on a specific cause. It was just. . .Minton.

And Zack. Sara looked forward to his morning calls more than she knew she should. Even when he had nothing more to tell her than that the situation remained at a stalemate, her mood brightened at the sound of his voice. Maybe it was his lighthearted enjoyment of life, so reminiscent of what Sara had come to call "the Minton effect."

Whatever the reason, Zack seemed to enjoy the calls, too, prolonging them far beyond the time it took to tell her nothing had changed.

Only yesterday, Sara had checked her watch after

hanging up from one of his calls and was mortified to realize she had spent over an hour on the phone. She hurried to the kitchen to find Aunt Esther rinsing the last of the breakfast dishes. "I'm sorry," Sara apologized, blushing profusely. "I had no idea I'd been talking so long."

Aunt Esther only smiled. "It must have been Zachary," she said, a knowing twinkle in her eyes.

This morning when the phone had rung, Sara had answered in a businesslike tone, intending to keep the conversation to a minimum.

"Good morning." Geoffrey's confident voice came clearly through the wire.

The receiver clattered to the floor. Sara picked it up, dropped it, picked it up again. This time she managed to get a firm grip on it. "Geoffrey?"

"What's going on?" he demanded.

"I'm. . .surprised to hear your voice. That's all."

Geoffrey chuckled, a rich, throaty sound. "I thought you'd enjoy hearing from the civilized world. A bit of a reprieve from your bucolic existence, eh? How is life among the rustics?"

"We're not quite in the backwoods here." Sara gritted her teeth and tried to maintain her temper. "And life's going along quite nicely, thank you."

Geoffrey laughed again. "Quite the little trouper, aren't you? Keeping a stiff upper lip while attending to auntie. I admire your spunk, darling, but haven't you had enough? It's high time you came home."

"Really?" Sara's tone should have quick-frozen Geoffrey on the spot.

"Of course," Geoffrey answered, unfazed. "That shabby little town is no place for you. You belong in St. Louis. With me."

"I don't belong to you, remember?"

"Don't be ridiculous. Some of the most important parties of the year are thrown during the holidays. People expect to see us together."

"No, they don't. When a couple is no longer engaged, their being seen together is the last thing people expect."

Geoffrey sighed the patient, long-suffering sigh that had irritated Sara so many times before. "I realize you had doubts. Many women do. But I have every confidence you'll come to your senses and things will be as they were before. When you do, I'll be waiting. Remember, I'm a very patient man."

"Dense" is more like it, Sara thought grimly. She gripped the receiver so tightly her hand ached. "Listen to me, Geoffrey. Listen carefully. There is no 'us' anymore. As for when I'll return to St. Louis. . ."

Her voice trailed off and she stared into the distance, allowing the hand holding the receiver to drift slowly to her side. A plan that had been nibbling at the edges of her mind now emerged full-blown. A plan she could hardly believe.

The insistent squawking from the phone caught her attention, and she raised the handset again. "I'm not sure I'm coming back," she said crisply and hung up.

The phone rang again almost immediately. Sara rolled her eyes. Geoffrey was not used to being thwarted. She yanked the receiver off the cradle. "You have to accept the fact that you won't always get your own way," she snapped.

"Huh?" Zack's normally cheerful voice held a touch of confusion. "Is everything okay?"

Sara resisted the impulse to scream. "Sorry." She massaged a throbbing temple. "I thought you were someone else."

"No problem. Listen, I have good news. Uncle Marcus finally agreed to talk things over with Esther. Will four o'clock this afternoon work for you?"

Chapter 6

Sara bent to pull the baking pan from the oven. "Are you sure you want to go to all this trouble for Marcus Taylor?" she asked doubtfully. "You had more planned for today than spending hours in the kitchen. I could have whipped up a cake mix in no time. Why do you have to feed the old grouch, anyway?"

Aunt Esther smiled serenely and continued bustling around the kitchen. "It's the right thing to do, dear. Trust me."

Sara cast a concerned glance at her great-aunt, wondering how much anxiety her placid appearance concealed. Sara had mixed feelings about the meeting. While resolving the situation with Marcus would be a relief, it also meant the loss of her daily conversations with Zack. Once the feud had been settled, there would be no more reason for the phone calls that started her days on such a bright note.

The doorbell buzzed, and Sara glanced at the clock. Four o'clock, on the dot. Trust a lawyer and his nitpicky uncle to be precisely on time. At least Marcus had come to the front door this time. And in broad daylight. She started for the door, but Aunt Esther waved her aside.

"I'll answer it." She hung up her apron, patted her silvery hair into place and headed for the door.

Sara followed, remembering the last time the four of them had met on a doorstep. Hopefully today's conference would bring a happier conclusion.

Aunt Esther swung the door open wide. "Marcus, Zachary, how nice of you to come." She smiled, while Sara stood at her elbow like a watchdog.

The two men entered. Zack gave Sara an encouraging grin, and some of her tension dissipated. Marcus removed his fedora and started to unwind the gray scarf from around his neck when he froze, narrowing his eyes.

Uh-oh, Sara thought. *Starting already?*

Marcus slowly pulled the scarf free and held it dangling at his side. He sniffed, his beaklike nose twitching.

"That can't be— Do I smell baklava?" His snapping brown eyes shone with a hopeful light.

Aunt Esther smiled demurely. "That's right."

The trace of a smile lit Marcus's face. Sara watched, fascinated. Without his habitual scowl, he no longer looked like the neighborhood Grinch.

"Ahh." He pursed his lips. "I haven't tasted your baklava in over forty years. I've never forgotten it."

A pale pink blush tinted Aunt Esther's cheeks. Zack stared open-mouthed, and Sara felt sure his bewildered expression mirrored her own.

"Do you mean to tell me you two have known each other that long?" Her voice came out in an incredulous squeak.

"That doesn't make sense," Zack put in. "Uncle Marcus, you only moved to Minton a year ago."

Marcus cleared his throat and shuffled his feet. He busied himself hanging up his hat, scarf, and coat. Sara turned to Aunt Esther, whose clear blue gaze never wavered.

"Actually, we've known each other even longer," she explained. "You see, Marcus moved *back* to Minton last year, but we both grew up here. We went to school together from the third grade all the way through high school."

Only the ticking of the grandfather clock broke the silence. It seemed an eternity before Zack spoke.

"I don't believe this!" he sputtered. "If you've known each other that long, then why—"

"Now, now." Aunt Esther shooed them toward the living room. "Marcus, you and Zachary make yourselves comfortable while Sara and I bring the refreshments." She slipped into the kitchen, picking up the dessert tray and managing to avoid Sara's urgent questions.

Sara loaded a tray with cups and a carafe of coffee and entered the living room in time to see Marcus lift a forkful of the dessert.

"Mmmm. Just as I remembered it. You always were a good cook, Essie."

Essie? Zack mouthed the name at Sara from his seat in the wing chair.

She shrugged and shook her head. She was just as much in the dark as he was. They had moved from *A Christmas Carol* to *Alice in Wonderland* without any warning.

Sara looked at her great-aunt, a suspicion forming in her mind. Aunt Esther sat at one end of the sofa, feet primly together, the picture of ladylike innocence. Had she deliberately chosen to make baklava to soften up Marcus? If so, it seemed to be working. The lines in his face had relaxed, and his expression was positively genial.

Sara turned her attention back to Aunt Esther. Underneath that fluffy exterior, Sara knew a shrewd mind was at work. She took a bite of her own baklava and closed her eyes, savoring its buttery, nutty richness. *Mmmm. No wonder Marcus remembered it all these years.*

Zack cleared his throat and Sara's eyelids flew open. "It's time we got down to business," he said. "We all know why we're here—"

Sara shot a look at Marcus, whose face still wore a benevolent glow. When he forgot to be angry, he wasn't bad looking. *Someone should feed him baklava in regular doses.*

"So let's air our feelings and see if we can't arrive at a mutually agreeable solution."

Marcus sprang into action, the baklava effect fading before Sara's eyes. "Air our feelings? All right, here's the way I feel." He aimed a penetrating look at Aunt Esther.

Sara sighed. Scrooge had returned.

"That traffic is a nuisance. Jefferson Drive was never intended to handle that many vehicles. Once the sun goes down, I can't even get my car out of my driveway." Marcus looked at Zack and gave a brief nod, apparently certain he'd won his point.

Zack looked at Sara and Aunt Esther. "Ladies?"

Aunt Esther's laugh tinkled like crystal. "But Marcus, you don't like to drive after dark."

Marcus glowered and appeared to consult a mental checklist. "What about those lights? They're blazing away until all hours of the night. How can a person sleep?"

"That's nonsense." This time Aunt Esther didn't laugh. "You know perfectly well I turn them off promptly at ten."

Sara nodded agreement. She had to finish cleaning the yard before ten o'clock to meet Aunt Esther's deadline.

Marcus tried again. "And she leaves it all up until after New Year's. This overblown production goes on for weeks on end." He turned a plaintive face to Sara, then Zack, in a blatant bid for sympathy.

Aunt Esther shook her head. "That's so I can add the wise men. They had to travel a long distance, you know. You'd be surprised how many people come back to see the changes I've made. It gives me another opportunity to talk with them."

Marcus cast an agonized look at Zack. "It's. . .it's just. . .impractical, that's what it is. And you know I am, above all things, a practical man."

Sara flinched, hearing an echo of herself.

"She, on the other hand—" Marcus gestured toward Aunt Esther. "She has been flighty ever since grammar school. Look at what she does. . .standing in the cold night after night, like a child with a lemonade stand. It's just another of her aberrations."

"Personal attacks won't solve anything," Zack

admonished, with a nervous glance at Sara.

"You wanted my feelings; I'm giving them to you," Marcus blustered, rising to his feet.

"I think we've accomplished all we're going to today." Zack grabbed Marcus and their wraps and herded his uncle out the door.

Sara glanced at the street sign. Dogwood Lane. She'd walked nearly a mile since leaving Aunt Esther's and was no closer to solving her dilemma than when she'd stepped out the door. She pushed her gloved hands deeper into her coat pockets and continued walking, careful to avoid the icy patches on the sidewalk. Three days had gone by since Marcus and Zack made their hasty exit.

And it had been three days since she'd heard from Zack. Sara hadn't fully realized how much she enjoyed his calls until they stopped coming.

Did that mean it was over? Had Marcus finally seen the error of his ways? *But if he had, surely Zack would have called to let me know.*

She sniffed the frosty air. Unless she missed her guess, the quiet residential block would be covered with snow by morning. She looked at the homes in the cozy neighborhood, picturing them under a blanket of white. They would look like something out of a Kinkade painting, especially the house just ahead on her right. Sara's steps slowed of their own accord.

The neat white clapboard with two bay windows seemed to call out to her. Sara surveyed the neatly-tended yard. The lilacs and redbuds would look glorious in the spring.

Without conscious thought, she turned up the brick walk and was halfway to the front door before she caught herself.

She halted in mid-step. *What am I doing? What if someone's watching from inside the house?* She turned back toward the sidewalk, then stopped, this time staring at a red-and-white sign. Hanson Realty. The house was for sale. Maybe no one lived there now. And if someone did and had witnessed her strange behavior, they might think she had been looking over the property as a potential buyer.

Sara took two steps toward the sidewalk, stopped again, and scrutinized the windows. On closer inspection, it appeared to be unoccupied. None of the curtains stirred, and there were no other signs of life. *A house like that doesn't deserve to be left vacant.* It was a friendly house, a welcoming house, and it needed someone to care for it. Someone who would appreciate its beauty and character.

The house sat neatly centered on its lot. It had at least two bedrooms, Sara decided, possibly three. *And I'll bet one of them would be just right for an office.* Her curiosity carried her back to the house, and Sara found herself peering through the windows, heedless of what the neighbors might think.

Most of the curtains were drawn, affording only narrow glimpses, but what Sara could see charmed her. Gleaming wooden floors and creamy walls cried out for rag rugs in muted hues. For an older house, there were an amazing number of closets and cupboards.

And in the living room, the huge stone fireplace looked like. . .home.

Sara pulled herself away from the house with an effort and continued her walk, wondering what had come over her.

Three blocks farther, she turned right and headed toward the main street to do a little Christmas shopping. Her wayward feet slowed again at the sight of the small office in front of her. The name Hanson Realty was emblazoned on the front window. Moving as though in a dream, she opened the door and went inside.

Two desks flanked the large window. On one, a computer monitor displayed an underwater screen saver. No one but Sara was in the room. She took a deep breath to calm her jangled nerves and prepared to slip back out.

"Good morning! I thought I heard the door." A plump blond woman entered from an adjoining room. "I'm Neta Hanson," she said, extending a hand that sported a ring on every finger.

Sara halted, her escape blocked. "Sara Jennings," she mumbled.

"How can I help you?" Neta Hanson's round face glowed with goodwill.

"I'm. . .really not sure," Sara stammered and flushed. She didn't usually babble like an idiot. She straightened her shoulders and looked Neta in the eye. Surely she could carry on a normal conversation.

"I saw a house a few blocks from here." Sara pointed toward Dogwood Lane. "Your sign was in front of it."

Neta's blue eyes lit up. "The Olsen place? Oh, it's a dream. Sixteen hundred square feet, three bedrooms, two baths. Central heating, wooden floors throughout, and a fireplace you have to see to believe." She fished in the desk drawer for a ring of keys with one hand and grabbed her coat with the other. "Come on, you'll love it."

"Wait," Sara protested. "I was only curious."

Neta's enthusiastic recital of the house's selling points continued nonstop. Sara found herself swept along to Neta's small blue hatchback and driven back to the Olsen house, where she was given a full tour. Neta waxed eloquent about each room.

"And just look at the backyard!" she exclaimed, opening the floor-length drapes with a dramatic gesture. "Isn't this a great place for kids?" She looked at Sara. "How many do you have?"

"None," Sara told her. "I'm not married."

Neta lost momentum for only an instant. "Not a problem. You'll have plenty of room for entertaining, but not so much you'll feel like you're rattling around." All the way back to the office, she touted the house's virtues. "Lovely landscaping, but easy to maintain, a great neighborhood. It's an incredible buy."

Sara stood her ground on the driveway, not wanting to be trapped inside. "Thanks for taking the time to show it to me."

"My pleasure. Think it over, but don't take too long. A place that great is sure to go fast." Neta gave Sara her business card and hurried back into the office.

Sara let out a whoosh of air that lifted her curly

bangs off her forehead. Dealing with Neta was a little like standing in a wind tunnel.

She resumed her walk downtown, trying to wipe thoughts of the house from her mind.

Chapter 7

Sara's attempt to forget the house proved as fruitless as her effort to pretend she didn't miss Zack. Every day that went by with no word from him seemed hollow.

She turned off Jefferson Drive and headed downtown, following the route that had become her favorite. Aunt Esther had decreed this a major baking day and sent her off to Greer's Market with a list of needed items.

Sara inhaled, enjoying the pungent scent of wood smoke. The walks that had become part of her morning ritual gave her a chance to renew the feelings of peace she had come to associate with Minton. There was a serenity here that answered a deeply felt need. If only she could hold onto that peace after the holidays ended.

Turning onto Dogwood Lane, Sara's steps slowed as she approached the empty Olsen house. Every day, she passed it on her walk. Every day, it seemed to call out to her. What would it be like to be part of this neighborhood, to call this place home?

Neta Hanson looked up at the sound of the bell above the door. "I knew you'd be back," she said, beaming.

❦

Sara moved along at a rapid pace, whether from nerves or a feeling of accomplishment, she didn't know. There was something exhilarating about making an offer on a piece of property. Exhilarating, and a bit frightening.

Had she lost her mind? Making an impulsive decision like that was utterly impractical. Or was it? Maybe capturing this sense of peace was the most practical thing she had ever done.

Zack's breathless voice came from directly behind her. "If you'll slow down a little, I'll walk with you."

Sara turned and laughed. "That's the trouble with you city boys," she teased. "All that sitting behind a desk leaves you out of shape." She grinned broadly, hoping he would think it was their banter and not his presence that brought her such pleasure.

Still trying to catch his breath, Zack settled for responding with an indignant look that made Sara laugh all the more. It was true. Life in the city kept people too busy for things that were truly important, but she would soon be a small-town girl. She hugged the knowledge to herself.

They lapsed into a companionable silence, broken only by the sound of their footsteps on the new-fallen snow. Sara compared it to the silences that often fell between her and Geoffrey. Those made her feel like Geoffrey's mind was a million miles away, working out the details of his next business deal.

This was a warm silence, a friendly one. One that

accepted and welcomed her presence. In some strange way, the bond between them seemed stronger for them not talking.

Sara knew without having to ask that Zack enjoyed himself as much as she did, skirting the drifts of snow piled deep around trees and against fences. They smiled together at the snowmen and snow angels in nearly every yard.

Zack helped Sara up and down the curbs, tucking her elbow protectively into the crook of his arm. She wondered at the feelings his actions stirred. He made her feel safe, cared for. . .wanted.

A block from Greer's, Zack spoke. "Are you in a hurry to get where you're going, or would you mind taking a detour? This seems like a good time to do some exploring."

Sara agreed and walked contentedly with Zack to the end of the street, where they crossed an open field.

Sara looked around, delighted. "I remember coming here when I was a little girl! See that hill?" She pointed. "I spent one entire day going up and down that hill with my sled. I came out after breakfast and never thought about eating again until it got dark. My dad finally came out to find me."

"Looks like it's still the thing to do." Zack nodded toward a group of youngsters, some trudging up the slope, towing their sleds, others careening downhill with shrill squeals of joy.

The snow deepened in the wooded area Zack led her to, and Sara appreciated the protection of her high-topped boots. He stopped under a massive oak tree, and they stared, rapt with wonder at the fairy-tale scene around them. Snow encased each branch and twig with a delicate tracery of glittering white.

Sara caught her breath. The effect Aunt Esther attempted to portray with her multitude of lights, God had gloriously created in one night's snowfall. Deep in the cover of the trees, the rest of the world seemed far away. Even the shrieks of the children were muffled. She and Zack existed in a world apart.

When Zack reached for her hand, entwining his fingers in hers, it seemed natural for her to return the pressure, enjoying his presence, delighting in this shared moment. The snow-covered morning was the kind meant to be enjoyed with a friend, and here she was, sharing it with Zack. Warm childhood memories and the anticipation of making a fresh start combined to create a wellspring of joy within her.

A sudden gust of wind sent a flurry of snowflakes showering down from the overhanging branches of the oak. Sara's feelings burst out of her in a gush of delight.

ॐ

Zack saw the spontaneous joy on Sara's upturned face. Her delighted laughter tugged at his heart. He knew he would always remember her as she looked just now—the unguarded laughter, the snowflakes sprinkled on her hair and eyelashes. Without conscious thought, he leaned down and kissed her.

He meant it as a friendly kiss, intending only to brush her lips casually with his.

ॐ

Sarah had seen the teasing light in Zack's eyes change

into something deeper, more serious. She was halfway prepared for his kiss when it came, but her own reaction caught her totally by surprise.

The feathery touch of his lips on hers strengthened. Zack's hands cupped her shoulders, and Sara found her hands reaching up to encircle his neck of their own accord.

They drew apart at the same moment, Sara dropping her gaze before looking up at Zack. He looked as confused as she felt. Sara tried to get a grip on her whirling emotions. It must have been meant as a friendly kiss, a platonic gesture. . .part of their joy in sharing this magical moment together. There was no rational explanation for the flutters in her stomach.

Geoffrey's kisses had never left her feeling like this. Zack's kiss and the electric current that had passed between them certainly didn't fall into the plain-vanilla category.

She followed his lead wordlessly, turning back toward town and trying to quell her longing to feel the warmth of his embrace once more.

Neither of them spoke during the short walk to Greer's Market. Sara barely noticed the silence, lost in her own turbulent thoughts.

The bell over the door jangled, and Emmett Greer looked up from the counter. He'd changed little from the genial shopkeeper Sara remembered. His shoulders stooped a bit more and an extra inch of scalp showed in front of his hairline, but she recognized him easily and smiled. Pale blue eyes peered back at her over wire-rimmed glasses perched on the tip of his nose.

"I know you," he said. Then his brow wrinkled. "Don't I?"

"It's Sara Jennings, Mr. Greer," she replied, laughing. "Esther Brown's great-niece. I'm impressed you remembered me after all this time."

"I never forget a pretty face. I try not to, anyway." The pale blue eyes twinkled, then he turned to Zack. "Don't believe I've met you, though."

"Zack Taylor." The men exchanged handshakes. "I'm visiting my uncle."

"Ah." Mr. Greer pushed his spectacles a quarter inch higher on his nose. "That would be Marcus Taylor, unless I miss my guess." He chuckled at Zack's look of surprise. "That wasn't much of a guess. I've known Marcus since we were boys. You favor him a bit, at least the way he looked years ago. Interesting man, Marcus. Strong-minded then, strong-minded now."

Zack laughed out loud. "You do know him, don't you?"

Sara left them deep in conversation and browsed the aisles for the items on Aunt Esther's list. When she returned carrying a heavily laden basket, she found the men bent over a pile of papers strewn across the counter.

"See here?" Mr. Greer pointed to a long paragraph in fine print. "The fellow wants to buy the property I have north of town, but I can't make head nor tail of all this legalese. Does he want this as recreational property for himself, or is he some big-time developer? And what's this about mineral rights?"

Zack nodded, his attention focused on the printed page. "You're right. It would definitely be worth your while to have a lawyer go over this to make sure your interests are protected."

"Thanks. I'll do that." Mr. Greer swept the papers aside and rang up Sara's purchase.

Zack carried two of the three sacks home, playfully moaning about the heavy weight. Sara led him up the back steps. "Let's take these in the kitchen door." She swung the door open and froze.

"What?" Zack plowed into her and did a gyrating dance step on the stoop, trying to keep from dropping the bags.

"Shh. Listen." Indistinct voices filtered through the closed door to the living room. Sara threw a wild-eyed look at Zack. "She wasn't expecting anyone. Do you think she's okay?"

"Marauders in Minton?" Zack lifted an amused eyebrow but moved silently to the door and pressed his ear against it. Sara joined him, trying to decipher the words, and gaped at Zack.

"Is that your uncle's voice?" she whispered.

Zack nodded slowly, looking as stunned as Sara felt. "Sounds like him," he whispered back. "But what's he doing here?"

"More to the point," Sara said, bristling, "what's he doing to Aunt Esther?" She burst through the swinging door with Zack behind her, still carrying the grocery sacks.

Aunt Esther and Marcus sat side by side on the couch, a large album spread open across their laps. Aunt Esther looked up, a pleased smile lighting her face. "How nice. You've brought Zachary with you."

"Good to see you, boy," Marcus said cheerfully. "I wondered where you'd gotten off to. We've been having quite a time, haven't we, Essie?"

Sara looked from her great-aunt to Marcus and back again. *How can these two be in the same room without the fur flying?* "What's going on?" she asked weakly.

"Only a bit of reminiscing." Aunt Esther's smile broadened. "Marcus and I were looking over some of my old albums. Look." She pointed to a faded photo. "There I am on Easter, just after the sunrise service."

Sara stared at the small, black-and-white picture of a much younger Esther. Her eyes still shone with that unmistakable joy, Sara noted, and her smile held the same gentle warmth.

"Here," Aunt Esther said, turning the yellowing page, "is one of my favorites, Zachary. Your uncle and me at a church picnic. Do you remember how you won the pie-eating contest, Marcus?"

Sara's mouth dropped open in astonishment. The handsome young man pictured there stared at the camera with an open, engaging smile. Try as she might, Sara could detect no bitterness pinching his mouth, no harsh lines creasing his face. She studied the present-day Marcus out of the corner of her eye. When did the change take place?

Zack set the bags down and stood next to Sara, looking over the older people's shoulders. He shook his head at her, shrugged, and grinned.

Sara grinned back at him, fascinated by Marcus's interest in pictures taken after he had moved away. Aunt Esther showed them photo after photo, many depicting situations she had used to share the story of Jesus with others.

"Here's the booth a group of us set up at the winter carnival," she told them. "And this is the puppet show we put on for vacation Bible school. One of the puppeteers got sick, and I had to play both Jonah and the fish."

Twenty minutes later, Marcus sighed softly and laid his hand over Aunt Esther's. "You always did have a heart for that kind of work, Esther."

Aunt Esther turned a gentle face toward his. "Once upon a time, Marcus, you enjoyed sharing the gospel every bit as much as I do."

"But I never understood how you could do some of the things you did." The frustrated note crept back into Marcus's voice. "Your behavior seemed. . .well, strange."

"And now?" Aunt Esther's voice prompted softly.

"It was your life's mission. Your calling. Looking at it from a more mature perspective, I can see that now. You always did fling yourself wholeheartedly into everything you were involved in."

Aunt Esther nodded, her eyes misting over.

"You never cared a whit back then what anyone thought of you," he continued. "Why should I expect you to start now?"

Aunt Esther stiffened, her sentimental mood evaporating. "Honestly, Marcus," she said, an exasperated quaver in her voice. "I've tried to make you understand. But even after all these years, you're still as stubborn and stiff-necked as ever. You always saw me as unconventional, but you never looked too hard at yourself. You told me then I didn't have enough regard for what others thought of me, but you had entirely too much."

Aunt Esther thumped the album closed and stood, leaning over Marcus to continue her tirade. "I knew what others thought of me then, and I know what you think today—that I'm nothing but a dithery old lady."

Sara saw Zack flinch when he heard Marcus's sentiments echoed so accurately.

"But," said Aunt Esther, pointing a finger at Marcus, "if it brings people to Christ, it doesn't matter what anyone thinks."

She stopped and drew herself upright. "That's the very reason I refused to marry you all those years ago. You wanted me to conform to society's expectations, and I couldn't do that, Marcus. I couldn't! It would have meant denying the person God wanted me to be."

She took a step backward. "It all came down to a matter of priorities. As important as your opinion was to me, what God thought of me mattered even more."

Aunt Esther's chin quivered, and to Sara's horror, for the first time in her life she saw the sparkling blue eyes fill with tears. Aunt Esther dabbed at her streaming eyes with a handkerchief she pulled from her sleeve.

Zack broke the tense silence, the shock in his voice reflecting Sara's feelings.

"Let me get this straight," he said. "You two were engaged back then?"

Aunt Esther only sniffled and dabbed harder. Zack gave his uncle a piercing look. Marcus rose with as much dignity as he could muster and walked out the front door, leaving a wake of confusion behind him.

Sara and Zack stared at each other. Aunt Esther blew her nose and folded the handkerchief.

"I apologize," she said, lifting her chin. "Goodness knows, I don't usually act that way." She pulled herself erect, and some of the old sparkle returned to her eyes. "Now, how about baking those cookies?"

Chapter 8

Sara surveyed the mounds of cookies, cakes, and breads spread over every available surface in the kitchen. She laughed incredulously. "I can't believe we managed to bake so much in one day. What are we going to do with it all?"

"That's no problem, dear." Aunt Esther drooped against a cookie-laden counter, mopping beads of perspiration from her forehead with a paper towel. "What we don't distribute to the evening visitors, we'll give to the senior center. And," she added, eyeing Zack, who was reaching for a cookie, "we won't have to worry about a good many of them."

"Quality control," Zack mumbled around a mouthful of macaroon. "An important factor that's often overlooked." He handed one to Esther with an impish grin. "Here. You haven't had one yourself in at least five minutes."

Aunt Esther swatted his hand playfully. "Just for that," she told him, "I ought to make you go without supper."

Zack groaned at the mention of food. So did Sara, who had sampled her own quota of treats.

"You mean no one's hungry?" Aunt Esther teased. "Then I vote we relax in the living room. Baking day is one time I don't go out to greet visitors. Since we washed up as we went along, there's really nothing to do except wait for those last loaves of nut bread to finish baking."

Sara was only too happy to comply after a day that had been an emotional roller coaster. *Aunt Esther has to be even more tired than I am. I hope she didn't overdo.* She sank onto the couch with a grateful sigh.

Aunt Esther, hovering in the background, touched Zack's sleeve. "Would you mind building up the fire? After a long day's work, curling up in front of a cheery blaze sounds like just what the doctor ordered."

Zack grinned at her fondly and did as she asked. "There," he said, sweeping his arm in a grand gesture. "A fire fit for a queen." He sprawled on the floor in front of the couch.

Aunt Esther beamed. "Thank you. It's perfect." She moved toward a recliner, then hesitated. "Actually," she said, "I'm afraid I'm too tired to enjoy it, after all. I think I'll go straight up to bed, if you two don't mind."

Sara started to push herself up off the couch, but Aunt Esther held up her hand.

"I'm fine, really. There's no need to concern yourself. It's just the aftereffects of all the excitement today."

Zack, too, looked concerned. "Maybe I should just head home and let you both get some rest."

"Oh, but Sara can't go to bed just yet," Aunt Esther demurred. "The nut bread is still in the oven, but I'm just too tired to wait for the buzzer to go off. You won't mind taking it out when it's ready, will you?" Without waiting for an answer, she added, "Zachary, you might as well stay and keep her company, since she'll be alone down here."

Sara squinted suspiciously at the guileless blue eyes. Aunt Esther paused at the bottom of the stairs and flipped off the living-room light.

"No point in wasting electricity, with that perfectly lovely fire providing plenty of light," she said solemnly and wagged at finger at Sara and Zack. "You young people may take these amenities for granted, but frugality is something I learned in my youth." She went up the stairs and disappeared down the hallway, leaving an uneasy silence behind her.

Sara mustered the nerve to look at Zack, wondering what he thought of Aunt Esther's transparent attempt at matchmaking.

"She's right you know," he said solemnly. "About being frugal, I mean. It would be a real shame to waste that fire." He held out his arm, and Sara slipped down off the couch to sit next to him. They settled back against the couch, watching the dancing flames in silence. The sap sizzled and popped, sending a shower of bright sparks up the chimney.

Zack's arm found its way around Sara's shoulders, and she leaned against him. This time, his kiss didn't take her by surprise. Sara searched Zack's eyes as his face drew nearer, seeing her own sense of wonder reflected there. Her eyes fluttered closed as his lips touched hers.

This time, there was no question in her mind about platonic gestures. This was a full-fledged, all-out, knock-your-socks-off, Fourth-of-July fireworks extravaganza. It put the sparks in the fireplace to shame.

Sara felt the pressure of Zack's lips even after he pulled away. She caught her breath in a quick gasp, trying to think of something appropriate to say. "Wow," was the only word that came out.

"Wow, indeed," Zack agreed. He traced the contour of her cheek with the backs of his fingers, sending a shivery tingle through her.

Sara rested her palm against Zack's face and closed her eyes once more, trying to sort out this maelstrom of emotions. What was happening? How could the utter contentment she felt in Zack's presence co-exist with such a dazzling, mind-boggling rush of electricity?

She felt Zack lean toward her again and lifted her face to his.

Bzzzzzz.

Sara stared at Zack blankly for a moment, trying to place the irritating noise. Recognition brought her scrambling to her feet. "The nut bread!" she cried, suddenly feeling awkward. "I need to take it out. I'll be right back."

Don't move, she wanted to say. She backed toward the kitchen, her gaze never leaving Zack's. *Don't let anything spoil this perfectly wonderful moment.* She bumped into the doorjamb. "I'll be right back," she repeated, grabbing the oven mitts and hurrying to the oven.

❦

Zack sagged back against the couch, feeling bereft. But Sara would return, and he could hold her in his arms again.

The phone's shrill ring jarred him.

"I need to take these out of the pans right away," Sara called. "Would you mind getting it?"

Zack picked up the receiver. "Hello?"

"Could I speak with Sara, please?" The clipped, male voice sounded in his ear.

Zack swallowed, his throat suddenly dry. *No reason to let this bother you. Sara has a business, after all. She must get a lot of calls for a lot of reasons.*

"She can't come to the phone right now. May I take a message?" Good. His voice hadn't betrayed his discomfort.

"Just tell her to call Geoffrey." The voice exuded confidence.

"Geoffrey," Zack repeated slowly. "Is there a last name?"

The smug voice responded with a laugh. "Just Geoffrey. Her fiancé. She'll know."

Zack hung up in slow motion. Her fiancé? Then what was that kiss all about? He would have stated under oath she felt the same way he did.

A sharp pang of jealousy stabbed at him. Was she playing games with him? Some version of "while the cat's away from the city fiancé, she'll play with the mouse in the country"?

Sara appeared in the kitchen doorway, her face flushed from the heat of the oven. "Was it anything important?" Her eyes shone, and her voice held a happy lilt.

Zack stared. He couldn't believe her capable of that kind of deceit. But then, there was the phone call.

"It didn't sound like an emergency," he said, finally

finding his voice. That much was true. That self-assured voice hadn't sounded the least bit concerned about a man answering the phone where his fiancée was staying. "I'll write the message down," he told her, scribbling "Call Geoffrey" on the notepad by the phone.

He looked at Sara, his heart melting at the soft light in her eyes. If he stayed one moment longer, he'd be kissing her again. Kissing some other man's fiancée. "I need to be going," he said, getting up and walking to the front door before he could change his mind. "I'll talk to you later."

Sara watched him leave, dumbfounded. What was going on? That kiss was like nothing she had experienced before. A few moments ago, she was sure Zack felt it, too. Sara slumped against the door frame, a sick feeling of dread forming within her. Had she read something into Zack's actions that didn't exist?

Maybe that's what comes of letting your heart rule your head.

Dejectedly, she turned off the kitchen lights. The fire's glow gave enough light to cross the living room to the stairs. Passing the couch, she felt drawn by the album lying on the cushion. She sat, pulling the large book onto her lap and turning on the small lamp next to her. She flipped through the pages idly, stopping at a group of pictures featuring a young Marcus.

I am, above all, a practical man. The words echoed in Sara's mind. She studied the photos, comparing the images of the person there to the man he had become. Her practical approach to life had been her security. Had she been wrong? Was she destined to become like

Marcus, embittered and lonely?

Her thoughts drifted to Aunt Esther and her joyous existence. Maybe what Marcus saw as foolhardiness was just living life exuberantly.

Sara let out a ragged sigh. How did Aunt Esther embrace life so freely? Such an open-hearted attitude was fraught with risks. But was the alternative winding up like Marcus?

Replacing the album, her elbow bumped the table. The notepad fell, unnoticed, to the floor.

Unsettled days followed. Sara threw herself into the evening activities, giving herself little time to brood. Zack's calls no longer brightened her mornings. Nor did he come by to visit. Sara missed his bright presence more than she could have imagined.

Her morning walks now took her past the Olsen place on a routine basis. Neta wouldn't have the owners' response to Sara's offer until after the holidays, but in her heart Sara felt sure the house would be hers.

Once her decision to relocate had been made, she knew she'd made the right choice. The location couldn't be better. She could easily keep in touch with clients in St. Louis via E-mail, fax, and phone. Plus, she now had the opportunity to build a new customer base in Minton and the surrounding area.

She would be in St. Louis on a semi-regular basis. It wouldn't be hard at all to get together with Zack. And he'd surely visit Marcus from time to time.

Wait a minute. With a pang, Sara remembered that Zack hadn't said anything about getting together again, regardless of who lived where. What a pipe dream she had built. She must have read more into those kisses than ever existed. Much more.

Chapter 9

Sara curled up in the wing chair, watching the tree lights blink off and on. She looked up when Aunt Esther came through the door, carrying two mugs and an insulated carafe.

"I made cocoa," she announced. "Let's just settle in tonight and enjoy our Christmas Eve." She lifted the carafe to pour the steaming drink, and a tentative knock sounded at the front door. "Would you answer that, dear?"

Sara pulled the door open to find a subdued Marcus on the doorstep. Zack stood behind him, avoiding Sara's gaze.

Sara opened the door farther, and the men stomped the snow from their feet before entering. Marcus took his time hanging up his coat, then turned to face Aunt Esther.

"Come on," Zack said, nudging his uncle with an elbow. "Speak your piece."

"All right," Marcus grumbled. "I suppose Christmas Eve is a good time to do this."

The two women stared at him without speaking.

Marcus shoved his hands in his pockets. "This nephew of mine has been talking to me like a Dutch uncle." He smiled briefly at his touch of humor, then sobered. "He's shown me I needed to look at this from God's point of view.

"I was wrong, Esther. Wrong to take the attitude I did and give you such grief." He fell silent, then flinched when Zack prodded him again. "You can relax," he said. "There won't be any lawsuit."

"Marcus!" Aunt Esther's face glowed with pleasure.

"I've always prided myself on being realistic. But maybe there's such a thing as being *too* pragmatic." The faintest of smiles touched his lined face. "After all, how practical did it seem for God's Son to be born in a manger?"

Aunt Esther smiled in return. "It wasn't exactly an orthodox approach, was it?"

Marcus sighed. "I. . .I guess there's room for your methods, too. I apologize for my stubborn blindness. I'd like it if we could be friends again."

"Oh, Marcus. What a lovely thing to say. Come, sit down. Sara, would you bring two more mugs?"

Sara glanced at Zack, who met her gaze and smiled. She felt lightheaded with relief. That smiling face looked more like the Zack she'd come to know and—

Don't even think it. She hurried to get the mugs.

They sat quietly, enjoying their cocoa. Aunt Esther broke the silence.

"I have something to say, too," she announced. "While my light display has been a great joy to me, I can see that perhaps my pride has been involved, as well.

"I've decided," she continued, "to make some changes. Starting tonight, I'll make sure the lights are off by nine o'clock. Most of the sightseers are gone by then, anyway. Will that help, Marcus?"

"I suppose," he muttered. "But the whole thing will only start up again next year."

"That's where you're mistaken."

Marcus stared in astonishment, and Zack turned to Sara for a clue. She could only shrug, mystified.

Aunt Esther went on. "I've decided the light display has served its purpose, so I am making plans for something different."

Marcus leaned forward with an unmistakable look of relief.

"A change," Aunt Esther continued, "won't hurt anything. In fact, it may bring back people who have already seen the lights several times." She sipped her cocoa, seemingly unaware of the other three sitting on the edges of their seats. "I've entered into negotiations with Mr. Brewster for the things I'll need."

"Brewster?" Marcus furrowed his brow. "That fellow with the farm just out of town?"

Aunt Esther nodded complacently and refilled his cup.

"What on earth could he provide that has anything to do with Christmas?"

Aunt Esther took another infuriatingly long sip. "Animals," she replied sweetly. "For the living crêche." Her face glowed with anticipation. "Picture it. Instead of all the gaudy lights—and I admit they might border on being gaudy—there will be a simple manger scene.

The high school shop class can build a stable, maybe a small inn adjoining it. There'll be a donkey, of course, and a cow, and sheep.

"I'm undecided about the goats," she continued, ignoring Marcus's stricken expression. "And I'm not sure whether to have one cow, or several."

Marcus's face worked convulsively, and Sara covered her mouth with both hands to stifle her laughter. She almost felt sorry for him, so obviously wondering which was worse—the multitude of lights or living, breathing animals sure to moo, bray, and bleat at all hours.

Aunt Esther went on. "The community theater director assures me there'll be plenty of volunteers to play the roles of Mary, Joseph, and the shepherds. The wise men, too," she added brightly. "The real challenge is getting the camels. Mr. Brewster has a friend who might—"

"Esther!" Marcus's anguished roar coincided with a most unladylike snort escaping Sara's lips. Aunt Esther stared in wounded dignity while Sara leaned back in her chair, arms dangling limply at her sides, shaking with helpless mirth.

Zack, too, succumbed to the laughter he'd tried to suppress, while Marcus sputtered about barnyard smells and prevailing winds.

Aunt Esther started to speak, but Zack intervened. "We had hoped we'd be able to resolve things in time to escort you to the candlelight service." He checked his watch. "There's just enough time to make it, if we hurry."

❦

"Wasn't that lovely? All those points of light flickering

while we sang 'Silent Night.'" Aunt Esther sighed happily.

Sara glanced at her great-aunt, sitting in the back-seat next to her former nemesis. She grinned, remembering how cozy they'd looked in the glow from their shared candle.

She lifted up a prayer that this might mark the beginning of a healed relationship for them. It would be nice to be sure her relationship with Zack had been healed, as well.

Marcus drove home alone after dropping off Sara and Aunt Esther. Zack remained, saying he would walk home later. Sara tilted her head and studied his profile. Silhouetted in the moonlight, he looked unusually somber.

"I'm glad you and Marcus are coming for Christmas dinner," she ventured.

"It was nice of your aunt to invite us. It looks like we can mark this one 'Case Closed,' doesn't it?" His light tone didn't match the solemn expression in his eyes. He focused his gaze on the house across the street and cleared his throat. "Heard much from your fiancé lately?"

Sara started. "What are you talking about?"

Zack continued to inspect the neighbor's house. "Geoffrey called the other night. I left a note on the table."

"I never saw it." Sara shook her head. "Our engagement ended months ago, but Geoffrey doesn't want to accept that. There's no reason I should call him."

A long moment passed. Zack turned and stared at her intently. "You're telling me you aren't engaged? To Geoffrey or anyone else?"

Sara nodded, then shook her head. "Yes. No. Yes, I'm not engaged." She heard Zack's slow intake of breath, felt his hands on either side of her waist.

"In that case. . ." His grip tightened and his hands slid behind her back, drawing her toward him. Their lips met, lightly at first, then with increasing pressure. Sara swayed when they finally drew apart.

Zack smiled, steadying her until she regained her footing. "I agree," he said softly. "There's something about those kisses that knocks me off balance, too." He brushed his lips against her cheek, then cupped her face in his hands.

"I'll see you tomorrow," he said tenderly.

❧

"Merry Christmas." Zack stood on the front porch, holding a large, cloth-covered basket.

Sara beamed at him. "What are you doing here so early?" she asked, trying to mask her delight. "Dinner won't be ready for hours."

"I came to help." He shifted the basket. "May I come in? This is getting heavy."

Sara waved him inside and eyed the basket curiously. "If you brought a turkey, you're a little late. It's already in the oven."

"Good. This is definitely not the main course." He set the basket on the floor and pulled back the cloth to reveal a yellow lab puppy with soulful brown eyes and a thumping tail.

"Oh!" Sara dropped to her knees. The puppy wriggled in delight and clambered into her lap. "Zack, he's precious! What's his name?"

"That's up to you. He's yours."

Sara gathered the little dog in her arms. "What a beautiful thing to do." She snuggled her cheek against the top of the puppy's head.

"Did I hear voices?" Aunt Esther bustled into the room and clapped her hands. "I see Mr. Brewster still had one available." She gave Zack a conspiratorial wink. "Bring him into the kitchen, Sara. I'll get some newspaper."

"Now that," Zack said, helping Sara to her feet, "is one practical woman."

❦

Aunt Esther swished her hands through the sudsy water and removed the stopper from the drain. "It's been a long time since I had a houseful of company at Christmas."

Sara gave a final swipe to the plate she was drying and handed it to Zack, who added it to the stack in the hutch. "That's the last one. It went quickly with everyone helping."

"Almost everyone, you mean." Zack nodded at Marcus, holding the puppy on his lap.

His uncle glared. "I helped by keeping him out of the way. You didn't want him underfoot, did you?" He turned his attention to Sara. "What are you going to call him? King? Rex?"

"I'm still working on that. It has to be a name that fits him."

Zack took the dishtowel from her and folded it over the rack. "How about a walk to help settle that incredible meal?"

"I'm busy watching the pup," Marcus answered.

Zack grinned. "I was talking to Sara. You can puppysit until we get back."

"Is that the same man who threatened a lawsuit?" Sara asked when they had gone a block.

"Amazing, isn't it?" Zack shook his head. "Shows you what a little change of heart can do. If only all conflicts could be resolved as easily as that one." Their fingers brushed together, and he took Sara's hand in his, twining his fingers through hers.

Sara gave him a sidelong glance. Did this mean things were back to the way they'd been before Geoffrey's phone call? And then there was the puppy. Would Zack go to the trouble of finding such a special gift if there were still distance between them?

They turned a corner, and she realized their meandering route had led them to Dogwood Lane. She tightened her fingers around Zack's. "I want to tell you something."

Zack returned the pressure. "A deep, dark secret?" he teased.

"Not exactly." She drew a deep breath. "What do you think of that place?" She pointed to the Olsen house.

Zack looked at the house, then at Sara. "There's a reason for this question, right?"

"I made an offer on it," she stated bluntly. "I've decided to move to Minton."

Zack blinked. "Permanently? What about your business?"

Sara tried to explain while they walked home. "My contact with my clients is mostly through E-mail and fax. I only see them in person when we discuss a project face-to-face or I deliver a finished product. Being here won't change that."

"What about St. Louis?"

"A few years ago, I thought it had everything I wanted. Now, I'm ready for a change. I'm tired of the rush, the need to constantly prove myself. This is where I want to be."

Zack seemed preoccupied the rest of the way to Aunt Esther's.

Sara stepped inside the front door and turned to Zack, a finger at her lips. She pointed to the recliners, where the two older people dozed. Gentle snores rippled through the room, one from Marcus and one from the golden ball of fur in his lap.

"What about calling him Sleepy?" Zack whispered.

"The dog, or your uncle?"

Zack's burst of laughter woke the three sleepers. "Sorry," he said, trying to keep a straight face.

Marcus yawned. "That walk didn't last nearly long enough."

"Would anyone care for more pie?" Aunt Esther offered.

"What I really want," Marcus said, "is to get into my slippers and my old flannel robe. Come on, Zachary, we don't want to wear out our welcome."

While Marcus pulled on his coat, Zack drew Sara into the kitchen. "Thanks for a memorable Christmas," he said, his breath warm against her cheek.

❦

The following morning, Aunt Esther pushed Sara

toward the door. "I've had enough of watching you mope around, listening for the phone," she said. "Get out, get some fresh air, and go spend some time with that young man of yours. Scoot."

Sara scooted.

It took several minutes to get an answer to her knock. Finally, Marcus opened the door.

"If you're looking for Zachary, he isn't here."

Sara smiled. "Where did he go, to Greer's? Maybe I can catch up with him."

"Not Greer's. St. Louis. He left before breakfast."

The smile froze on Sara's face. "What happened?" she managed to say through stiff lips. "When is he coming back?"

"He didn't say. Just said something about making a bad choice and took off."

Chapter 10

A re you sure this is what you want to do, dear?"
Sara set her bags at the foot of the stairs
and wrapped her great-aunt in a warm hug.
"I'm sorry for leaving on such short notice."

"Have you changed your mind about moving here?"

Sara drew a ragged breath. "No," she answered,
squaring her shoulders. "I'll be back. I'm going home to
pack and. . .I just need some time alone." Her gaze fell
on the puppy at her feet.

"Except for you, little guy," she murmured, settling
the pup into his travel crate. "It was nice of your neighbor to loan me this."

"Still no name for him?"

"Not yet," Sara said with a wry grin. "I want something that fits his personality, but so far all he's done is
look adorable and go through stacks of newspaper every
day."

She carried her luggage out to the rental car on the
driveway, then bent to kiss Aunt Esther's cheek. "I'll
come back as soon as I can."

❧

Sara taped down the last cardboard flap and stood, trying to ease the stiffness in her lower back. Neatly labeled boxes filled with her belongings littered the floor. Stuffed garbage bags and heaps of clothes destined for Goodwill completed the maze.

She stood, hands on her hips, surveying the chaos with weary satisfaction. As soon as she picked up the rented trailer, she could load it and leave. She'd paid an extra month's rent in lieu of giving thirty days' notice, which meant she'd have to cut corners for a while, but it would be worth it. Soon, she would be leaving all the things she disliked about the city and heading for the things she really wanted. . .with one notable exception.

The puppy scampered to a newspaper spread open in the corner, then ran to Sara and whimpered. She picked him up and cradled him in her arms. "That's what comes of not being practical," she whispered, rubbing her cheek against his silky fur. "It's best to forget the razzle-dazzle and settle for plain vanilla instead. It's bland, but it's predictable."

She ticked off a mental checklist, wanting to leave nothing undone. Her customers had been notified of her change of address. So had the post office. Her packing was finished. Good-byes had been said.

A knock at the door broke her concentration. "Probably the landlord," she told the puppy.

"Come in," she called.

The knock sounded again. Irritated, Sara set the puppy down and maneuvered through boxes and bags to get to the door. She flung it open.

"May I come in?" Zack asked, with unaccustomed uncertainty.

Sara stepped back, her stomach clenching in knots.

Zack closed the door behind him, and Sara took another step back. If she could keep her distance physically, maybe she could control the attraction that surged anew at the sight of him. She folded her arms protectively across her middle.

The puppy ran to inspect Zack's ankles, tail wagging madly. Zack bent to scratch the little dog's head, then straightened, seeming at a loss for words. "Have you found a name for him yet?"

"Noah." Sara nodded at a stack of newspapers. "Somehow, the idea of floods kept coming to mind."

A grin flickered across Zack's face, then faded. He shoved his hands in his pockets. "I owe you an apology," he said. "Again."

Sara raised a questioning eyebrow, saying nothing.

"I never should have left Minton without letting you know. I thought you'd still be there when I got back."

Sara swallowed. "I left the same day you did."

Zack's eyes widened. "I didn't know that. I called you the next day, and the day after that, but all your aunt would say was that you couldn't come to the phone. After awhile, I got the impression you didn't want to talk to me."

Sara rubbed her hands along her arms. "So how did you find out I was here?"

"I went back to Minton to see you and wound up having a long talk with Esther. She gave me your address. And here I am," he said, spreading his hands and stepping forward.

Sara sidestepped a garbage bag, putting it between them.

"Actually," Zack continued, pushing the bag aside with his foot, "I spent some time in Minton before I came back here. I even went by the Olsen place."

Sara corrected him silently. *You mean, my place.*

Zack tilted his head. "Would it be a huge disappointment if you found out you'd been outbid?"

Sara's jaw dropped. "Do you know. . ." She swallowed, trying to moisten a throat that had suddenly gone dry. "Do you know how much higher the other bid was?"

Zack nodded. "One dollar."

"A dollar?" Sara sputtered. "That can't be ethical. I can't believe Neta would do this!" She turned away from Zack, trying to control her emotions. "Do you happen to know who the other buyer is?"

"Uh-huh. Me."

Sara whirled and gaped at him. "You? *Why?*"

"Well," Zack said, "it seemed. . .practical." He narrowed the gap between them by one more step. "The reason I, in all my thoughtless, impetuous haste, left Minton so abruptly was to come back here to turn in my resignation."

Sara raked her fingers through her thick hair. "You lost me somewhere. I don't understand the connection."

"I went into law school as an idealist, ready to fight all the odds to see justice done. When I came out, full of fire and vinegar, I joined Schuyler, Temple, and

Wells. What I thought was my big break turned out to be just so much corporate paper pushing."

Sara shook her head. "So where does my house come in?"

"Spending time in Minton helped me rediscover something I was afraid I'd lost forever. Remember Mr. Greer and his land contract?" Zack inched nearer. "That's the kind of law God called me to—helping people who don't otherwise have an advocate. I finally realized the only solution was to leave the firm. I won't make as much money, but I won't need as much in a small-town setting. And I'll be able to sleep nights."

"And you've decided to do that in Minton?"

"Right. Tying up all the loose ends took longer than I thought, what with the holidays and all." He moved even closer.

Sara tried to back away, but this time the wall blocked her retreat.

Zack cupped Sara's shoulders in his hands. "After years of chasing the brass ring, I'm finally getting my life back on track. I'm ready to pursue the things that matter—serving God, serving people, raising a family. You know, that house is plenty big enough to start a family."

His hands slid behind her shoulders to pull her to him in a warm embrace. "I'd like to start with you," he whispered against her hair, his voice husky. Tilting her chin up, he studied her face intently. "Sara, will you marry me?"

Sara's practical mind went into high gear. It wasn't rational to enter a lifetime commitment based on such a short acquaintance. No one in her right mind would consider such a thing.

Smiling radiantly, she whispered, "Yes," and raised her lips to meet Zack's.

Zack stood holding the phone and shook his head. "No answer at Uncle Marcus's," he reported. "He may be at Esther's house. I gather the two of them have been spending a lot of time together. Making up for those lost years, I guess."

Sara raised an eyebrow. "They aren't arguing?"

"Apparently not." Zack punched in Aunt Esther's number. "Let's keep hoping for the best." He turned his attention back to the phone. "Hi, it's Zack. Is Uncle Marcus there?" He gave Sara a thumbs-up.

"No, I don't need to speak to him right now. I'm at Sara's. . . . Yes, I found her. Thanks for the directions. She has something she wants to tell you." He handed the phone to Sara.

"Aunt Esther?" Sara could hardly stand still while she shared the good news with her great-aunt.

"Is she telling Uncle Marcus?" Zack asked during a pause. "Are they taking it well?"

Sara nodded, her face shining. "Yes, to both questions. They sound excited. They're doing a lot of talking, but I can't make it all out. What? Say that again, Aunt Esther. I didn't quite hear you." Her face paled.

Zack leaned forward. "What? What is it?"

"Oh. Yes, I got it that time. Um, we'll see you in a day or two. We can talk about it then." She hung up the phone mechanically and stared into space.

"Sara?" Zack gripped her shoulders, his face a mask of concern. "What's going on? Is Uncle Marcus stirring up trouble again?"

"No." She took a deep breath. "That's not it at all. They seem to be getting along beautifully." The corners of her mouth twitched. "She said. . .she asked. . . she wanted to know how we'd feel about making it a double wedding."

Zack stared at her in disbelief, then Sara threw her arms around him and they collapsed on the couch in helpless laughter.

"One thing's for sure," Zack said when he finally caught his breath. "Life will never be dull with those two around. And," he added, stroking her hair gently, "I want you to know I'm truly sorry about taking off like that without letting you know."

Sara grinned and traced his cheek with her finger. "That's what comes of not being practical. It can get you in big trouble."

Zack chuckled. "And would you say we're acting in a practical manner now?" he murmured, rubbing his cheek against her hair.

"Nope. Not in the least."

"So?"

Sara tilted her glowing face and braced herself for one of those all-out, knock-your-socks-off, Fourth-of-July kisses.

"So maybe it's overrated."

CAROL COX

A native of Arizona, Carol's time is devoted to being a pastor's wife, home-school mom to her teen, active mom to her preschooler, church pianist, youth worker and 4-H leader. She loves anything that she can do with her family: reading, traveling, historical studies, and outdoor excursions. She is also open to new pursuits on her own including gardening, crafts, and the local historical society. She has had two historical novels published in Barbour Publishing's **Heartsong Presents** line *Journey Toward Home* and *The Measure of a Man*, and novellas in *Spring's Memory*, *Resolutions*, and *Forever Friends*. Her goals for writing inspirational romances are to encourage Christian readers with entertaining and uplifting stories and to pique the interests of non-Christians who might read her novels.

A Most Unwelcome Gift

by Pamela Griffin

Dedication

Dedicated to all of those believing God for
the restoration of their marriages. He is able.
And to the Lord, my continual source and
the restorer of all things,
Who makes ALL things new.
Also, with special thanks to Tracey B. and
to my parents, John and Arlene T.,
for their abundant help and support.
You guys are the best!

*"However, each one of you also must love his wife as he
loves himself, and the wife must respect her husband."*
EPHESIANS 5:33

Chapter 1

Tessa slammed the phone down, tears filling her brown eyes. Almost immediately it rang beneath her fingertips and she jumped, startled. Wary, yet hopeful, she picked up the receiver again and croaked out a stiff, "Hello?"

"Tessa? Tessa, dear, is that you?" Strains of "We Wish You a Merry Christmas" played in the background.

How ironic.

"Are you there, dear?"

Tessa blew out a soft, disappointed breath and tucked a long strand of straight, honey-blond hair behind one ear. "Yeah, Mom. It's me."

"What's wrong? You don't sound well."

Inwardly Tessa gave a sarcastic laugh. Well? Why shouldn't she "sound well"? Her storybook marriage was only crumbling to dust around her feet. . .

"Tessa?"

"Sorry, Mom. I was off in my own world for a minute there." Tessa wiped away a couple of stubborn tears with her fingers and angrily rubbed the moisture onto the leg of her jeans. She took a deep breath. "I'm fine. What's up?"

"Dad and I want to invite you and Jared to the cabin tomorrow night."

Tessa grimaced. "Sorry. Jared can't make it. Work. . . you know how it is."

"Doesn't he get Christmas vacation this year?"

Tessa's lips turned upward in a bitter smile. "Yes, but he's already made plans. He wants to get a jump on the Pearson commission," she explained for probably the tenth time that week. They had been invited to a number of parties already.

"I really wish you'd ask him for me, dear. It's very important. Please, tell him I said so."

Instantly Tessa straightened, her brow puckering into a worried frown. "Are you and Dad all right?"

"Well. . .there is a problem."

"It's about the doctor's appointment Dad had last week, isn't it?" Tessa closed her eyes with dread. "Oh, Mom, tell me it's not his heart again?"

"No, dear. Just please be here tomorrow—both of you. Plan to come at six o'clock for dinner. I have to go now. Your father is calling. Bye, honey."

"Mom. . .?"

Tessa blew out a breath. She lowered her hand and looked with frustration at the humming receiver, finally dropping it into its cradle. Barefoot, she rose from the white leather divan and padded over the lush carpet to the kitchen. She turned off the oven, shook the meat out of the pan back into the tin foil and stuck it in the freezer. Resigned, she retrieved a TV dinner for one from the stack and tossed it into the microwave, preparing herself for another lonely night.

Jared wouldn't appreciate this intrusion into his preconceived plans, but her mother had sounded so strange over the phone. *Besides, if he can stay for the office Christmas party—which he's always claimed a strong dislike for—then he can certainly spare his wife a few hours,* Tessa thought, clamping her lips together tightly.

Memory of the earlier phone call and the sound of sultry feminine laughter in the background, alarmingly close to Jared, pricked at Tessa's mind. Perhaps there was a reason her husband had developed a sudden liking for office get-togethers. . . .

An insistent "meow" at her feet shook Tessa from her disturbing thoughts, and she looked down at the silver tabby brushing against her ankles. "Well, Cinders, it looks like it's just you and me again. Time for another rollicking night at the Baker household."

Several strong "meows" followed, and Tessa reached up to the high shelf for the cat food. "Yeah, I know, I know," she muttered as she stuck the can under the opener and pressed the lever down. "Your love is conditional."

Was Jared's? Or did he even care anymore?

🐾

Dully, Tessa watched the stark branches of oaks, hickories, maples, and other trees fly past the passenger window. Cold drizzle fell, matching her mood, as the sports car sped up the incline. She hazarded a glance at her husband.

Jared looked straight ahead, one hand on the wheel. Laughing, he wrapped up the conversation with his boss on the cell phone, assuring the woman he would have the finalized plans for the high-rise office building on her desk next week at the latest. Finally, complaining of the possibility of weather interference producing a bad connection, Jared said his goodbyes, punched a button with his thumb, and set down the phone.

"Did you have a good time at the party last night?" Tessa asked, unable to keep the hurt note out of her voice.

Jared's hand gripped the wheel, and a nerve ticked near his clean-shaven jaw. He threw a suspicious glance her way. "Okay, Tessa. What's this all about?"

"About? I just asked a perfectly simple question."

"Yeah, right. The first time you've opened your mouth since we left home"— he shot a look at the digital clock on the console—"exactly forty-three minutes ago."

She shrugged and pulled her leather bag hanging from her shoulder close, clutching it on top of her lap in a defensive gesture. "It's a bit difficult to talk to a man with an instrument attached to his ear most of the time."

"I've been talking to Sharon for the past four and a half minutes. That still leaves thirty-eight and a half minutes unaccounted for."

Tessa blew out a frustrated breath. "Okay, okay, no need to get so analytical, Jared. I was just trying to make conversation. That's all."

"Which in and of itself is pretty remarkable."

"What's that supposed to mean?" Her brows drew

together in a frown.

He shot her another look, his sable eyes hard. "Take it any way you want it, Tessa. You usually do."

Too hurt to reply, she whipped her head around and stared back out the window. A hand-lettered wooden sign atop a weathered post with the words "Old Acorn Lane" raced past.

"Jared! We missed the turnoff."

The tires squealed as he slammed on the brakes, and Tessa was amazed that the car didn't skid on the wet pavement. He spun the wheel to the left and made a quick U-turn, narrowly missing the trunk of a thick oak, then steered the car onto the uneven dirt road—now slick with mud.

"Don't know why your parents decided to get a place in the middle of nowhere and can't live in town like normal people do. Makes it impossible for a person to find a place," Jared grumbled, as the car bumped up the long lane thickly flanked with towering trees, oaks being predominant.

Tessa kept her mouth shut, biting down on her tongue to keep from making a stinging reply. He'd know exactly where her parents lived if he didn't always have an excuse every time an occasion to visit came up. Since her parents had bought the cabin in the woods a little over a year ago, after Dad had had his heart attack, Tessa had been the only one to traverse these back roads. Except for the solitary time Jared had accompanied her last Christmas.

Christmas. . .did he even remember their fourth wedding anniversary was coming up in a matter of days?

Probably not. Unless a business memo was attached to his desk or a note was written in his book of appointments, he would have forgotten. Yet since only work-related items found their way to those honored spots, the chance of his remembering their special day was practically nonexistent.

Holding back a sigh, Tessa watched as her parents' cabin finally came into view. The simple building looked peaceful in the midst of the heavily forested area, with its lazy trail of white smoke uncurling from the stone chimney. Not for the first time, Tessa wished she and Jared could live in the country, with the Appalachian Mountains their only neighbors, instead of residing in the overcrowded city. Somewhere between here and her great-aunt Ginny's tourist cabin would be perfect.

Jared steered the shiny car beside her father's dirty black pickup truck and turned off the ignition. Tessa waited, but the door to the cabin didn't swing open, and no one came flying out with arms wide to greet them. Her brow wrinkled in concern as she got out of the car and hurriedly followed Jared to the covered porch.

Before she raised her hand to knock, Tessa couldn't prevent herself from muttering, "Let's not weigh Mom and Dad down with our problems. And I'd appreciate it if you'd throw a smile my way now and then—just to act as if you actually like me." She firmly knocked on the door then, leaving Jared no chance to respond to her acid words. However, she didn't miss the angry glint that lit his dark eyes.

Silence.

Tessa frowned and tried to see through the brown and gold plaid curtains of the window overlooking the porch. Incandescent yellow light glowed through the material, but she couldn't detect any movement from within. She knocked again.

After about a minute had elapsed, Jared shouldered her aside. "Let me try." But even his insistent banging didn't bring anyone to the door.

They looked at one another, puzzled; then Tessa put her hand to the knob and turned it. The door swung inward.

Warily, she entered, Jared close behind her.

Everything appeared normal. A huge stack of wood rested near the fireplace—a crackling fire greeting them. A folded newspaper lay near Dad's easy chair, and the usual scent of cinnamon potpourri mixed with the acrid-sweet smell of wood smoke and pine tantalized Tessa's nostrils. In the corner stood a small, live tree decorated with old-fashioned glass bulbs and tinsel, with wrapped gifts underneath. Gaily decorated boughs and wreaths flecked with red velvet bows hung over the mantel and on the walls.

However, her parents were nowhere in sight.

Confused, Tessa pushed open the swinging door to the kitchen. The small blue-and-cream-colored room was sparkling clean. Too clean. No pots with delectable foods simmered on the gas burners of the stove, and the oven was ice cold.

"Jared. . .?" She turned to look at him, her puzzlement evolving into worry. "It's not like Mom not to have dinner started by now. We're late as it is."

He frowned and shot a glance at his gold watch. "I'll check outside at the back. You look in the rest of the house."

Tessa headed for her parents' bedroom. The door stood open, revealing a perfectly made bed covered with a colorful quilt in the wedding ring design her mother had pieced together before she married. Everything else stood neatly in its place.

Heart thudding against her chest, Tessa rushed to the adjoining bathroom. Only gleaming porcelain, pine green rugs, and a shower curtain decorated with tiny fish swimming through waving seaweed greeted her.

She stepped into the hall and had just put her hand on the glass knob of the guest bedroom, when Jared came in the back door, noisily wiping his feet on the mat. She hurried to him.

"Well?"

He shrugged, looking as confused as she felt. "Nothing."

"But Dad's truck is here. Where could they be?"

All of a sudden a motor revved up, then another, followed by the sound of tires swiftly crunching on small wet rocks.

Jared's eyes widened. "My car! I'd know the sound of that engine anywhere," he yelled as he bolted for the front door and swung it open, with Tessa close behind him.

Dumbfounded, they both came to a stop on the porch and watched as the red taillights of her father's pickup truck and Jared's sports car bounced down the lane through the icy drizzle.

"What the. . .?" Jared's voice trailed off as he stared at the two departing vehicles—now moving blobs of blue and black in the waning light. As if awakening from a dream, he sprang into action and bounded from the steps to take off after them—right onto a patch of mud. His feet flew up as he landed with a hard thud on his bottom.

"Jared, are you all right?" Tessa managed. She swallowed a laugh as she looked down at her city-boy husband in his brushed flannel gray slacks and leather loafers, sprawled out and sitting on the cold ground, blinking up like a confused owl.

"Call the police! Someone stole our car—and your dad's truck, too!"

At last the gravity of the situation fully dawned on Tessa. She hurried to the phone and snatched up the receiver. It came up easily. Too easily. The springy cord usually attached to the mouthpiece wasn't there; nor was it connected to the cradle of the phone.

Eyes widening, she stared down at the device in her hand, puzzled, then looked toward her husband, who painfully made his way up the porch stairs and through the open front door. "Uh, Jared? The cord is missing."

"What do you mean 'the cord is missing'?" he growled, taking the few steps toward her and snatching the disabled instrument from her hand.

He stared down at it and slowly shook his head, his eyes turning her way again. "The cord is missing."

"I know," Tessa calmly replied. "That's what I said."

Jared pushed a frustrated hand through his dark hair. "Is this some kind of practical joke? What's going on here?"

Tessa shook her head, giving a slight shrug of her shoulders. "I'm just as much in the dark as you are."

Brows drawn together in a frown, Jared turned away from her and put his hands on his slim hips. "Okay, everybody out!" he yelled. "Joke's over!"

The soft ticking of the mantel clock and the crackling fire were the only sounds in the room.

"I'm not kidding! This isn't funny anymore."

Tessa bit her lip and walked up behind him, putting a hand to his broad back. "Jared. . .? This is getting really creepy, and I'm starting to get scared."

He turned her way and looped a strong supportive arm around her waist. "I'm sure there's a logical explanation for everything, Hon." Suddenly he snapped his fingers and beamed a smile her way. "My cell phone."

He reached for where he kept the device in his inside jacket pocket—to find it empty. Groaning, he shook his head. "I must have left it in the car."

"What are we going to do?" Tessa asked, her horrified voice barely above a whisper. "Do you think something awful has happened to Mom and Dad? Maybe whoever took the car and truck harmed them, then ran away." Her eyes widened, and she swallowed hard. "The spare bedroom. I didn't get a chance to check there earlier."

He frowned. "I'll go with you."

Stealthily they walked to the door of the guest room, Tessa right on her husband's heels. She kept a tenacious hold on his muscular upper arm, her heart racing. Jared shot an unreadable look her way before opening the door.

The old-fashioned room was in perfect order, the double bed made—a small, white folded sack sitting on the end.

Tessa let out a relieved breath, not realizing she'd been holding it. Working up her courage, she peeked into the main bathroom, which also opened out onto the hall. The room was dark and empty.

Turning to her husband, she frowned. "What do we do now?"

"Where's the nearest neighbor?"

"I don't know. A couple of miles off the main road, I guess. I know there's a five and dime several miles north of here, though—off the highway."

Jared drew a whistling breath through his teeth. "Great. Just great. Your parents would have to live out in the boondocks!" He swiped a hand through his hair to the back of his neck. "I guess I'll just have to walk down the lane until I hit the main road, and hope a car comes by."

"In those shoes?" Tessa said, with an incredulous lift of her eyebrows. "And in this weather? Besides, it's dark now, and I don't want to be left here alone. And I can't walk in these." She cast a rueful glance at her high-heeled, fur-lined boots. They were nice for show, but not very practical, otherwise.

"Well, then, what do you suggest we do?" Jared bit out.

Tessa shook her head helplessly. "I don't know. I can't make any sense out of this. It's all too crazy. Why would Mom and Dad invite us up here for dinner and then not be here when we showed up? And what happened to their phone? And who would steal both cars?" She voiced the questions buzzing around like maddening flies inside her mind.

Slowly she exhaled a loud breath. "I'm going to make a cup of hot tea or coffee or something to help me calm down so I can think straight. Want anything?"

Lips narrowed, Jared only gave a curt shake of his head.

Tessa went to the kitchen. She filled the kettle with water then put the pot on the burner and turned up the flame. As she took a ceramic mug from the high shelf, Jared walked in. He pulled out a chair next to the kitchen table and sank onto it.

Tessa relaxed a bit, grateful for his presence. Right now she needed his company more than ever. "Likely Mom and Dad took a walk and lost track of time—or got caught in the rain and are waiting it out somewhere dry."

"That still doesn't explain what happened to the car, the truck, or the phone."

Tessa shrugged, her brow wrinkling into a frown again.

"Think your mom has any of those oatmeal cookies like the ones she made last Christmas?" Jared muttered. "I haven't eaten anything since breakfast."

"I'll check."

Tessa opened the well-stocked freezer. The red tin of cookies sat on the rack, as did something else: an envelope addressed to her and Jared in her mother's handwriting.

Eyes widening, Tessa plucked the green paper rectangle from the ice tray and brushed away the frost. "Jared?"

"Hmmm?"

"I think I may have solved the mystery," she said, her voice trembling as she tore open the gummed flap and withdrew a Christmas card. A dove holding an olive branch covered the front. Instantly Jared was at her side.

"What are you talking about?"

Tessa ignored him and silently read the note:

My Dears,

I told Tessa over the phone that there was a problem, and there is. You.

Dad and I know you love each other, but somehow you've forgotten what's really important in life, and your priorities have gotten all out of kilter. You must think us fools if you didn't suspect we knew all along that you've been having marital problems this past year. Now, I know it's not my place to interfere, but on your wedding day, when I heard the minister say, "What God has joined together let no man put asunder," I took it to heart. And I won't let you two "put your marriage asunder" without a fight.

This is the only way I could think of to get you two alone and together without any outside interference. Your car is fine, and we'll take care of Cinders. Enjoy the coming week, treat the cabin as if it were your own, and please take this gift in the spirit it was intended.

The freezer and refrigerator are fully stocked, and we've left plenty of firewood. Please tell Jared not to get any foolish ideas about walking down to the main road to find a phone, though. Sleet is forecast tomorrow, with the possibility of snow.

Oh, and in case you're worried, we're fine. We're spending Christmas week with Aunt Ginny. We'll see you on New Year's Day.

Happy Anniversary and Merry Christmas!

Love,
Mom

Chapter 2

Tessa had the crazy desire to laugh hysterically and nearly choked, trying to stem the fierce tidal wave of emotion. Tears filled her eyes as she turned to Jared, who looked at her with a concerned expression on his handsome face. His worry was warranted. She felt like she might crack any moment.

"Tessa?"

"All this—" She swung her hand around the kitchen and shook her head still unable to believe the lengths to which her parents had gone to "help" them. "It seems all this is my parents' idea of getting us alone for a romantic getaway."

His brows drew together in a frown. "What do you mean?"

"Just what I said. They're responsible for the phone being out of order, and apparently they've also taken your car—"

"What did they do—hot-wire it?" he interrupted. "I've got the keys."

"Well. . .uh. . .remember last May when you were on a business trip and I borrowed your car while mine was in the shop?" He nodded, and she offered a faltering smile. "I locked myself out and had to call a locksmith. After that I made a spare set of keys for both cars and the apartment and gave them to Mom. . ."

Jared's mouth narrowed. "Go on."

She shrugged. "Mom wrote that this is their gift to us. She must've hidden the card in the freezer, not wanting to risk the chance we'd spot it right away." Her smile grew wider. "Otherwise we might have caught them red-handed and spoiled their little gift."

"Some gift!" Jared exploded. He turned on his heel and took a few steps from her, running a hand through his damp hair. "Are your parents completely loco? I left all my work at home. I have plans to write up, blueprints to look over. . . Besides, I told Sharon I'd meet her at the site the day after Christmas. I don't need this kind of hassle right now, Tessa."

Any mirth lingering inside Tessa quickly died, as the pain of his words lanced her heart. "I completely agree, Jared. This is a most unwelcome gift, but there's nothing we can do about it now. We're stuck here for a week. So we might as well make the best of it."

"A *week?*" He shook his head and frowned. "No. For tonight—okay. But tomorrow I'm heading for the nearest phone, even if I have to slide down that muddy lane, barefoot. I didn't get to be tops in my field by sitting on my hands and letting others get a jump on me." He stormed from the room, slamming the swinging door against the wall.

"No, you didn't, did you, Jared?" Tessa replied under her breath to the door still madly swinging to and fro.

"Instead you sacrificed our relationship to climb your corporate ladder."

The teapot began to whistle, and Tessa quickly took it off the heat, grateful for the momentary diversion.

A small part of her appreciated her parents' gift. But the logical part of her mind couldn't help but feel their efforts had been wasted. Tessa was certain Jared blamed her for their present set of circumstances. Would he even listen if she tried to share with him what had been bothering her all these months?

Tessa's lips firmed with determination. Another opportunity might not present itself in the near future. Whatever her husband's reaction might be, the time had come for them to talk.

She hesitated. But first she should probably make him dinner. Better to feed his stomach before delving into serious issues. Food to tame the savage beast.

A faint smile tipped her lips. Jared could hardly be called savage, but he *was* irritable when hungry. More like a grouchy Doberman without teeth. The picture in her mind made her chuckle wryly as she set about preparing dinner.

❦

Tessa found an untouched turkey casserole her mother had previously baked—obviously for them—and popped it into the preheated oven. Rolling up her sleeves, she again scanned the contents of the refrigerator, then grabbed the jug of milk, poured the liquid into two tall glasses, and headed for the den.

Jared sat in the easy chair in front of the fire—glaring into it and still wearing his wet jacket.

Tessa inwardly sighed. "Dinner will be ready in about twenty more minutes. I brought you something to drink while we wait."

His gaze swung her way, and one black brow sailed upward in incredulity. The horrified look he gave her was almost comical.

"Milk?"

"It was either that or cola. It's diet, though."

"Of course it is," Jared muttered, taking the milk from her outstretched hand. He took a swallow then hastily set it on the nearby coffee table, a grimace covering his face. "Yuck! I can't believe I liked that stuff as a kid."

"It's skim milk. Mom's on a bit of a diet right now."

"Oh, great! I can't wait to see what other goodies she's lined up for us."

Choosing to ignore his sarcasm, Tessa sank onto the adjoining sofa and stared into the dancing fire, cradling her cold glass. A log cracked and flames spit. Other than that they slipped into uneasy silence.

With each movement of the minute hand on the mantel clock, Tessa grew more and more tense. Her emotions began to simmer and boil like a heating kettle as she replayed scenes from the past year over and over in her mind.

"Jared, what's wrong with us?" Tessa blurted after ten empty minutes had passed. All intentions of waiting until after dinner for their talk fled.

He turned his head her way, his eyes blank. "What?"

She sighed. "I asked you 'what's wrong with us?' "

A look of irritation covered his features. "Tessa, I

don't want to go down this road right now."

"You never do." She shot to her feet and began to pace, unable to contain her feelings any longer. "But I think we should. We really need to talk, Jared. We've needed to talk for some time now."

He blew out a lengthy breath. Slowly shaking his head, he turned to look back into the fire.

Tessa rapidly covered the distance between them, her heels tapping a staccato on the wooden floor. She came to a stop in front of him and planted her hands on her hips.

"Look at me, Jared! I'm your wife. You once thought me attractive and wanted to spend time with me. . . ." Her voice trailed away to nothing as his sober gaze turned her way, dropped, and roamed over her slim form, before returning to her face. A long-buried flame kindled in his dark eyes.

"I still do," he said quietly after a few electric moments had passed.

Tessa's heart did a somersault, but she was too upset to give heed to the warm tingles spreading throughout her body.

"Then why don't you?" she implored. "You spend countless hours at the office, and then—when you do choose to come home—you close yourself off in your study, and I barely get a peek at you. Or you come home so late that I've already gone to bed. You've even started leaving the house before I wake up and eating breakfast out. And now that we finally have a rare opportunity to be alone, you sit there and sulk like a little boy who didn't get his way."

A nerve ticked near his jaw. "Getting to the top—and staying there—requires some sacrifices. You know that, Tessa."

"Our marriage, for instance?"

"I didn't say that."

"You didn't have to."

She crossed her arms against her soft pink angora sweater. "Tell me, Jared. Do these 'sacrifices' you mention include entertaining your boss at office parties?" She kept her tone level, though she really wanted to scream the accusation at him.

His eyes narrowed, the expression in them now guarded. "What are you talking about?"

Tessa looked at him steadily, her face grim, though a burning ache had formed in the center of her chest. Strange, since she suddenly felt like a block of ice.

"I noticed the lipstick smudge on your collar last night—dark red—definitely not my color, Jared. More of something a brunette would wear, I think. Like Sharon."

He exhaled loudly. "Trust you to immediately suspect me of foul play! One of the secretaries had a little too much to drink and stumbled onto my lap. Her head fell against my shoulder when it happened. It was all perfectly innocent—"

"And that's another thing," Tessa interrupted, her chin going up into the air as she stared him down. "Since when did you develop a sudden liking for office Christmas parties?"

"A little 'P. R.' never hurt anyone," he ground out between clenched teeth. "There were several clients there, as well."

"Oh, how convenient," she shot back. "But the truth is any excuse will do as long as you don't have to go home to the wife. Right, Jared?"

Too late, she realized she'd pushed him too far.

Grabbing her wrist, Jared gave a hard yank, and Tessa fell awkwardly across his lap, stunned. The smell of his spicy aftershave pervaded her senses, and she felt herself slipping into an emotion-filled whirlpool— long withheld feelings beginning to surface and slowly spin out of control.

His hands gripped her upper arms, his serious face now only inches away. His dark eyes seemed to burn into hers, and she forgot how to breathe.

"Just what do you want from me, Tessa?" he rasped. "Proof I still want you and need you? Will that make you happy?"

His dark eyes intently scanned her face then he lowered his gaze to her parted mouth. All the anger drained away from his features as suddenly as it had come.

"Well, I do," he admitted hoarsely. "Maybe too much. . ." His warm breath fanned her cheek as he slowly lowered his head. "Way too much," he whispered against her mouth.

Dazed, Tessa lay frozen in his arms, the present not fully registering. In past months, Jared had only given her a cool kiss on the cheek or an unsatisfactory peck on the lips for "hello" and "good-bye." She hadn't been kissed like this in a long time. A very long time.

A glowing ember burst into flame deep inside her,

completely melting any ice left. She twined her fingers in his silky hair, eagerly returning his warm kiss. He groaned and grabbed her jeans-clad legs, sliding her closer to him, his other hand moving down her back.

Somewhere in the distance a shrill beeping invaded her mind. Tessa tried to ignore the noise and clutched Jared's shoulders, wishing they could remain like this forever, wishing the sound would go away, wishing the world would just leave them alone. . . .

Her eyes flew open and she pushed hard against his chest, breaking the kiss. "The casserole," she said, voice hoarse. "I need to get it out of the oven before it burns."

Jared allowed her to rise from his lap, though he loosely clasped her forearm as though unwilling to let her go yet. His gaze never once broke contact with hers. Tessa awkwardly took a few steps backward—Jared's hand sliding down her arm to her wrist and then to her hand and fingertips, before dropping away.

She turned and moved toward the kitchen, feeling his stare on her the whole time. Her legs felt as wobbly as gelatin, and her arm and hand tingled from the trail of fire his fingers had produced. She swallowed but her throat was dry.

Tessa went through the swinging door, punched the button of the insistent timer, and turned off the oven. Leaning her forehead against the flowered wallpaper, she closed her eyes.

Well, that definitely was one area she and Jared didn't have a problem with. Yet there was so much more to marriage than just the physical. So much more. . .

As she spooned out creamy noodles and turkey mixed with vegetables onto blue stoneware plates, Tessa's annoyance that the timer had interrupted them turned to gratitude. If they were going to get those difficult areas in their marriage worked out, she couldn't let her mind get clouded with her husband's nearness. And Tessa knew from past experience that once she melted into Jared's arms she would forget everything—and later probably wouldn't broach any unpleasant subjects so as not to shatter the fragile intimacy between them. And certainly her closemouthed husband wouldn't introduce any painful topics; of that Tessa was sure.

No, they needed to talk—which meant she needed to keep a clear head. And keep her distance.

She took the plates to the den, her firm resolve weakening when Jared's mesmerizing gaze locked with hers. He'd taken off his jacket and now sat on one end of the couch in front of the fire. His dark blue patterned sweater enhanced his broad shoulders and chest. One arm lay casually draped along the back of the sofa. Playing racquetball with the guys from work several times a week had certainly kept up his fine physique.

Hurriedly Tessa set the plates on the coffee table in front of him with a loud clatter and grabbed up his half-full glass.

"I'll get you some more milk."

She swung around and escaped to the kitchen, almost sloshing the liquid out of the glass. Once she was safely behind the door, she set the milk down and sank onto a chair.

"Oh, Lord," she moaned, propping her elbows on the table and lowering her head into her hands, while smoothing down the top of her tousled hair. "Give me the strength I need so I won't buckle under—so that Jared and I can work things out first. Please. And help me know what to say to him."

Tessa felt a measure of peace. She was ashamed to realize this was the first time she'd sought the Lord in months. But regardless, she felt God had heard her plea for help.

Tessa poured about a half cup more milk into Jared's glass. Then, holding the bluish-white drink in front of her like a shield, she took a deep breath for courage and re-entered the den.

Chapter 3

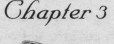

Warily, as though approaching a sleeping tiger, Tessa walked across the room and handed Jared his milk. He took it and set it on the coffee table, next to his untouched plate. She backed up a few steps and sat a couple of feet away from him on the sofa, ignoring his raised brow. Looking down at the coffee table, she shot to her feet again.

"Oops! Forgot the forks and napkins."

"Tessa. . ." Jared grasped her below the elbow, stopping her mid-flight. Slowly, he pulled her down beside him. "I'm really not all that hungry. Relax. . . ."

She swallowed hard as he moved to nuzzle her neck. "But you said you hadn't eaten since breakfast." Was that funny croak her voice?

"I lost my appetite."

Tessa closed her eyes at his low words and nervously flicked her long hair behind one ear. *Lord, help me here.*

Intending to broach another subject, she moved away from his warm lips and faced him with a half smile. Instantly she saw her mistake. The look in his dark eyes practically melted her. Feeling her traitorous body lean toward his, she scooted to the opposite end of the couch, putting distance between them again.

His brows slanted into a frown. "What's wrong, Tessa? I thought you wanted to be with me."

"I did," she squeaked, then cleared her throat and tried again. "I do. But first I think it's important that we resolve some issues in our lives."

Jared inhaled deeply then blew out a harsh breath. Putting his hands up as though in surrender, he fell back against the cushion. "All right, okay, fine. We'll talk."

He took a swig of milk, grimaced, and then faced her. "Now, just exactly what issues do you think need to be resolved? My attendance at the office Christmas party? At least I called you and told you I wouldn't be home for dinner."

Her mouth dropped open and she stared. "You really have to ask that question? This isn't just about the party, Jared. Think about it for a minute. I can count on one hand how many evenings we've spent alone the last five months—since you received that stupid Merriweather commission and got promoted. We never do anything together anymore. We don't even go to church together like we used to."

A nerve jumped in his cheek. "That 'stupid Merriweather commission' is what's been putting designer clothes on your back and got you that little blue sports car you wanted—"

"And I'd trade it all in a heartbeat, if it meant I could have a week alone here with you," she interrupted softly.

He shook his head in frustration. "I can't stay, Tessa. I'm leaving in the morning. I've got to if I want to get the new plans on Sharon's desk by January second. I know life is hectic right now, but things won't always be like this."

"Oh, really?" Tessa's voice increased a couple of notches, despite her desire to remain calm. "And when will that wondrous day be, Jared? When I have to put color on my hair and am too old to bear children?"

She felt the telltale burning in the bridge of her nose, signaling tears, but ignored it and went on. "I want us to try again, Jared. But first I want us to work on building our relationship. We were once so happy."

He rocketed to his feet and strode to the window, rubbing an unsteady hand along the back of his neck. Almost immediately he turned on his heel, his brown eyes pained.

"Just what is it you want from me, Tessa?" he implored. "God knows I do my best. But you're never satisfied. This is an important time in my career. You know my dream is to one day operate my own architectural firm. But first I have to establish myself in the business, make a few contacts—but do I get any support from my wife? No way! She's too busy hiding at home, feeling sorry for herself. . .and making me feel bad for things that can't be helped."

Tessa averted her eyes, a small thread of guilt worming its way through her.

"You claim you want time with me, Tessa. But whenever I asked you to come with me to an office function, you refused to go—which is one reason I stopped asking."

Tessa's fingernails dug into the upholstery. "That's not fair. You know I don't like those parties. I tried going with you once—remember the man with the octopus arms who followed me all over the grounds at the summer picnic? There's always alcohol at those get-togethers and that bothers me."

"For crying out loud! You don't have to drink. I don't."

"You did last night," she shot back.

His eyes narrowed. "Yeah, maybe I did have a couple. . . . I'm not used to having my wife slam the phone down in my ear."

"But I am used to my husband coming up with one excuse after another of why he won't be home at night," Tessa said, her fervent words sounding strange to her own ears, as they echoed off the walls of the cozy room.

Jared continued to stare at her, his brown eyes hard. Muttering something under his breath, he whipped around and wrenched open the front door. It slammed shut behind him, jarring loose one of the red ornaments in a wreath on the wall. The shiny bulb fell to the floor, shattering into hundreds of shard-like fragments.

So much like my marriage, Tessa thought, tears trickling down her cheeks. She ran to her parents' bedroom, slammed the door, and locked it.

❦

Jared took three swift steps off the covered porch, not sure where he was going and not really caring. His furious stride came to a sudden halt as icy droplets hit his head and shoulders. He looked up and scowled at the dark sky.

Brilliant move, Baker. Now what?

A freezing wet missile hit him in the eye, and he impatiently brushed it away. Shivering without his warm fur-lined jacket, he tucked his hands under his armpits and relented enough to move onto the covered porch. But what he really wished he could do was jump in his car and go for a drive like he usually did when they fought.

His mouth thinned. He wouldn't go inside. No way. Tessa was being obstinate. Completely pigheaded. There was no reasoning with her when she was like this. He was only doing what was best for both of them. And that meant doing what he could to get ahead in his career. One day she would see that and thank him.

Jared stamped his feet for warmth and briskly rubbed his hands together then blew on them. Remembering the tears in her eyes, he frowned. He hated it when she cried. It made him feel like a royal jerk.

Okay, so maybe it hadn't been such a great idea to do the party thing last night. He hadn't enjoyed himself that much anyway. Only good thing about it had been the tasty spread. And what would it hurt to share breakfast with her once in awhile? The Pancake House, for all its great food, wasn't as good as Tessa's ham and tomato omelets with two kinds of cheese. He'd only eaten at the restaurant because it was directly across the street from the firm. And those crispy golden hash browns she cooked were out of this world. . . .

Terrific. Now he was hungry.

Jared eyed the door, grudgingly swallowed his pride—or what pride a man could possess while standing in freezing drizzle without a coat—and turned the knob.

"Tessa?"

The room was empty.

He eyed his plate of untouched food with deep longing, sighed, and went in search of his wife.

Muffled sobs came from behind her parents' bedroom door.

"Tessa?" He tried the handle. The door was locked. "Tessa, open the door."

The crying trailed away, sniffles taking its place, but the door didn't budge.

"Tessa?"

"Go away, Jared. I don't want to talk to you right now." Her soft but firm voice clearly reached him through the thick layer of wood.

Mouth thinning, Jared tried the door once more then gave up. He was hungry, and he'd tried to make amends. But *now* she didn't want to talk. Women!

He grabbed a fork from the kitchen then returned to his cold food, took a couple of halfhearted bites and stared at the rest. Losing interest, he wrapped up the leftovers and stuck them in the fridge. He seized a thick blanket and pillow from the hall closet and hurried back to the warmth of the fire. Wrapping the blanket around him, he rubbed his hair dry with one corner of the soft wool and sat, glum, staring into the flames.

❦

Tessa woke the next morning, feeling as if a truck had run over her—repeatedly. Groaning, she divested herself of her uncomfortable clothes, then padded into the bathroom and turned on the taps to the shower. She stepped inside the tub, pulled the curtain closed, and adjusted the spray until it steamed.

Closing her eyes, she let the water gush over her body, erasing all tension from the previous evening. Tears mixed with the hot water, and she briskly began to shampoo her hair, as if by doing so she could erase all memory of last night from her mind.

Jared would be gone by now, she dully thought as she rinsed her hair. *Maybe it's better this way.*

With an angry twist of her wrist, Tessa turned off the faucets and stepped out of the tub. She dried off with a long coarse towel, until she was certain she'd taken off a layer of skin along with the droplets of water, then wrapped and tucked the terry cloth around her rosy body.

She blinked in shock. She had no clean clothes!

Moaning, Tessa looked toward the floor where her wrinkled jeans, sweater, and under-things lay. What was she supposed to do—put them back on?

The thought wasn't appealing, and she headed for her parents' walk-in closet, deciding she would borrow something while she washed her things. Again she blinked. Where were all of Mom's winter clothes? Her mother must have taken them with her to Aunt Ginny's. Great. Now what?

She spotted a beige wool skirt hanging in a dark corner with a matching patterned sweater and grabbed it. It was four sizes too big for her. Of course. Nothing she wore of her mother's would fit her size eight frame.

Her eyes flicked to her father's side of the closet and she grinned. Dad's old robe! It would swallow her up, but at least the belt could be cinched around her waist. Thankful her dad rarely parted with anything, Tessa wrapped it around her and rolled up the frayed sleeves a couple of times until they hit her wrists. She glanced in the full-length mirror on the door.

Wet-darkened hair hung in snarls past her shoulders, almost to her waist. With her unmade face, she looked like a little girl in the huge robe, the light freckles on her nose doing nothing to detract from the picture.

Lovely.

Tessa stuck out her tongue at the image then swung the door closed. Picking up a large-toothed comb, she ran it through her hair, breaking up the tangles. No blow dryer, either.

Sighing, she scooped up her dirty clothes and wet towel, unlocked the door, and opened it. Padding barefoot down the hall, she tried vainly not to stumble on the trailing material. She stopped short when she entered the den, almost dropping the small bundle of clothes in shock.

Hands in his pockets, his back to her, Jared stood at the window and stared at the falling sleet.

Tessa involuntarily gasped, and he turned her way.

Chapter 4

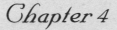

I thought you'd be gone by now." Tessa clutched the bundle of clothes tighter to her breast, heart skipping a beat at the unreadable look in Jared's eyes. She felt strangely shy and vulnerable, standing in her dad's robe—though it did cover every inch of her and then some.

"Disappointed?"

"You know better than to ask that, Jared. I'm the one who wanted you to stay. Remember?"

He gave a curt nod, his dark gaze taking full inventory of her attire. "The sleet stopped me...you look cute. Like a little girl dressed up in her mother's clothes."

Flustered, Tessa looked down. "One thing Mom forgot was our need of clean things. This is Dad's old robe," she added, moving to the kitchen and pushing open the swinging door. A part of her mind registered the fact that the broken ornament had been swept up and the uneaten turkey casserole was nowhere in sight. "Have you had breakfast yet?" she threw over her shoulder.

"I had a sandwich. It's past noon, Tessa."

She whirled to face him and almost tripped on the

hem of the robe. "You're kidding. I slept that long?"

He nodded, and she shook her head in disbelief, letting the door swing shut. How could she have slept so long? She hadn't even taken anything last night. . . .

Tessa went to the corner of the room and pulled open the wooden accordion door that secreted her mother's washer and dryer in a small storage closet. Propping open the lid of the washer, she then tried to pour detergent into the cup, but her long sleeves kept coming undone and getting in the way.

"Here, let me do that."

At the suddenness of Jared's low words directly behind her, Tessa spun around in shock, again catching her foot in the folds of material—but this time she lost her balance and pitched forward. Jared closed the short distance between them, catching her against his chest. The plastic cup of liquid soap went splattering to the linoleum floor, a gooey, blue mess.

Her cheek against the rough material of Jared's sweater, Tessa swallowed hard and closed her eyes, allowing herself a few blissful moments next to his comforting, solid warmth, before she must force herself to move away.

"Thanks. I better wash my clothes now, so I can get out of this getup before I do myself serious bodily injury," she joked, though her voice came out strained.

"Tessa. . ." His arms tightened around her, not letting her go. "I'm sorry. That's what I wanted to tell you last night. I was pretty upset by what your parents had done, but I shouldn't have taken it out on you. I hate it when I say things to hurt you and make you cry."

She lifted her head then, her heart doing double-time at the soft look in his eyes. "I'm sorry too, Jared. We both said some pretty cutting things to one another. And I'm sorry I locked you out, but I was just so upset—"

"Shhh." He laid a finger across her mouth then bent his head. His lips brushed hers for a few heart-stopping seconds before he straightened and grinned. "Apology accepted. Now go dry your hair before you catch cold."

"Can't. No blow dryer. They must have taken it with them."

"Then go sit in front of the fire until it dries."

"The laundry—"

"I'll take care of the laundry and the spilled detergent." Uncertain, she tilted her head. "Are you sure?"

"You still wash everything in cold, right?"

She nodded.

"I washed my things early this morning. So I've had experience using your mom's washer and dryer," Jared continued in a matter-of-fact tone.

But Tessa still wasn't thoroughly convinced. He'd never washed her clothes—well, maybe once, during their first year of marriage. She had ended up giving the dress to Goodwill, hoping the talented people who worked for that organization could somehow fix it. She'd thought about bleaching the dress back to ivory, but was afraid she would do it worse damage.

Her brows drew together in a troubled frown. "Jared, I'm not sure. . ."

Putting his hands to her shoulders, he turned her to the door and playfully swatted her backside. "Go on with ye, wench! The laird of the castle will take care of the wifely duties this time 'round."

Tessa turned and gave him a hesitant smile. "Well, uh, okay. Only this time don't wash your black socks with my clothes—even though I know you said it was an accident last time and that sock just somehow managed to slip in. And definitely use cold water only. . . ."

Not looking at her, Jared nodded, waving her away with one hand. Tessa watched from afar as he set the dials. Only then did she head toward the den.

Noticing a rumpled blanket on the couch, she folded it and returned the cover and pillow to the linen closet. She felt bad that she'd forced Jared to sleep on the couch by keeping her parents' bedroom door locked all night. Idly she wondered why he hadn't used the guest room instead. Probably because of the fire in the den. The nights were cold when you didn't have someone to snuggle up to. How well she knew.

Sighing, Tessa sank to the plush rug next to the hearth and finger-combed her wet hair. Jared did seem different today—as though he really wanted to work things out with her. Had their heated talk last night opened his eyes? Hope flickered anew. Maybe her mom's idea would work after all. . . .

Jared reappeared through the swinging door, threw a wink Tessa's way then headed down the hall. Puzzled, she watched him enter her parents' room. Within minutes he returned, comb in hand. Tessa felt unexplainable heat touch her cheeks when he stopped in front of her, his gaze roaming her face.

"Turn around, Tessa."

Swallowing hard at his husky tone, she awkwardly did as he asked, her pulse fluttering as he lowered his tall frame to the floor behind her. With every slide of the comb through her damp hair, his warm hand followed and pleasant sensations zinged through Tessa. This was so much like the first year they were married. He used to brush her hair often then.

"I'm glad you never cut it," Jared said from behind, his voice deep. "You have beautiful hair."

Tessa wasn't sure how to respond, wasn't even sure she'd be able to find her voice, as sweet memories blended with the present. Jared continued moving the comb through her drying hair, and when he quit, she almost asked him not to stop.

There was a long pause.

Tessa waited, nervously catching her bottom lip between her teeth. Electricity charged the air between them. It took every ounce of willpower not to turn his way.

He stood, and she heard the clatter as the comb hit the coffee table. "You must be starved. You didn't eat last night. I'll get you a sandwich," he said quietly.

She looked over her shoulder and watched his retreating form. Things appeared to have changed, but had they really? If it weren't for the icy rain outside, would Jared be here with her? Or would he be in his study at home, drawing up plans and talking business over the phone with Sharon?

᪗

Starved, Tessa ate every bit of the turkey sandwich and the orange Jared brought her. Afterward, fed and warm, with the soft velour of the robe caressing her body and the flames of the fire producing their own cozy warmth, she stretched her arms above her head and settled back like a contented cat.

She heard the swinging door move to and fro, signaling Jared's return from the kitchen. When silence followed, Tessa opened her eyes and looked his way. He stood by the door, his dark gaze locked on her, his face expressionless.

Tessa straightened and averted her eyes, feeling suddenly uneasy. Her gaze landed on the Christmas tree in the corner and the three wrapped presents underneath. On the large, bulky package, she could make out a T and what looked like two S's, a J, and a D.

Curious now, she scooted toward it. The package bore her and Jared's names. The other two were identical in size—one addressed to her, one to Jared.

She pulled out the shimmering, red foil package, her eyes turning upward to her husband. "It's for us. They all are. . .do you think we should open them?"

He shrugged. "Why not? It *is* Christmas Eve." He strode across the room and took a place on the fur rug beside her.

"Here. Let's open these first," she said, handing him the rectangular package wrapped in pine green paper with gold Christmas trees. She took the silver foil one, pulled aside the curly ribbon and poked her fingernail under the flap, tearing the decorative wrap away.

A small Bible, embossed in gold with her name on the front, rested in her hand. She opened the cover to the flyleaf. In caps her mother had written: USE IT,

TESSA! Jared held an identical one bearing his name with the same message to him.

Tessa arched a brow, throwing a guilt-ridden look his way. "Think she's trying to tell us something?"

"Probably," he answered with a wry grin. "Let's see what's in the other package."

She pulled at the metallic gold bow holding the wrapping together and pushed the paper aside. A round decorator basket, filled with fruit and a bottle of sparkling juice, sat nestled in green excelsior, along with two crystal wine goblets. Containers of aromatic bath salts and body lotion sat propped up on one side. Tessa's cheeks burned.

Jared spoke into the uncomfortable silence. "Nice of your mom. Maybe she's not as much of a nut as I thought."

Feeling his stare on her, Tessa didn't dare look at him.

"Would you like to save this for our anniversary?" he asked softly, plucking up the bottle of sparkling white grape juice.

Tessa's head shot up, her startled gaze meeting his steady one. "Our anniversary?"

He cocked a teasing brow. "Did you forget?"

"I thought maybe you might have," she said before she thought about it.

"A Christmas anniversary would be a little hard not to remember," he joked. "Have I ever forgotten one?"

"No, but you've been so busy this past year. I—I thought. . .I thought maybe. . ." Tears clouded her eyes, and she looked down, unable to go on.

His hand went to her face, and he brushed a single

tear from her cheek with the pad of his thumb. "Tessa, Tessa." Gently he drew her to him, holding her close. "No, I hadn't forgotten."

He kissed her forehead then looked down at her, his dark eyes soft. "At this moment a diamond and emerald tennis bracelet is sitting in a velvet box in a drawer in my study. Don't know when I'll ever get it to you though," he said ruefully. "This wasn't exactly the way I'd planned to spend our anniversary."

"Oh, Jared," she said, her voice trembling. "It doesn't matter. I know I'll love it. But I love having you here with me more. That's all I really want. You and me together."

"Tessa," he whispered, his hands moving to her temples, his fingers weaving into her long hair. His mouth lowered until it met hers in a kiss that soon sizzled. His hands traveled down to the middle of her back, and she felt herself being gradually lowered to the rug.

Wrapping her arms around his neck, Tessa felt as if she were drowning in a wonderful sea of sensation. She tightened her hold around him. His fingers went to the sash of her robe. . .

BZZZZZZZZZZZZZZ!

The loud buzzer startled them both apart. Jared blinked down at her. "Your clothes are dry," he said, his voice hoarse.

"Who cares," Tessa whispered, pulling his head down to hers. Again she thrilled in his kisses, in the feeling of being in her husband's arms. How long had she dreamed of this moment. . .prayed for it. . .wondered if they could ever be like this again. . .?

Beep! Beep! Beep! Beep!

At the intrusive noise, he again broke their kiss and Tessa frowned. She knew that piercing sound only too well.

"Please, don't look at it, Jared. You can't do anything about it anyway. Just turn it off and come back to me."

Indecision marking his face, he looked at her, then toward his jacket hanging over the chair. "It may be important."

"We don't have a phone. There's nothing you can do," she stressed, unconsciously tightening her hold on his shoulders. The beeping continued, cruelly demanding his attention.

"Maybe so. . .but I really should check to see who it is." Gently he pulled her arms away and disentangled himself from her. "No one would be paging me on Christmas Eve, unless it has to do with work. Something might have gone wrong. At least I want to know. . ."

Disappointment filled Tessa as she watched Jared retrieve the beeper he carried as a backup to his cell phone, turn off the irritating noise, and look down at the message in the window. Shakily, she pulled the folds of her robe together, clutching them tightly against her throat. She'd been a fool! She'd thought— because of his tender actions toward her today and the words he'd spoken earlier. . .

She shook her head at her stupidity, tears blurring her vision. Nothing had changed. Nothing at all.

Jared stuffed the intrusive gadget back into his coat pocket. His sober gaze went out the window to the icy rain, which still fell from a lead gray sky.

"Jared?"

He looked at her then, his dark brows drawn together. "It was Sharon. Her message said she needs me and it's urgent. It must have to do with old man Pearson. I can't think of any other reason she'd contact me on Christmas Eve when the offices are closed—especially since I talked to her only yesterday."

Tessa could think of another reason. At the office picnic a year and a half ago, she'd seen the longing in Sharon's dark gaze as it had brazenly roamed over Jared's athletic build. Sharon likely knew Tessa and Jared were having marital problems. After all, he spent more time in the company of his boss than he did his wife. Tessa wouldn't put it past the voluptuous divorcée to make a play for Jared. If she hadn't tried already.

Tessa cleared her throat. "I'm sure there's no problem with Mr. Pearson. You told me over the phone last week that he was excited for you to represent his company and loved your unique ideas for the high-rise."

"You can never tell with him. He's a bit of an eccentric." Jared slowly shook his head. "My whole career may be plummeting downhill, and I'm stuck here in the middle of nowhere and can't do a thing about it!" He slammed an open hand against the wall. "I wish your parents would've picked another time for their little surprise. This is really bad timing."

"What difference would it have made?" Tessa replied dully, rising to her feet and holding the robe around her like a protective mantle. "There will always be an important commission—always a reason for you to rush back to the office." *And to Sharon,* she added silently.

He frowned. "This is my job we're talking about, Tessa. Not some insignificant hobby. Just what is it you want from me?"

"A little of your undivided attention and time would be nice for starters. But apparently that doesn't rate top billing in our marriage." Her voice rose a notch. "For crying out loud, Jared, you're supposed to be on vacation. Everyone else is!"

Indignation left her like a sudden change in climate, leaving defeat in its wake. She sighed and looked away, shaking her head. "Forget it, Jared. Just forget it. I can't make you care—wouldn't want to. I want you here with me because you really *want* to be. Not because bad weather conditions force you to stay and are keeping you away from what you'd rather be doing."

She turned toward the hall, then stopped and looked his way again. "I think, under the circumstances, it'd be best if you slept in the guest room tonight—or you can sleep on the couch again. Whichever you prefer. I'll sleep in my parents' room."

His eyes widened. "You have got to be kidding."

She regarded him sadly. "No, Jared. I'm perfectly serious. Nothing's been resolved between us, after all." Wanting to say more, but not trusting herself to speak, Tessa hugged her arms tightly around her waist and hurried down the hall, head down.

"What you really mean is that you want everything your way. And since you can't have that, you're gonna make me suffer for it. Right, Tessa. . .?"

His frustrated words followed her all the way to her parents' room, but Tessa quickly closed the door, cutting them off with a soft click.

Chapter 5

After counting the furry white polka dots on one side of the curtain—247—and mentally redecorating her parents' room three times, Tessa chastised herself. *This is silly! I can't stay in here all day.*

She looked at the round face of the old-fashioned bell alarm clock. Two hours had passed. It felt more like two years.

Remembering her clothes were still in the dryer, she went to the kitchen to retrieve them, ignoring Jared, who sat by the fire, reading an old *Newsweek*.

Eyes widening in dismay, she looked at her soft wool sweater—now a miniature of the one she'd worn to the cabin—and groaned. She'd been so determined to make certain he understood what temperature to use, as well as a bit flustered by his changed behavior—not to mention his kiss—that she'd forgotten to tell him not to wash her dry-clean only sweater. She should have never brought it in with the other clothes. Now what was she supposed to do?

She scooped up her blue jeans and once white satin

under-things—now an interesting shade of bluish-gray—and headed back to her parents' room to change, again not looking Jared's way. Finding an old flannel shirt of her dad's, she rolled up the sleeves a couple of times. It would have to do.

Needing something to help while away the hours, Tessa located a scenic winter puzzle on the top shelf of the hall closet, grabbed it, and hurried back to the kitchen. Soon she was fully engrossed in putting together the outside frame. When the door swung open minutes later, she jumped, managing to knock several puzzle pieces to the linoleum floor with her elbow.

Jared's serious gaze locked onto her for a few pulse-racing moments before she broke eye contact and looked down at her puzzle.

Without a word, Jared moved to the refrigerator and rummaged through it. He pulled out various items, setting them on the counter with pointed bangs and clunks—obviously resorting to preparing his own meal. The silverware drawer squeaked open, then shut with another bang.

Feeling guilty, Tessa turned sideways in her chair and addressed his back. "I'll get you something to eat. Go read your magazine."

He turned, but before his magnetic gaze could capture hers again, Tessa faced front and stared back down at her puzzle. The clank of a utensil being flung into the enamel sink made her heart skip a beat. Rapid steps stomped away. The swinging door banged against the wall, creaking as it swung to and fro.

Sighing, Tessa rose from the chair and put the

sandwich stuff back into the refrigerator. She preheated the oven for the leftover turkey casserole and retrieved some frozen corn to cook in her mom's steamer. Her stomach protested the idea of food, so she would just prepare Jared a plate, then head back to her parents' bedroom and find something to do there.

It would be a long night.

ॐ

After a lonely meal in the kitchen, Jared searched the den for something to do. Sleet again pattered the roof. It didn't really matter. Where would he go if he could escape the confines of the cabin? Especially with night approaching?

He had read everything he could lay his hands on and now scanned the shelves of the bookcase at the far end of the room, hoping to find something—anything—to pass the time. His fingers brushed against a small object on the highest shelf. Withdrawing the paper box, he was elated to find a card deck. He hadn't played Solitaire since he was a kid, but right now the idea more than appealed. It was better than staring endlessly into the fire all night.

How long was Tessa planning on giving him the cold shoulder anyway? And what had he done to deserve it? Wasn't it only natural he should be concerned about his job and his need to get ahead, since he was the breadwinner?

Sitting on the couch, he tipped the cards into his hand, counted them, and frowned. Thirty-four cards. Well, what else should he expect in a house that contained year-old magazines, month-old newspapers, and no TV? What was one incomplete deck compared to that? Glowering at the cards, he wondered what to do now.

Thirty minutes later Jared sat perched at the edge of the couch and concentrated on balancing the remaining card atop his makeshift building. Task accomplished, he fell back among the cushions, crossed his arms against his chest, and glared at the multi-leveled card house.

Tessa just didn't get it. Without his place at the firm, they would probably be living in some dump and driving a rusty used car—like his mama had done. Why couldn't Tessa see he was doing this for her?

For her or for you? The soft words seared his brain.

He clamped his lips tight. "Okay, for both of us then," he muttered. He shot up from the couch, feeling suddenly restless. His leg jarred the table. The house of cards went toppling.

"Terrific." Jared eyed the red-backed cards, disgusted. Should he waste another hour rebuilding a flimsy card house that would eventually come down anyway? What else was he supposed to do to pass the time?

His gaze roamed the room and stopped on the Bible Tessa's mom had given him. He looked at it wryly, chewed his lower lip, then blew out a resigned breath. Oh, well. Why not? He had nothing better to do.

Giving a disparaging glance to the lumpy couch, he opted for the bed in the guest room. It was probably more comfortable than the piece of furniture he'd slept on last night—which would have fit well inside a medieval torture chamber. He picked up his new Bible from the chair and headed down the hall.

🍂

Tessa sat back among the pillows, pulled the sheet and blankets over her legs, and picked up her new Bible. First she would try reading herself to sleep. And if that didn't work, she'd resort to the other method.

Where should she start? With a guilty twinge of conscience she realized she hadn't opened a Bible in a very long time. She flipped through the book, noting with surprise several pages throughout had verses highlighted in yellow. Her mother's doing, no doubt.

Tessa read a few passages then skipped to other highlighted pages. An uneasy feeling settled in the pit of her stomach. The highlighted verses all had to do with a wife's role to her husband. Knowing she was sadly lacking compared to the Proverbs 31 woman, Tessa shut the book, feeling like a complete failure.

A tapping sounded, and she watched as Jared pushed the door ajar without waiting for a response. His enigmatic eyes studied her, and she felt heat flame her cheeks. He tossed a folded white sack her way. Her name was printed on the front in bold red letters.

"That was in the guest room, on the bed. You might be interested to see what's inside."

Tessa stared at the sack as if it contained a rabid skunk. She was tired of her mother's surprises.

"I'm really not up to it right now—"

"Open it."

His commanding words left no room for argument. Swallowing hard, Tessa reluctantly peeked inside the bag. Her heart plummeted.

"Obviously your mother wouldn't approve of the

sleeping arrangements, either."

Biting the inside of her lip hard to stop the tears, Tessa shook her head and closed her eyes. "Please, Jared, just go."

"I'll go," he said, his voice low. "But do you honestly think your decision to sleep apart is helping our marriage any?"

She pressed her lips together, refusing to take the bait. There was an eternal pause before the door harshly clicked shut.

Tessa grabbed up the white sack and threw it as hard as she could against the wall, next to the door where Jared had stood. A rose negligée slipped out to puddle in a shimmering pool of soft color on the beige carpet.

How could Tessa make him understand? She didn't want to always come second to his career. She wanted to be the most important priority in her husband's life—needed to be—but work was Jared's mistress and had been for some time. Tessa didn't want to share a few nights of passion with Jared, then return to the same old life upon leaving the cabin. She desired more. So much more. Like the marriage her parents had.

Tears blurred her vision and ran down her cheeks. Her heart felt as if it had been rolled in ground glass. Sleep would be an elusive stranger to her now.

Snatching up her large handbag, Tessa rummaged through its crowded interior, her hand shaking. Unable to find what she wanted, she dumped the entire contents onto the night table then threw her purse to the floor. She spotted the prescription bottle and, relieved she'd left it in its hiding place, plucked it up, and popped the cap.

☙

Tessa cried out, kicking off the heavy sheet and blankets as she thrashed around. Feeling black despair, she reached out, trying to grab hold of something that seemed always out of reach, always disappearing around another corner. No matter how hard or fast she ran she couldn't quite catch up to the phantom object. But she knew it was the only thing that could bring her happiness. . . .

Warmth pressed against her back and in the midst of the darkness, she heard an insistent voice coming from a distance.

"Tessa, honey. Wake up. You're having a bad dream."

Sensing bright light behind her closed eyelids, she turned her head away and burrowed closer to the soothing warmth. Gentle fingers trailed over her face, pushing back long strands of damp hair, and she relaxed, drifting back into her dream world. The warmth left, and she groaned, leaning forward and trying to find it. It returned and she gave a small, contented sigh. The warmth pressed hard against her, as if reaching beyond her, toward the light. . . .

"What the. . .?" a deep voice trailed off, sounding strangely disembodied. Bedsprings creaked, and then there were clatters and clinks as objects were pushed around. Groaning, Tessa buried her head deeper in the pillow, wishing the strange echoing noises would stop and the warmth would return.

"Tessa!"

Strong fingers grabbed her upper arms and shook her. Uttering a moan of protest, she vainly tried to turn away, to burrow her head further into the pillow.

"Tessa, wake up!"

She felt herself hauled to a sitting position, but too weary to care, she allowed her head to loll to one side. Again she was shaken. She heard a muttered oath, then was hauled to her feet and brought close to the hard warmth.

"Tessa, wake up! How many of these did you take?"

She tried to lift her eyelids but they felt like heavy weights. She was roughly shaken again. This time she managed to open her eyes and tilt her head back. Jared's blurry face stared down at her, filled with alarm.

"What?" she said groggily, her eyes sliding closed. Her head felt like a block of lead. She couldn't hold it up, didn't even bother to try. . . .

He shook her hard. "Wake up, Tessa! The bottle's empty! Did you take all the pills? Tessa!"

A thread of coherency reached her brain. "No," she said, her words coming slurred. "Took two. . .I think. . ."

He blew out a shaky breath. "You *think?* You mean you don't know for sure?" He shook her again. "Tessa, answer me!"

"Took two. Bottle empty. Need to get more. . ."

Her knees gave way. Instantly Jared's muscled arm went under her legs, and he scooped her up. "Dear God, what do I do?"

She nestled against his solid chest, wanting to return to the empty blackness. He held her close for a long time then lay her down on the now cold mattress. The weight of the cool sheet and blankets covered her form, causing her to stir again. His warm lips touched her forehead then she felt him move away.

Tessa reached out, a hint of reality piercing her fogged mind. "Don't go," she murmured.

"Nothing could keep me away now," his deep voice came back.

The bright light was extinguished from beyond her eyelids, then there was a creaking of bedsprings, and soon she felt pleasant heat at her back and the welcome weight of Jared's arm go around her waist. Sighing with contentment, she drifted back into her dream world.

Tessa opened her eyes to daylight flooding the room. Her head dully throbbed and her stomach felt vacant. Staring at the ceiling, she tried to recapture the pleasant dream of lying in the warmth of Jared's arms. She turned sideways. Heat flooded her cheeks. The pillow shoved close to hers showed a deep imprint where a head had lain.

Then it hadn't been a dream.

Inexplicably flustered, Tessa stumbled out of bed and staggered to the bathroom. The sound of water dripping on tile attested the fact that Jared had recently showered. Only a hazy memory of the previous night existed in her mind, and though she struggled to remember everything, facts eluded her. Why had he come when she'd made it perfectly clear she wanted to sleep alone?

Unwilling to deal with a shower before breakfast, she found a fresh flannel shirt of her dad's, pulled on her jeans, and ran a comb through her hair. Her stomach clenched with hunger pangs as she padded barefoot into the den.

Sitting in the easy chair, Jared looked away from the

fire to her. His unshaven face was an unreadable mask, his red-rimmed eyes solemn. He looked like he hadn't slept much. Her dad's robe covered his trim form—the sleeves hitting him several inches above the wrists.

Still miffed that he'd gone against her wishes last night and sneaked into her room, Tessa lifted her chin and gave him a frosty "good morning."

"Sit down. We need to talk."

His low, demanding words filled her with dread. "Can't it wait until after breakfast?" she asked, making a move toward the swinging door.

"No."

Reluctant, Tessa took a seat on the sofa, pulling her legs up beneath her. She arched a curious brow, though her rapidly beating pulse belied her seeming indifference. "Well?"

Jared slipped a hand into the pocket of the robe and withdrew an empty prescription bottle, holding it up so she could see it.

Her heart sank to her toes.

"How long has this been going on, Tessa?"

Feeling like a hunted animal, she averted her gaze to the window. The sleet hadn't returned; though the day was bleak as ever. More so since he'd discovered her secret.

"Tessa. . .?" he prodded.

She grabbed up a square throw pillow and clutched it to her breast like a protective barrier. Exhaling loudly she forced herself to look at him. "After I lost the baby. Okay? Around the time we started having problems."

His eyes widened in alarm, and he tried to keep his

voice steady. "You mean to tell me you've been taking prescribed drugs for almost a year?"

"I've had trouble sleeping sometimes. And the over-the-counter stuff wasn't working anymore." She fidgeted. "Dr. Graves is the one who issued the prescription, Jared. It's all perfectly legal. You make it sound like I'm a druggie or something."

"Are you?" he asked very softly.

"Of course not! I only take them when I need to."

"And how often is that, Tessa?"

She shrugged and looked away. "It's not a big deal. Don't worry about it. I have it under control."

"You wouldn't say that if you'd seen yourself last night."

Frowning, she turned to face him again. "If memory serves me correctly, you weren't even supposed to be there. Just why did you sneak into my room?"

One dark brow lifted. "Sneak in? You were having a nightmare. You cried out my name."

"Oh." Tessa looked down at the pillow. That was odd. She usually didn't dream when she took the pills.

"You also asked me to stay."

Her cheeks went hot. "I don't remember."

He ran a hand through his already tousled hair. "From what I saw last night, it's no wonder. Do the pills always affect you like that? They must be some pretty powerful stuff."

"I took the last two in the bottle because I was really upset, okay?" She blew out a frustrated breath. "I guess at the time I thought two would do more for me than one would. It was stupid—I realize that now. Especially since I took them on an empty stomach. I usually only take them after I've eaten something. But I wasn't thinking too clearly last night. Like I said, it's not a big deal. I won't do it again."

She looked down, intently analyzing the burnt orange threads in the pillow and running her finger along their tracks.

The chair creaked as Jared rose. He took the few steps separating them and sank next to her, putting an arm around her shoulders. "I'm not trying to be unreasonable, Tessa. I care about you, that's all."

Words of denial rushed to her lips, and she sucked them in and bit down hard, trying to stop them from tumbling out. She wouldn't bring up Jared's work or his neglect of her again. She wouldn't!

"Before we came here," he said softly, "I had no idea how hard this past year has been for you. After you lost the baby, you were so quiet and withdrawn, and I didn't know how to reach you. I know I threw myself into my work more than usual—"

She lifted her head and gave him a level look. "You've always been a workaholic, Jared."

He blew out a rapid breath. "Yeah, okay, you're right. Blame that on seeing my mom raise five kids single-handedly and work herself to her grave doing it." His mouth narrowed and a nerve ticked in his cheek.

Tessa's expression softened. "You're not your father. You've proven that many times over." She reached up and smoothed her fingertips over his bristly jaw. "I know it was hard on your mom not having any financial support from your dad all those years, and I'm sorry you had such a painful childhood. . .but, Jared, you can't go the other extreme, either. There has to be a line drawn somewhere."

She felt him stiffen and hurried on. "I know your job is important. But there has to be more. There has to be time for us, too. A relationship too long neglected will eventually shrivel up and die."

He looked into the fire, his expression grim. At last he gave a curt nod, his eyes closing shut. "You're right, Tessa. I know you're right. Maybe we can start going to church again on Sundays. I can take time off for that. And I'll start eating breakfast at home again. Would that make you happy?"

"Yes. That would be nice," Tessa said in a small voice. Well, what did she expect? Instant change? For him to promise her that the greater percentage of his "off hours" would be devoted to her? At least it was a start.

Suddenly she smiled. "I just realized it's Christmas Day."

"Merry Christmas," Jared said, drawing her close, "and Happy Anniversary."

"You too." She accepted his gentle and all too brief kiss. "It seems strange not to go to Christmas services, though. Don't you think? This will be the first year I haven't gone in I don't know how long."

"Tell you what. . .we can snuggle in front of the fire, and I'll read the passage about Christ's birth from the Bible your mom gave me."

"All right." She beamed at him. "And afterward I'll make wassail. I noticed Mom has cans of fruit juice and a bottle of apple cider in the cupboard. And we can listen to Christmas carols on the radio—"

"And maybe eat some of your mom's oatmeal cookies?" Jared put in hopefully.

She laughed. "Of course. Christmas wouldn't be Christmas without Mom's famous oatmeal and raisin nut cookies."

He cocked his head to the side with an answering grin of his own. "Well, then. . .what're we waiting for, Mrs. Baker?"

"Oh, I don't know," she teased. "Breakfast first, maybe?"

He gave a firm nod. "I can deal with that. I'm starved—haven't had anything to eat yet. Oh, and while you're in there, could you check and see if my clothes are dry?"

She rose from the sofa, an imp of mischief taking over as she thoughtfully eyed him, her head cocked to the side, one brow raised. "Maybe. I kinda like what you have on, though. You look. . .cute. Like a little boy wearing his younger brother's clothes."

"Just for that," he growled, making as if he was coming after her.

She squealed and sped to the kitchen, the door swinging shut behind her. The smile didn't leave her face. The past few minutes were so much like the way things used to be in their first year of marriage. Would it last?

After taking Jared his clothes, Tessa returned to the kitchen and put a frying pan on the stove, deciding she would make a special omelet to celebrate the day. She opened the refrigerator, studying possible contents for her culinary surprise.

"Tessa! Come here—quick. You gotta see this."

Curious at the undercurrent of excitement in her husband's voice, Tessa shut the refrigerator door and hurried to the den.

Chapter 6

J ared looped his arm around Tessa's waist as they stared out the window.

"Just like our wedding day," she said in awe, watching while powdery flakes floated to the slick brown earth like a soft sprinkling of talcum powder from a giant hand. She turned to Jared, her expression hopeful. "Do you think it'll stick?"

He grinned. "I'm no weatherman. But I guess it depends on how cold the ground is."

Wistfully, Tessa looked back out the window. "Remember how Uncle Mark tried to talk us into waiting until after Christmas to get married?"

"How could I forget? He took me aside a few days before the wedding and said, 'Son, I'm right honored to marry you two, Tessa bein' my niece and all. But it might be better to wait 'til the week after Christmas. Don't ya think?'"

"He didn't!" Tessa's mouth dropped open in shock, though she was laughing at Jared's realistic impression of her uncle.

Jared put a hand over his heart. "As God is my witness."

"I'll bet he was afraid he'd miss out on the good food at his wife's family reunion. It's an annual Christmas tradition, and Aunt Elise and all the women in her family are superb cooks. Gourmet quality," she explained. "But I think Mom outdid herself by hiring those caterers. Uncle Mark looked satisfied with the way things turned out. I noticed he sat near the banquet table and helped himself to thirds."

Jared's grin grew wider, though his eyes were curious. "I never did understand why it was so important to you that we get married on Christmas Day."

Tessa cocked her head and looked back out the window at the softly falling snow. "I've always thought it a time of important beginnings. We celebrate the birth of our Lord that day, and I thought it fitting we also celebrate the birth of our marriage then, too. Plus, my great granny was married on Christmas."

Feeling suddenly playful, she turned to him, the little girl in her rising to the fore and begging to come out. "Let's go catch snowflakes on our tongues."

"On an empty stomach?" Jared protested. "Won't that ruin our appetites?"

Laughing, she pulled his arm. "Come on, you nut."

"I'm the nut, huh? Haven't you forgotten something?"

"What?"

With deliberate slowness, Jared's eyes traveled downward.

Tessa followed his gaze to her bare toes topped with coral nail polish. She gave him an embarrassed grin. "Guess I better put my boots on first, huh?"

"I can't believe your feet don't freeze like that."

"Well. . .this wooden floor *is* cold this time of year. Guess I should at least wear socks while we're at the cabin."

"Tessa, my Tennessee gal." He winked and drew her close. "You can take the girl out of the country, but you can't take the country out of the girl," he quipped.

She cocked an eyebrow. "Mind very much?"

Jared's smile grew. "Not one bit." And lowering his head, he proved it to her.

❦

The temperature had dropped at least ten degrees compared to yesterday, and much to Tessa's delight the snow stuck to the muddy ground though it was only a light dusting. The brilliant white covering the dark earth and limbs of barren trees reminded Tessa of newness, of purity—of the desolate past being erased with fresh hope.

So much like her marriage.

They only spent a short time outdoors—neither of them dressed appropriately for the weather. Once inside, Tessa flicked on the radio, turned the volume down to pleasant background music, and prepared breakfast. They enjoyed the food and each other's company, bantering and laughing with one another.

Afterward, not wanting to spoil the moment, Tessa ignored the breakfast dishes and sat across from Jared to work on the puzzle, humming along with the carols on the radio. Soon the image began to take shape beneath their fingers. To Tessa's surprise, it wasn't the snowy mountain that appeared on the front of the box, creating even more of a challenge to discover the mystery picture.

After about an hour of interlocking small pieces, Jared stretched then gave her a lazy grin. "Didn't I hear you say something earlier about wassail?"

"A man and his stomach," she teased, though the idea did make her mouth water. "I'll get right to it."

She found a large kettle and poured the ingredients into it, adding cloves and cinnamon sticks with a dab of honey. She had just turned the heat to simmer, when she felt Jared's arms slide around her waist.

"Dance with me," he murmured against her ear.

Funny little tremors played havoc inside Tessa, and she felt her smiling face go warm. "We're in the kitchen, Jared."

"So?" He turned her around. His arms locked around her waist, and they began to leisurely move to the nostalgic strains of Bing Crosby's "White Christmas" coming from the den.

Tessa melted against him, wondering how life could be any sweeter. They danced through two stanzas, shuffling in tight circles in the confined space. Jared's hand traveled to her chin, lifting it.

"I love you, Tessa," he murmured. His lips touched hers several times, brushing soft as eiderdown against her mouth.

Tessa wrapped her arms around his neck. The kisses lengthened and deepened, sending her mind into a whirl. Uncertain if it was the heat of the nearby stove or Jared's kisses that made her feel comfortably warm— or maybe a mixture of both—Tessa clung to him, returning kiss for kiss.

In the far regions of her mind, she hazily heard the

sound of tires crunching, a car door slam. A knock sounded far away. Jared continued to kiss her, and she became oblivious to everything else—until the banging started.

Jared was the first to break away. "Someone's here," he said, his eyes a little unfocused. She nodded, just as dazed.

Taking her hand, he led her to the den. He threw her a curious look before opening the front door.

A skinny young man in a shabby coat stood on the wooden porch. His panicked brown eyes filled with relief upon sight of Tessa and Jared. "Thank God! I saw the smoke from the chimney but wasn't sure anyone was home. It's my wife. She's having a baby. I need to use your phone to call an ambulance."

"Sorry. The phone's out of order," Jared said.

The man's eyes got that panicked look again. "I don't know what to do. We're not from around here. We live in Millington. We were on the way to visit Sandy's folks in North Carolina when her pains started. She's not due for another two months and this is our first," he rambled, pushing a trembling hand through his cropped brown hair.

"The hospital is about twenty minutes from here," Jared said. "I'll go with you."

A pang stabbed Tessa's heart.

The young man looked so relieved Tessa thought he might kneel down and kiss Jared's feet. "Thank you, sir. My wife's not strong, and I'm really worried."

"I'll get my jacket," Jared assured him and turned away.

"I'll get a blanket for your wife," Tessa said, her voice flat. She knew she was being selfish. Under the circumstances, Jared's decision to go with the couple and direct them to the hospital was the right thing to do. She knew that. But things had finally been going so right between her and Jared. Yet now that he'd found a way into town, Tessa was certain his work on the Pearson high-rise would take top priority again.

So much for Christmas vacation—and for their anniversary.

She took a thick blanket out to the anguished girl in the front seat of the old sedan. She looked much younger than Tessa—possibly seventeen or eighteen. Bright blue eyes full of pain regarded Tessa, and the girl managed a soft, "Thank you, ma'am," before she closed her eyes and clenched her teeth against the pain.

In an attempt to comfort, Tessa smoothed a gentle hand over the girl's brow then turned to face Jared, who'd just exited the cabin.

"Are you coming with us?" he asked softly, though the expression in his eyes told Tessa he already knew the answer.

"I'm staying. For the rest of the week."

His sober gaze held hers, then he gave an abrupt nod. "I'll see you New Year's Day then. . . Tessa, you know I can't come back. I wish I could, but I can't. I have to get back to work. Maybe we'll go out to eat the night you come home and celebrate our anniversary then."

"Maybe." She didn't trust herself to say more.

He bent to brush a kiss against her unresponsive lips. Tessa swallowed hard against the painful lump in her throat and watched while both men helped the woman to the backseat where she could lay down. Then Jared coaxed the shaky young man into giving him the keys. Tessa's last view of her husband was of his dark head behind the wheel of the rusty old sedan.

Jaw clenched tight, fingernails biting deeply into her palms, Tessa forced herself to turn and enter the empty cabin.

❦

Tessa gazed into the fire, took another sip of the now cold wassail, and looked back down at the open Bible in her lap. For the past few hours she had delved into the Word, reading the highlighted passages, comparing them to her life.

The results were disturbing.

She was as far removed from the Proverbs 31 woman as Alaska was from the tropics. Respect her husband? Look up to him? Revere him? When had she done those things? She'd always been too busy nagging him and making him feel guilty about his devotion to his job and his lack of time spent with her, to show him any appreciation.

Condemnation threatened to settle over her like a hundred-pound weight, but her mother's words "the Holy Spirit convicts; the devil condemns" flitted through her mind.

How could she fix her four-year mistake? And yet. . .wasn't it just payment for the indifference Jared had shown her this past year—when he deigned to spend time in her presence, their short time at the cabin excluded?

Tessa shook her head and tucked a long strand of hair behind one ear. She wasn't a vengeful person and had no idea why these random thoughts kept popping up. She flipped to the book of Matthew. Her eyes went to the thirty-seventh chapter and the words written in red.

Love the Lord your God with all your heart, with all your soul, and with all your mind. This is the first and greatest commandment. . . .

Tessa again stared into the fire, as the truth slowly dawned on her. She had accorded Jared the place in her life she should have given God. Was that why she'd grown so despondent concerning their faltering relationship? Because she hadn't put God first and had put Jared on some sort of exalted pedestal she'd made for him, depending on her husband to fill the empty spots in her heart? Loving him wholeheartedly and sweeping God into some back corner of her life? That wasn't fair to her, to Jared, or to God.

Just when had she pushed the Lord out of her marriage? The answer came immediately: after she lost the baby. Yes. That's when their relationship had begun to sour, and she and Jared had quit going to church as much as they used to. Tessa still went, but only occasionally.

With a huge growl, her stomach let her know it was past time to eat. Tessa reluctantly closed the Bible, the truths she'd just read taking root deep inside her mind. And her heart.

❦

The rest of the day went by in a haze of internal questions and in-depth personal inventory, as well as more Bible reading. By the time dusk approached, Tessa felt deeply convicted. She asked the Lord's forgiveness for her shortcomings as a wife and put God first place in her life and her marriage again.

She couldn't wait to see Jared, to tell him of her spiritual awakening, to confess her failures and ask his forgiveness. She longed to tell him how proud she was to call him her husband and express her gratitude for the hardworking man he was. She'd never once had a material need.

Frustration filled her when she realized she would have to wait until New Year's Day to talk to him.

Sighing, she put out the fire, made sure all electrical appliances were off, and locked both doors, front and back. Before leaving the kitchen, she glanced at the now finished puzzle on the table.

A pale pink rosebud, bejeweled with sparkling dewdrops, gently unfurled in the middle of a smoky gray background.

"Newness arising out of the ashes of the past," she said softly, running a finger along the delicate flower.

Strange how that puzzle had been in the wrong box. Or was it a mistake? Maybe an angel had put it there for just such a purpose—to encourage her in the midst of her problems with Jared. Looking at the flower gave her assurance that God could restore her life and her marriage.

Tessa readied herself for bed, her mind going to the sleeping pills when she caught sight of her purse on the floor. She had no need for the pills tonight—she felt such peace—but wondered if she might need them again in the future. The thought of being without them scared her. For the first time, since she'd begun taking the prescribed medicine and relying on its power so heavily, Tessa admitted she might have a problem. She would talk to her pastor about it when she went to church again and see what he thought she should do.

Again Tessa reached for her Bible, realizing she'd not yet read the Christmas story in Luke today. Christmas just wouldn't seem like Christmas without doing that.

Chapter 7

Tessa jerked awake, her eyes flying open. What was that?

She straightened, letting the Bible slide off her lap. The bedside lamp still gave off its soft yellow glow, and nothing seemed out of place. She tensed. There it was again!

A crunching sound—footsteps—coming from outside, next to the cabin. A wild animal? A bear?

Tessa quickly doused the light, though she still felt vulnerable. Were bears attracted to sight or smell or both? Had she just brought the beast's attention her way?

She held her breath, afraid to move, afraid the animal would hear her. *Oh, don't be so silly,* she inwardly chastised herself. *You're safe within these four walls, and he's out there.* Still, her heart beat a staccato against her rib cage—and the rapid drumming in her ears surely could be heard by anything within close proximity—inside or outside. Oh, why had she stayed at the cabin alone?

She heard a scraping on the den window and her heart jumped to her throat, lodging there. She hadn't even thought to check the windows when she locked the doors! But surely bears weren't intelligent enough to break into cabins. . .were they?

Furtively, she made her way to her parents' closet and grabbed the closest weapon she could find. A battered tennis racket left over from Dad's high school days. The strings were no longer tight as a drum—several dangled loose—but if the bear tried to gain entrance, she would give it a good swat on the nose. She'd heard somewhere that such an action often caused the creatures to turn tail and run. Tessa had no idea if this were true. But she sure hoped it was.

Heading toward the den, she groped her way in the dark, putting her hand along the wall for guidance. A huge shadow at the curtained window blocked out the illumined light from the moon. Tessa's heart again lurched when she heard the unmistakable sound of a pane being raised.

Noiselessly, she padded across the room, tennis racket raised above her head and waited. Her hands shook and her heart beat fast, but she didn't loosen her grip on the sweaty rubber handle.

The curtains bulged as the creature stuck its upper body through the open window. Tessa bit her lip then came down hard with the racket.

"Yeoowwww!" The bulge disappeared and the curtain flattened as the creature fell backward.

A remote part of Tessa's mind thought it odd the bear had sounded almost human in its cry of pain. She rushed to the window, intending to slam it shut and throw the lock. Her hand wavered on the curtain as she glanced at the large intruder on the frozen white ground next to the porch. Mouth going wide, she dropped the racket and rushed out the door and down the steps.

"Jared! Are you hurt?"

Rubbing the top of his head, he sat sprawled in the snow, regarding her warily. "I take it you're still mad."

"No—I thought you were a bear." Her bare feet stung from the thin layer of snow on the ground, and she hopped up and down on one foot then the other, arms wrapped around her, trying to relieve the pain. Her legs didn't like the cold much, either.

"A bear?" Jared asked incredulously, then, "Get inside before you catch pneumonia. I'm all right. Just stunned."

Tessa gladly obeyed and rushed into the cabin. She flicked on the light switch and made her way to the couch. Pulling up her bare knees to her chest, she began to rub her feet briskly.

Jared moved stiffly through the door, still rubbing the top of his head. "I'll make a fire," he muttered. "It's cold in here."

Soon a cheery blaze burned, and he took a place on the sofa next to Tessa, his gaze going to her hands. "You okay?"

Sheepish, she nodded and stopped rubbing her feet. "I should be asking you that question. Do you need an ice pack or anything?"

"No—no ice." He put a hand to his scalp. "My head's sore, and that dive I took off the porch didn't help much, but I think I'll live. I don't see any blood," he muttered after pulling his hand away and looking down. "Lady, you sure pack a wallop! What did you hit me with, anyway?"

"Dad's old tennis racket," she mumbled, her gaze going to the floor. "I thought you were a bear. I mean, what else was I supposed to think? I had no idea you'd be back. And I heard something try to get in the house. . . ."

"A bear." He shook his head, still dazed. "I didn't want to wake you and both doors were locked."

"Didn't you see the bedroom light on?"

He shrugged. "This late at night I was sure you'd be sleeping. Besides, you fall asleep with the light on all the time. And I wanted to surprise you. Guess I'm the one who got the surprise. Definitely not the reception I had hoped for." His gaze went to the racket on the floor.

Embarrassed, Tessa began to rub her feet again just to have something to do.

"Here, let me," Jared said, reaching for her feet and placing them on his lap. His hands were warm from the fire, and pleasant tingles rushed through Tessa as he moved his hand along the inside of one foot with gentle but deliberate strokes.

"How did you get here?" she murmured. "I didn't hear a car."

"Ray—the new proud papa—dropped me off. Since I wanted to surprise you, he didn't drive up to the cabin." Jared's brow furrowed.

"Something happened to me while I sat in that hospital waiting room with Ray," he said, his voice low. "Poor guy was about to lose it, so I stayed with him. While we waited, he told me how he almost lost his wife in a six-car pileup last year. She was in ICU for days, and the doctors gave him little hope."

Jared looked up at her, his dark eyes solemn. "It got me to thinking—like the pill scare did last night—if I lost you, then everything I'm working for just wouldn't be worth it. It wouldn't matter what income bracket I was in, or that I drove a new car every year, or that I lived in the nicest part of town. If you weren't there to share those things with me, then I wouldn't want them. They wouldn't be important anymore."

Jared managed a grin. "But your mom's little surprise really opened my eyes and showed me where I've been missing it."

"Mom's surprise?"

"Yeah. By the way, Sandy had a girl, and mother and baby are doing fine. Thought you'd want to know."

"I'm glad. But you're changing the subject on me, Jared. What do you mean 'Mom's little surprise'?"

He withdrew his new Bible from his jacket pocket. "Your mom highlighted all the verses in here dealing with a man's role to his wife—one of the most important being, 'Husbands love your wives just as Christ loved the church and gave himself for her.' " He shook his head. "Can't say I've done much of that in our marriage. I got to thinking, 'I love Tessa, but I've never really given myself up for her—put her needs ahead of my own.' I've always focused on what I wanted, never what you needed. And for that I'm really sorry, Hon."

Tessa put a hand to his arm. "You're not the only one at fault here, Jared. I haven't been a very good wife. I never once thanked you for providing a living for us or told you how proud I was of the firm's star architect.

So I'm saying it now. Thank you. You have a lot of talent with designing. I've always thought so, and deep down I've always been proud of you, though I've never shown it."

Jared arched a surprised brow. "Really?"

She nodded. "I'm ashamed I never told you before. I began to see your work as your mistress and I felt jealous. That's one reason I nagged you about it so much. But that's in the past. Today I saw how wrong I was—thanks to my new Bible."

Jared grinned. "Your mom?"

"My mom," Tessa affirmed with a smile.

She wondered if now was the time to broach the other subjects. Yet, if not now, when? "Jared, somehow we got off track this past year. And I want to put God first place in our marriage again."

"I agree. I'm the one who suggested going to church, remember?"

She nodded. "But I think it needs to be more than that. I want us to have daily devotions together—like Mom and Dad do—and really pray with one another when the need arises. Even when it doesn't. Maybe we should consider joining a Bible study. We could sure use it. At least I could. There's a lot in the Word that I didn't even know was there."

He thought a moment then nodded. "Yeah, you're right."

"And," she paused, working up her courage, "I would also like to start working for Aunt Ginny in the spring—helping her with the tourist cabin."

Jared's brows drifted downward. "Tessa—"

Hearing the warning note in his voice, Tessa hurried on, "Oh, I wouldn't be doing it for the income. I understand how you feel about me helping out financially after the kind of childhood you had—really, I do."

Tessa took a deep breath. "But I get lonely at home with little to do. And until we start a family I would like to help my aunt out. Her arthritis has been flaring up lately, and sometimes it's been hard on her to wait on customers. That's all I'd be doing really. Waiting on customers and taking care of the store—dusting souvenirs—that sort of thing. And it would only be three days out of the week. I'd get home in plenty of time before you got off work and it wouldn't interfere with anything—"

"Whoa! Whoa! Whoa!" Jared exclaimed, throwing up his hands, palms outward. He shook his head as though to clear it.

"I can see you've given this a lot of thought," he said at last, "and I don't want to sound unreasonable. But that's almost a two-hour drive there and back." When she remained silent he added, "Is it really that important to you?"

"Yes, it is. I've been thinking about it a lot today. Maybe if I had more outside interests, I wouldn't be so dependent on you," she explained. "And I've lived near the mountains all my life. I know the road to Aunt Ginny's like the back of my hand."

He thought awhile then nodded. "Okay. I guess we could try it out, but I meant what I said about spending more time with you, Tessa. I also thought we might visit my brothers and sisters in Amarillo during the spring—maybe at Easter."

Her eyes shone. "That would be wonderful. I'd love to go to Texas with you and see your family again."

"And I know they'd love to see you, too," Jared said, wrapping an arm around her and bringing her close. "They loved you from the start. I've got smart siblings. I loved you from the start, too. . . ."

He kissed the top of her head and for a companionable moment they stared into the fire.

Tessa snuggled up against him. "I know there'll be times when you can't make it home, and I promise I'll try to be more understanding. You're the young star of the firm; I know you're in demand. The Merriweather commission proved it."

"Well, they'll have to do without me for a week."

Tessa's heart leapt. "What do you mean?"

"I'm not going back until after Christmas vacation, and I'm not working on any plans yet, either. I called Sharon while I was at the hospital and found out her 'urgent' message wasn't so important after all. I also told her the finished blueprints won't be in her office until the week after New Year's—which was the original plan anyway."

"You did?" Tessa looked up at him and blinked.

"Yeah. She sounded disappointed—especially when I told her she wouldn't be able to reach me for a week because I was spending that time at the cabin with my wife."

"You are?" Tessa's eyes grew round and her mouth parted.

"Your mom's note did say they wouldn't be back until New Year's Day. Let's see. . .that gives us six more days alone together." He gave a roguish laugh.

Tessa only blinked again. "You're really here," she breathed. "You came back." Somehow in all the commotion with mistaking him for a bear the fact hadn't fully registered. Until now.

"Yeah, I came back." He grinned and glanced at his watch. His dark eyes lifted to hers again, a sparkle in them as he turned his wrist her way. "And I made it just in time. See—it's 11:47. It's still our anniversary."

She smiled. "Yes, it is, isn't it?"

He pulled her close and his mouth found hers. Heat swamped her and all weariness fled. She'd never felt so alive as she did at this moment. Suddenly he pulled away, his hands going to her upper arms.

"You don't have anything in the oven, do you?"

"This late? Of course not." Tessa stared at him, confused, still reeling from his kiss.

"What about in the washer or dryer?"

Catching on, she felt her cheeks grow hot, but shook her head. "I suppose, though, we'll have to wash our clothes every day until Mom and Dad get back."

A wicked gleam lit his eyes. "Oh, I don't know. You could always wear the new negligee and trade off when you need to with that robe of your dad's. It definitely proved useful." He pulled her closer. "It got you into my arms."

She grinned. "Jared, you're terrible."

Smiling, he retrieved a familiar black device from his inside pocket. He flicked the switch to turn it off, then tossed it to the coffee table.

"Jared. . .?"

"For the rest of this week, it's just me and you. I don't want any interferences—beepers, buzzers, or timers—to get in the way this time."

"Guess that means burnt food and wet clothes, huh?" she teased.

He gave a dramatic sigh. "If it has to be, it has to be." His expression turned serious. "Today I discovered just how important you are to me, Tessa. And nothing tops that," he said, lowering his head to hers.

Elated, she returned his warm kisses, feeling as if everything—her marriage, her life, and her husband—had been restored. Thank God for new beginnings!

He moved her onto his lap, cradling her. "You know what, Hon? I think your parents' 'most unwelcome gift' turned out to be the best thing that's ever happened to us."

She tilted her head and grinned. "You know what, Jared? I can't agree with you more." And again she pulled his head down to hers.

Silence reigned throughout the night. And Tessa had never been more grateful.

Be kind and compassionate to one another, forgiving each other, just as in Christ God forgave you.
EPHESIANS 4:32

PAMELA GRIFFIN

Pamela juggles her time between writing, parenting her two sons, and engaging in all the activities that make a house a home. She fully gave her life to the Lord Jesus Christ in 1988, after a rebellious young adulthood, and owes the fact that she's still alive today to an all-loving and forgiving God and to a mother who steadfastly prayed and had faith that God could bring her wayward daughter "home." Pamela's main goal in writing Christian romance is to help and encourage those who do know the Lord and to plant a seed of hope in those who do not. Her first novel, '*Til We Meet Again,* released from **Heartsong Presents** in 2000.'

The Best Christmas Gift

by Veda Boyd Jones

Dedication

To Jennifer and Landon, with love and appreciation
for the great tour of the Big Apple.

Chapter 1

Elaine Montana concentrated on the road ahead of her, ignoring the seven girls who were belting out Christmas songs at the top of their lungs. Who would have thought these loud junior high girls had sung like angels in their white robes at the new church at Beaver Cove, Arkansas, just an hour ago? Now they were clowning around, singing off-key harmonies, and laughing in high-pitched giggles.

Elaine didn't share in their frivolity. The girls seemed oblivious to what was going on outside, and she didn't want to alarm them. By keeping the defroster on full blast, she was able to keep the windshield clear, but the fine mist that had started when they had climbed into the church van in Beaver Cove was now freezing rain.

She'd watched the weather forecast before she'd picked up the church van that afternoon, but the call was for just rain, not ice. Those critical few degrees between 34 and 30 made the difference. She glanced at the outside temperature display on the dash and saw that the temperature had fallen to 28.

Beaver Cove had been excited about the girls coming

for the performance, even though it had been a last minute type of arrangement, only put together the day before. Elaine had been surprised that seven of the twelve girls in the choir were still in Rockwood instead of having left to visit out-of-town relatives for Christmas. The girls had met at the church parking lot at four, just an hour after school had let out for the holidays. The plan was to have plenty of time for the hour drive over Boston Mountain and still allow time for the girls to get a hamburger and relax before their seven o'clock performance.

The church van had been returned to the parking lot at 4:15, so they hadn't even taken time to unload craft supplies that had been used at a senior citizen's center. The choir robes were hung on a rod at the back, and the girls had piled in, all in high spirits now that school was out for Christmas vacation.

The candlelit program had been a huge success, even though there were only forty-some people in the sanctuary to hear the girls. The candles made a difference, Elaine had decided. It gave just the right feel to the beautiful Christmas melodies. With clear bright voices, the girls sang "O Holy Night," "Joy to the World," and other Christmas favorites. They'd sung longer than their normal program because of requests from the audience. And getting the girls away from the performance had also taken longer than she'd planned. But the raves of the audience were things the girls needed to hear. That told them their time was well spent practicing and performing. Their songs had touched the hearts of their listeners in the small church at the Christmas celebration.

If only those listeners could hear them now. Elaine

smiled at the antics of the girls but didn't take her eyes from the road ahead. Slowly the van climbed the twisting mountain road. Surely the road ahead was okay or the authorities would have closed the road, which they did whenever the weather was hazardous.

Now that she thought of it, they had met no traffic for the last ten minutes. The road ahead must be closed. About five miles farther was a wide spot in the road with a convenience store, which had been the place where the roadblock had been put up before and where travelers had been marooned. That had never happened to Elaine, but she'd had friends who had spent a day there before, and it had not been a pleasant experience. Keeping seven girls cooped up like that wasn't something Elaine could even imagine.

She had one alternative. She could take the back road. It was gravel, and it was narrow, but it was a way over the mountain. Surely gravel would not ice over like pavement, and it would be a safe way to deliver these girls home.

She peered through the windshield at the night. She would not gamble with these girls' safety, but she wanted to get them back to Rockwood. They couldn't be twenty-five miles away. Surely she could make it.

The gravel road was just around the bend. Still there had been no traffic coming toward them. And, she reasoned, there had been no highway patrol, either. If it were really dangerous, they would come down from the roadblock to stop traffic. With a quick prayer for a safe trip, she turned on her left signal. A glance in the rearview mirror assured her that the turn signal was from habit, not necessity. No cars were behind her.

The girls continued their high-spirited singing and didn't seem to notice that Elaine had taken a detour, even though the van jostled more on the gravel surface than on the highway.

Elaine knew this road. Although she had only lived in Rockwood for three years, she had explored the by-ways and lanes in the area. This one wound around the mountain in a series of switchbacks that weren't much tighter than the ones on the main highway. It was a longer way over the mountain, but it didn't appear icy.

"Where are we, Miss Montana?" Tiffany asked from the seat directly behind her.

"On the back road," she answered, keeping her eyes fixed ahead. "We've run into some weather, so we're taking a safer route."

"You think they've closed the highway?" Allison asked in a loud voice.

The singing ended abruptly as the girls stared out at the dark night, apparently assessing their situation. Elaine was assailed with questions.

"Is it slick?"

"Can you see to drive?"

"How far are we from home?"

"Is that hail?" Tiffany asked.

"It's freezing rain, and I suspect the main road is closed. But we're nearly home and shouldn't have any problems. Are you all wearing your seatbelts?"

There was a little shuffle behind her, and she heard the click of several belts. The girls must have unbuckled so they could turn around in their seats for the songfest.

"I've been on this road before," Ollie said. "It's slow. It'll take us all night to get home."

"Oh, I think we'll be fine," Elaine said. She glanced at the clock on the dash. Already nine. She'd told the girls' parents that she'd have them home by nine-thirty at the latest. Well, it would be later than that. She hadn't realized how slowly she'd driven on the highway. Ollie was right; it would take them awhile to get home now.

The girls were to call their parents when they got back into Rockwood so they could be picked up. Now she needed a new plan. When she got to the crest of the mountain, she'd let each girl use the cell phone to call home. That way she could report their position, and the parents could judge when to come to the church parking lot.

Elaine relaxed her white-knuckled grip on the steering wheel. This road was much better than the highway. There wasn't the broad shoulder that she liked on the main road, but she didn't need to worry about that. She wasn't meeting any traffic, and there was no one behind her, so she didn't need to pull over to let faster traffic pass.

☙

Clay Stevenson opened the door of the old home place, as he and his relatives called the stone house that his great-grandparents had built around the turn of the last century. Freezing rain pelted the tin roof of the porch with loud pinging sounds, and he shined his powerful flashlight on the flagstone sidewalk to see if small hailstones were making all that racket. He had always loved the sound of rain on the tin porch roof, but this was a different sound. More lonely. More threatening.

Just that morning he had driven to the old home place from Rockwood to escape from what? Holiday fever, that's what it was. Didn't psychologists say that the Christmas holidays made many people depressed? Well, he wouldn't say he was depressed, just. . .disgusted. He couldn't handle all the parties and all the tinsel and all the commercialization of Christmas. His way to escape was to take to the country. And just as he had for the last four years, he found his sanctuary at the old home place. Except this year something seemed missing.

The beam of his flashlight found ice, a solid sheet on the large flat stones that served as a sidewalk from the house to the fence gate. The wind was picking up. This was going to be a huge ice storm. He'd watched the weather before coming to the mountain house, but he'd expected rain and lots of it from the front that was moving in from Oklahoma. The meteorologists had sure missed the temperature. A few degrees lower than expected meant the rain would form ice on every surface.

By morning he knew he'd wake up to a winter wonderland with ice glistening on limbs of trees, bushes, and brown tufts of grass. In town, there would be problems. In his mind's eye, he visualized how paralyzed Rockwood would be. Probably lose power with iced-over electric lines. That wasn't a worry here. There was no electricity.

He'd built a cozy fire in the pot-bellied stove in the living room, and he'd filled the back porch with wood from the wood pile before the storm hit. He'd unloaded his perishable groceries in the old icebox and stuck in a block of ice he'd brought up in the cooler. The rest of the groceries he'd stuck in the big tin storage box or in the glass jars that kept staples fresh. Sometimes he came to the old home place on the spur of the moment and relied on supplies that had been laid in earlier, so when he made a longer trip like this one, he stockpiled the place. He had plenty of kerosene for the lamp in the living room and the one in the kitchen, and there was another lamp in the spare bedroom if he needed it. He'd be fine.

And he'd have his down time, his R and R, that always restored him. Too bad he wouldn't be able to hike around the place as he'd planned tomorrow. Being in nature restored him, too. Made him see God's world from a different perspective than life in Rockwood. Not that it was some bustling metropolis, but the day-to-day worries of running a company that employed two hundred workers consumed his mind when he was in town. Out here was different. It was quiet and serene.

Well, that wasn't the case now. It was noisy and ominous. Rain hit the tin roof with loud and constant pings, and he thought there must be hail mixed in with it now. One more glance into the darkness showed no hailstones, just ice coating everything.

A huge gust of wind that made the rain slant sideways drove him inside. Must have been a fifty-mile-an-hour flat wind, he mused, as he leaned against the door to shut it.

Here inside he was snug as a bug in a rug. He smiled at the memory of his grandpa using that old saying. He'd been a corker. He still missed him, and he'd been gone for nearly twelve years. Out of the five siblings, he was the one who had been closest to Grandpa.

The family would be gathering this weekend, and he would show up on Christmas Eve as always. They'd chastise him for not being there earlier, when after all, he was the one who lived in Rockwood. Why did he escape each holiday?

Grandpa would have understood, but the others never would. It wasn't that he disliked his family. He loved them. He just didn't need them in big doses. Quiet. That's what he liked, and with his three sisters and brother and their huge broods of kids, there was constant noise. Well, by coming to the old home place, he found his quiet, and then he returned for their festivities.

He settled down in the green upholstered recliner by the stove. That piece of furniture didn't belong in this old place, but he'd brought it there because it fit him. He could doze in it, or he could read in it, or he could just sit quietly and think.

Tonight there was no quiet to think in, so he opened the new mystery he'd brought with him and read in the flickering light from the kerosene lamp on the table next to his chair.

※

Tension filled the van. Elaine glanced in the rearview mirror and saw the girls leaning forward in their seats. They weren't even whispering to each other now, as they had when they'd first discovered their treacherous situation. It really wasn't so bad, Elaine told herself. They were still moving, albeit slowly, and every mile moved them closer to home and safety.

What she wouldn't give to be safe in her warm bed

right now. Out of the weather, away from the responsibility of these girls. It had been a busy week as school had wound down. Nothing had been accomplished today in her high school classes. The Christmas choir concert was over; the demand for performances by her small groups had been met. It was time for the holiday vacation, and how she wished she'd said a resounding no when the pastor had asked her to take the girls' church choir to Beaver Cove. Three months ago, she'd taken on the additional load of being choir director at church until a new one could be found. Of course, with her taking the job, the search had slowed.

Elaine gripped the wheel as a darker spot appeared on the road. It was ice as she had suspected. The back wheels slipped, and she correctly turned the steering wheel into the skid. But at the same time, a strong gust of flat wind wailed through the pine trees along the roadside and hit the van broadside with a powerful force. The van slid into the ditch. The girls' shouts turned into screams as the van teetered, then toppled onto its side.

Chapter 2

"Everyone all right?" Elaine yelled. She pulled the key out of the ignition, turned on the interior light, and then worked to release her seatbelt. She was dangling on her side, held in place by the belt. Once she heard the click, she braced herself against the wheel with her hands and put one foot out to the seat beside her.

"What happened?"

"What are we going to do?"

"Get me out of here."

"Is anyone hurt? Check the girl beside you," Elaine said in her teacher voice that commanded attention.

"I'm all right. I'm okay," resounded from the girls.

"We're okay back here, but there's junk all over." Jennifer's voice was muffled from the backseat, and Elaine watched her dig out from under choir robes.

"That craft stuff is everywhere," Sara said from beside Jennifer, and Elaine remembered the senior citizen project boxes that hadn't been unloaded before she had grabbed the van for their trip.

The passenger door to the van was flat against the

ground. There was no escape in that direction. The back doors might work, but there was so much junk there. Elaine decided to use the driver's door. One by one they would climb out. She didn't smell gasoline, but she wasn't going to take any chances on a fire.

Elaine stood on the tilted front passenger side window. "We're going to climb out the driver's door in this order," she said. "I'll boost you from behind if you can't make it out. "Allison, you first, then Tiffany, Ollie, Megan, Holly, Jennifer, and Sara. Until your turn, stay in your seat. Jennifer when you come to the front, bring those choir robes. We may need them."

If memory served her right, there were some houses along this stretch. They weren't close together, so they'd have to walk some distance, but at the sight of the first one, they were going in, whether the occupants liked it or not.

"Now hurry, girls. Let's do this in an organized fashion, but quickly."

She still didn't smell gas, so that danger was receding in her mind, but she wanted these girls in a safe, dry place. "How many umbrellas do we have? Hand them forward."

Elaine unlocked the driver's door and pushed it open above her head. She tossed the umbrellas outside. "As soon as you get outside, grab an umbrella, but don't worry about getting wet. We'll get you dry in a few minutes."

"Where are we going, Miss Montana?" Jennifer asked.

"To one of the houses along here. Move, girls. Let's go."

There was nothing fast about the evacuation. The girls squealed and yelped when the freezing rain hit them as they climbed out of the van using the steering wheel and arm rests as if they were rungs of a ladder. Allison stayed on the top side of the van and tugged the girls out one by one. Jennifer had bundled the robes under plastic cleaner bags and handed those out ahead of her. Finally it was Elaine's turn. As soon as she was on the side of the van, she allowed the driver's door to slam shut. She and Allison jumped down to the slick road. Allison's feet went out from under her, but she claimed she was all right.

At least the girls all had coats. Those with hoods had them up.

Those without huddled under the umbrellas, but they weren't much help because the wind was so fierce.

"Which way, Miss Montana?" Tiffany asked.

She didn't have the slightest idea. Although she knew approximately where they were, she couldn't remember which way the houses would be.

"Ollie, what do you think?" Elaine asked. Hadn't Ollie said she'd been on the slow road before?

"I don't know," Ollie said. "I don't know."

Elaine peered through the rain first in one direction, then the other.

Was it a light she saw not a hundred yards away? She couldn't imagine that it could be, but there it was again and it was coming toward them.

"Oh, thank you, God," she said softly, then in a regular voice said, "This way, girls."

She led them toward the light that bobbed ahead.

"Hello. Can you help us?" she called.

"Is anyone hurt?" a man's voice yelled from behind the flashlight.

"No. We're just cold and wet," Elaine called back.

In less than a minute, they had closed the gap between them. Or rather, the man had closed the gap. He was bundled against the rain with a heavy coat and a hood drawn close around his head, and he was much more surefooted than the girls, who slipped and slid around on the ice in their black one-inch heels.

"Follow me," he said.

The girls clung to each other and marched along after him as best they could. Elaine brought up the rear of the motley group.

Soon they were walking up slippery flagstones to a house. Through the window, Elaine saw a flickering light that made shadows. An old lamp. Obviously the power lines had already snapped under the weight of the ice.

The man opened the door and stepped back for the girls to file inside. After Elaine slipped into the living room, he entered and shut the door.

"Thank you so much for helping us," Elaine said. "You don't know what this means."

✧

Oh, yes, Clay knew what it meant. He'd known when he first heard the odd sound outside and had gone to investigate. It meant the end of his serenity. It meant the end of his peaceful holiday. Unless he was mistaken, these girls could be here at the old home place for a couple days. He'd turned on his battery-operated radio and heard the latest news. The roads leading up and down Boston Mountain had been closed. He had no clue how this woman and her young charges had gotten to his place, but they were here, and he knew that he couldn't turn them away.

The woman was drenched, but she didn't take off her wet coat. Nor did the girls. They stood around the stove, their hands outstretched to its warmth.

"I'm Elaine Montana." She held out her cold hand.

Clay took off his glove and shook her hand. "I'm Clay Stevenson. Why don't we get your wet things off and hung up to dry. Then we'll go from there."

"We skidded, and there was a terrific wind. The combination sent us into the ditch. I was afraid to keep the girls in the van because of an explosion or fire."

Some of the girls gasped. Apparently that possibility hadn't occurred to them. They had not said a word, not to him or to each other. But they unbuttoned and unzipped coats. Now where could he hang nine dripping coats?

"You four, hang your coats on those hooks by the door. The rest of us will put them on the backs of the chairs." He motioned toward the kitchen table, which was visible through the wide doorway.

The girls moved away from the stove and silently followed his orders, and then they returned to stand by the stove again.

"Girls, are you all right? Has anyone found a bump or a bruise or something you overlooked before?" Elaine asked.

"I broke my fingernail," Holly said, and the others laughed with relief.

"We're okay, Miss Montana, but what are we going to do?" Tiffany asked.

She looked expectantly at him.

"I guess you're going to stay the night here," Clay said. "The roads are closed. And if the forecast is right, there's going to be a lot more ice before this is over."

"Where will we sleep?" Tiffany asked. She seemed to have made herself speaker for the group.

"We'll figure something out," Elaine said. "Let's get those robes out of that plastic. We can use them as blankets."

So Elaine Montana was the take-charge kind of woman. He liked that. She was looking around as if making decisions on where to place each girl.

"There are two bedrooms, and it might be best if I used one and you all used one as headquarters, but you'd probably be warmer out here by the fire." That said, he realized it would be hard to get all the girls stretched out in the living room. They'd need the kitchen as well. Good thing he'd already built a fire in the old wood cookstove. At least it wasn't bitterly cold outside or it would have been hard to keep the house warm. It was just cold enough to turn rain into ice.

He started toward the kitchen, then turned back.

"Why are you out on a night like this?"

Elaine explained about the choir performance.

"Well, make yourselves at home while I get more heat in here." He quickly opened the kitchen door and darted outside to the wood porch. How glad he was that he'd had the foresight to load that porch before the storm hit. He filled his arms with chunks of wood, then went back inside. The girls and Elaine Montana hadn't moved away from the fire.

Of course they were cold. They sure weren't dressed for an ice storm. They all wore dresses and hose and those ridiculous shoes. He added wood to the fires, then went into one bedroom, and then the other.

"Take off your shoes, and as soon as your feet dry, put on these socks." He distributed eight pairs of socks. Most of them were his, some he'd brought up for this trip, but some had been stored in drawers for a long time. Two pair were army green, but the rest were white, and all would be warmer than what they were wearing.

"We'll get our shoes mixed up," Tiffany said. "They're all alike for the choir," she explained to him. "Oh, wait. We'll each get one area. We can put our purses down to claim our spot with our shoes."

Purses! Elaine had left her purse in the van. She hated to admit that the girls had kept their heads better than she had since they had all brought their purses with them. Her cell phone was in her purse. She'd have to go back and get it. The girls' parents should be notified immediately. They were probably worried sick already because the girls weren't home.

"Uh, I left my purse in the van," she said. "I'll be right back." She reached for her coat from the hook by the door.

"Do you really need your purse tonight?" Clay asked.

"Yes. I need my phone."

"I'll get it," Clay said in what Elaine discerned was a begrudging voice.

"No. I left it. I'll get it." She slipped into her coat.

He picked up a cell phone from a side table. "You can start making calls while I'm getting yours. Then the girls can call twice as fast."

"Can I call my folks?" Tiffany asked.

"All right." He handed the phone to her, put on his coat, and trudged out into the storm.

"Tiffany, see if your folks will call some of the other girls' parents. I'll be right back." Elaine wasn't about to let this man get her purse. He might be dressed for the storm while she was not, but she could tell he didn't want them staying with him. And they didn't want to, for that matter. But there was no way around it. They were stuck.

He had already made it past the gate when she got out on the porch. The rain on the tin roof made an incredibly loud pinging noise.

"Wait. I'll get it," she said as she held onto a support post and stepped gingerly off the porch.

He swung around, pointing his flashlight at her. "Are you crazy? You don't even have a hat."

Good point, but she didn't appreciate him calling her crazy. With determined steps, she made her way to his side. "We'll go together. You might need me, and I'd like to see the van. I must call the pastor and report the damage."

He grunted something she didn't hear, but he waited for her to join him by the gate. They walked side by side toward the van, which was about the length of a football field away. The gravel road was still rough in places, but in others it was a solid sheet of ice.

Clay played the light over the van. It didn't look too bad, almost as if it had carefully laid down for the night. It wasn't flat on the ground as she'd thought when they were climbing out. It was leaning against an embankment at a thirty-degree angle. It was impossible to tell what the passenger side looked like, but she was hopeful that it wasn't beyond repair. She had left the interior lights on. How had she forgotten to turn them off? She'd thought she'd been cool in the face of danger, but now she reassessed her behavior.

Clay leaned against the van and reached over it for the door handle. It wouldn't budge. "Iced over," he said.

"I may have locked it," Elaine said. She reached in her pocket and was relieved to find the key.

He climbed onto the side of the van, inserted the key, but still the door wouldn't budge. He knelt on one knee on the area beside the door, using his other foot for leverage, but still the door remained shut.

"We could try the back," Elaine suggested through chattering teeth. That area wasn't taking a direct hit from the freezing rain.

Clay climbed down and tackled the back doors. He unlocked them and with a great jerk got the upper door open. A few papers, some Styrofoam cups, and an empty cardboard box flew out. The door on the bottom remained wedged shut.

"What is this?" he asked, picking up the junk and tossing it back into the van.

"Craft supplies. Sorry. Let me go in. I know where my purse is."

He stepped back and let her climb over the other boxes, over the backs of seats, and make her way to the front. The interior lights allowed her to find her purse in the narrow area between the passenger seat and the door. She was on her way back to the door when she remembered the interior lights and returned to click them off.

Finally she was back in the freezing rain, with her purse stuck under her coat to protect it. Clay carefully shut the door, and together they started back toward the houseful of girls.

Chapter 3

"D o you have anything hot to drink?" Elaine asked once they were back inside the house.

The girls had made themselves at home, all right. Where earlier they had been reticent, now they reminded Clay of a gaggle of geese with several talking at the same time, while one spoke on the phone. They all wore his socks and each had staked out an area for herself with shoes and purses scattered in a somewhat orderly fashion.

"I'll draw some water," Clay said. He didn't pause to take off his coat but took two buckets from the counter in the kitchen. *Better have a good supply of drinking water.* He stomped out to the well, lowered the rope, then pulled it back up and released the plunger to fill the bucket with water. He repeated the process three times until both buckets were brimming full. That should last them until morning.

Back in the kitchen, Clay put water on the stove to heat for instant coffee. He had an old coffeepot, but it wouldn't make enough for all of them—if these girls drank coffee. He didn't have any tea or hot chocolate, which would probably be more to their liking.

"Can I help?" Elaine Montana had broken away from the group by the living-room stove and was at his elbow. "You don't have plumbing?"

"No plumbing and no electricity." Roughing it was what appealed to him about this place, but she made it seem unbelievable that in this day and age he did without those conveniences.

"That makes it a bit difficult at times, doesn't it?" Now her voice had a ring of sympathy. Did she think this was his permanent home?

"I like to come to the old home place for relaxation. No bright lights, no pressures."

"No bathroom?" she asked.

"There's an outhouse. I've got another lantern we'll use for out there." He hadn't thought of that problem. Eight females brought a lot of trouble with them.

She nodded. "I'll start that process and take each one out, as soon as all the calls are made."

He glanced at her feet, still in those ridiculous dress heels. She hadn't changed to his socks yet.

"Stay here. I'll see what I can find."

While she stayed in the kitchen, he rummaged in the closet of the second bedroom. It wasn't much of a closet, no closet door, just a curtain dividing the three-foot square from the small bedroom, but it contained old shoes and some clothes. His grandpa had liked coming up here just as he did and had kept some things permanently at the old place.

A short time later, he returned with two pairs of heavy work shoes and an armload of shirts and pants.

He handed one pair of shoes to Elaine and dumped the clothes on the table. There were no women's clothes, but they would have to do with what he had.

"Put on these shoes before you go out, and the girls can share this pair. Once each girl returns, she can change to these old clothes, which should be warmer."

"You're very generous," Elaine said. "We'll launder these when we are able to get back to Rockwood." She sat down in one of the ladder-back kitchen chairs and put on socks and men's high top shoes that were several sizes too large for her.

"Did you call the pastor?"

"Not yet. The girls are still talking to their parents."

As if she knew they were talking about her, one of the girls wandered into the kitchen. "Miss Montana, Mom wants to talk to you."

Elaine let out a long breath, then sat up straighter and took the phone.

Clay tried not to listen, since he felt Elaine was in a ticklish situation and needed privacy to explain the circumstances. He got cups from the freestanding cupboard and lined them up on the table. From another cupboard he extracted a large jar of instant coffee and a gallon glass jar that protected a partially used sack of sugar. The top had been folded down, and a rubber band held it closed. He kept most of his provisions in glass jars to keep bugs out in the summer.

"Clay?"

He looked up at the sound of his name.

"Sorry. I've forgotten your last name."

"Stevenson." So she didn't know who he was. His

name wasn't a household name in Rockwood, but most people knew of Stevenson's Wood Products. Different divisions in the company made everything from fine bookcases to wooden strawberry containers.

She said his name into the receiver, her eyebrows shot up, and she glanced at him again. Obviously the parent on the other end of the phone knew of the company.

"He's being very kind. . . . Yes, I'll tell him. Holly's in good hands here. . . . Thank you, and I'm so sorry about the accident. God was with us and kept us safe. Actually Holly suffered the worst with a broken fingernail." She laughed. "All right. Holly will call you again tomorrow, but if you need her, you can reach us at this number. Got a pencil?" She gave her cell phone number, then handed the phone back to Holly, who carried it back to the living room.

"Have you been talking to the other parents?"

"Just one other. The girls are having long conversations. I doubt they talk to their parents this much when they're at home."

He laughed and saw her eyes brighten at the sound. Was she afraid of him? That possibility had never crossed his mind. Okay, he hadn't shaved this morning in anticipation of being alone for a few days. He hadn't even brought a razor along. His usually neatly combed hair probably looked wild from being in and out of the hood of his coat. He ran his fingers through his dark hair in an attempt to control it and be presentable.

"Miss Montana." Now it was Jennifer with the phone.

Again Elaine went through an apology for the accident, an assurance that all was well, and mentioned the broken fingernail as a humorous end to her conversation. She was very good with people, and knew she should leave them feeling positive about a difficult situation.

"Is choir director your job?" he asked, after Jennifer had returned to the living room to pass the phone to another girl.

"Temporarily for the church, but I draw a salary for teaching music at the high school."

"So that's why they call you Miss Montana."

"I'll probably have some of these girls in class in a couple years, and I don't want them to be too familiar. A little distance helps keep discipline in the classroom. Are you tied in with Stevenson's Wood Products?"

"It's the family business, but I run it now."

"So why are you out here? At Christmas?"

"As I said, it's my relaxation place. The holidays are pretty tension filled, so I come up here each year for a break. Are we ready to start that outhouse run? Then they can come in and have some coffee."

❦

Elaine called in the girls who had completed their phone calls and explained the outhouse procedure complete with the men's shoes routine. She started to put on her coat, but when Clay offered his heavy coat with the hood and his gloves, she accepted.

Carrying a lantern in one hand and Clay's large flashlight in the other, she ducked under the umbrella that Tiffany carried and escorted her to the outhouse. She let Tiffany take the lantern inside, and with the flashlight to light her way, she returned to stand in the shelter of the porch until Tiffany opened the outhouse door. Then she slipped and slid her way back to Tiffany's side and walked her back to the house. She repeated the process six more times, then took her turn before returning to the warm kitchen.

Six girls, in an odd assortment of men's clothing, were sitting around the kitchen table, some sharing chairs. As Elaine shrugged out of Clay's coat, Megan joined them in a sweatshirt and pants that were rolled up several times.

"More sugar, please," Holly said. "This is bitter stuff. No offense, Clay."

"I'll never have them in class," he offered as explanation to Elaine's glance his way. "Your first coffee, Holly? Are you ready for some, Megan?"

So, he had already learned their names. He was a quick study. The girls were at ease with him, something that Elaine hadn't managed to feel. Now that she knew he ran a big industry in town, she felt she understood him better, his need for escape from the pressures of business, but she also felt a bit in awe of him. Earlier she'd felt nothing but relief that he had rescued them. Then she'd felt leery of him because he seemed put out that they were there. She was completely confused by this man.

"You get what's left," he said and motioned toward the living room. The last of the extra clothes hung on the recliner by the fire.

"Be right back," she said. The bedroom was cold, so she hurriedly changed into the warm clothes—a plaid flannel shirt and a pair of men's nearly worn out khaki pants. How were the girls holding up these pants? They were way too large around the waist. She slipped back into the big shoes and made her way to the kitchen, holding the pants up by bunching the extra material in one hand.

"Here's your belt," Clay said when she joined them, and he handed her a three-foot length he had cut from a ball of twine.

"I wondered how you all were holding them up," she said. While still holding the pants, she one-handedly threaded the twine through the belt loops and then tied it in front.

"Coffee," Clay said and put a cup down in front of an empty chair, obviously for her.

She took a long sip and felt the warmth flow through her. "Hmm. This is wonderful."

The girls laughed.

"You're the only one who thinks so," Clay said with a chuckle. "The girls are drinking sugar water with a bit of coffee flavoring."

"It's an acquired taste," she said. "Did you all call your parents?" They all nodded.

"Okay, then I guess it's my turn to call the pastor."

"Actually, I already did that," Clay said. "I figured by now he'd already know it from their parents, so I wanted to assure him that everything was under control. I told him you'd call when you came in from outside, but he said there was no need. Things are getting pretty hectic in Rockwood. Power lines are falling, people are without heat, and he was just leaving to turn the fellowship hall into a place of refuge for those who needed a warm cot.

Elaine wasn't sure how she felt about Clay usurping her responsibility. A part of her felt relieved that she didn't have to talk to the pastor, like a teen not wanting to confess to a parent that he'd hit a car in a parking lot. Another part of her felt that she should have the right to explain the situation. She had chosen to take the side road, not stay on the highway, and she should have had to tell him that.

"How many blankets do you have, Clay?" Ollie asked.

"Not enough. We'll have to share. Are we ready to call it a night?"

Elaine glanced at her watch, surprised to see that it was closing in on eleven. She felt tired, yet not sleepy. Too much had happened for her to close her eyes and rest.

But there was a lot to do before that could happen anyway.

"Okay, girls, have you settled on your beds?"

In the end, the girls pushed the table back against one wall and helped drag the mattress from the spare bedroom to the kitchen. Three of them piled on it, sharing one quilt and adding choir robes as covers. They voted that Elaine take the recliner. The other four girls spread coats on the floor as a pallet, covered them with sheets and shared two quilts. Clay headed for the main bedroom.

"Shall we say our prayers?" Elaine asked the girls, once they were all settled. "I'll start, then everyone can add a line of thanks, starting here with Tiffany and going around." She paused a moment to let the girls gather their thoughts. "Father, thank You for giving these girls such positive attitudes that they are turning a negative experience into a positive one."

"Thank You for saving us in the wreck," Tiffany said.

"Thank You for Clay rescuing us," Allison added.

"Thank You for Clay being a nice guy," Ollie said.

"Thank You for Clay sharing his house with us," Jennifer said.

"Thank You for the warm kitchen and the sugar coffee," Sara said.

"Thank You for Miss Montana taking care of us," Holly whispered sleepily.

"Thank You for these good socks," Megan said.

"Amen," Elaine said with a chuckle, and the girls echoed her word.

She lay awake for a long time, listening to the freezing rain hammer on the tin porch roof. This was not how she had intended to spend this evening. She had planned to be packing and taking off first thing tomorrow morning for her parents' home in central Missouri.

Well, tomorrow she'd call them and explain that she'd be a few hours late. Surely the light of day would bring the tow truck and warmer weather that would melt the ice and let her get home to her family.

Chapter 4

E laine awoke around two when Clay opened the door of the stove. Rain still pounded on the roof, and she knew instantly where she was and why. In the flickering of the flames, she could see intensity on his face as he added wood to the fire from the pile of wood he'd brought in earlier. He shut the door and moved silently around the pallets on the floor to the kitchen and fed that fire, too.

"Clay," Elaine whispered.

"Sorry. I didn't mean to wake you," he whispered back.

She waved away his apology, but doubted that he saw it in the darkness. "Thank you so much for taking us in. I don't know what we would have done without you here."

"You're welcome. Now get some sleep."

"Good night," she whispered, but for some time she twisted and turned in the recliner, trying to find a comfortable position before she fell asleep again.

The next time she awakened, she pushed the light on her watch and saw that it was only two hours later. Could she feed the fire so that Clay wouldn't have to get up?

She pushed aside the coat she was using for cover and tried not to squeak the chair as she got up. It was pitch black in the room, so she opened the door of the stove to get light from the flames. Now she could see a bit. She stepped around the sleeping girls to the wood pile and picked up a couple logs. She stuffed them in but left the door open for the light. She stumbled into a side table but managed just a gasp, not a cry, so hoped she didn't awaken anyone. When she made it to the kitchen, she opened the top of the cookstove and added a couple chunks of wood and then put the top back in place.

She smelled smoke. Not just a little smoke, a lot.

What had she done wrong? As fast as she could, she moved to the pot-bellied stove and closed the door.

A beam of light caught her full in the face, blinding her.

"What?" she exclaimed

Tiffany was coughing, or was it Allison?

"Elaine, what did you do?" Clay asked from the bedroom door. In the flashlight beam, Elaine could see thick smoke coiling around.

"What's going on?" Ollie asked.

"Hey, who's that?"

"That's my leg, Tiffany. Turn loose."

"I fed the fire," Elaine explained.

"Did you turn the damper before you opened the door?"

"Oh, no."

Now another girl was coughing.

"We're going to have to clear out this smoke," Clay said. "Maybe it won't take too long. Open the front door; I'll get the back."

With both doors open, the wind whistled through the house, taking the smoke with it but lowering the temperature a good twenty degrees.

The girls huddled around the stove, except for Holly, who slept peacefully through the excitement. With the doors opened, the sound of rain on the tin porch roof resounded through the house.

"It's still raining," Ollie said.

"Yes." Clay played the flashlight through the opened front door. The slick flagstone sidewalk glistened back.

"Miss Montana," Allison whispered. "I need to go to the bathroom."

"Okay," Elaine said, but inwardly she cringed. She deserved this, she decided as she put on the large shoes, for smoking up the house and waking the girls. Without even asking, she donned Clay's warm coat while Allison got ready. "If anyone else needs to go outside, be ready when we come back."

Clay lit the lantern and handed it to Elaine. By the time they returned, the doors were shut, but three more girls needed to make the trip outside.

It was nearly five when everyone was dried out and settled back down, but it was still as dark as midnight.

The phone woke Elaine around eight. She reached for it, punched the button, and answered in a groggy voice, "Hello."

"I'm sorry. I must have the wrong number. I was calling Clay Stevenson. I'm terribly sorry to disturb you," a female voice said.

"No, no, you're right. I'll get Clay."

"Who is this?"

"Elaine Montana. Just a moment, please."

He was coming out of the bedroom with his hand held out for the phone. "Yes?"

There was a long pause on the other end, and Elaine could just imagine what was being said.

"She's a music teacher and has seven junior high choir girls with her. Their van went off the road last night." He held the phone away from his ear, and even from a distance, Elaine could hear laughter.

"We're managing," he finally said. "How are things in town? And when did you get in?" A long pause followed. "Very funny. I'll be sure to keep you informed. See you."

He had no sooner clicked off the phone than it rang again.

"Yes? . . . What does it matter?" He looked straight at Elaine and winked, then said, "Hard to tell an age, probably late fifties, gray hair, plump, motherly type." Again he held the phone away from his ear. "I'm only kidding," he said into the phone. "She's beautiful, late twenties, blond hair, average height, nice figure. . . ." He moved closer to Elaine. "Yes, blue eyes. Bright eyes. Intelligent eyes. . . . No more questions. Bye."

"Who was that?" Tiffany asked.

"My sister from Atlanta got in yesterday afternoon. She thinks it's hilarious that my quiet retreat has been. . . interrupted. But right now she doesn't know what to believe."

"Do you like your sister?" Tiffany asked.

"Of course. She's just a bit nosy, so I wanted to

throw her for a loop."

Elaine was still recovering from his description of her—both of them. Did he really think she was beautiful? She ran her tongue across her teeth. Right now she didn't even feel presentable.

"Ah, Clay, do you have any toothpaste we could use?"

He looked at her a long moment, then nodded and headed back to the bedroom. He returned with a half-used tube.

"Girls, we need to get organized," Elaine said. "First we'll all brush our teeth—with fingers and a tiny bit of toothpaste. Then we'll start the trips outside."

"Miss Montana, look!" Allison exclaimed, pointing at the living room window. "It's snowing."

Just when the freezing rain had changed to snow, Elaine didn't know, but now every surface was covered with about two inches of the white stuff, judging from the amount on the wooden fence posts.

Just what they needed. Snow would insulate the ice. Who knew when they could be rescued from the mountain. Well, she wouldn't think about that right now. There were too many other things to be done.

The girls neatly folded up their pallets. The mattress was carried, shoved, and pulled back to the bedroom, and the kitchen table was put back in place.

"Now what?" Ollie asked.

With a dishpan for a sink, the girls took turns with the toothpaste and a small amount of water. Clay went to the well for more water and returned to heat some for coffee. Elaine started the outhouse routine. Although she went out the first time to take the kerosene lamp, she didn't wait for each girl. Now that it was daylight, they could make their own way.

"The girls are probably a little hungry," she told Clay. "I have a granola bar in my purse. Maybe they each have something they could add to the food collection."

"We can manage breakfast, but we need to conserve our food." He opened a large tin box and pulled out a new box of pancake mix he'd put in there just yesterday. "Let's use water to make this instead of milk. I only brought a half-gallon, but I have a dozen eggs."

"That's great," Elaine said. "Just point me toward a big bowl and I'll get started."

In a short while, Elaine stood at the cookstove flipping pancakes. The first batch was nearly black from a too-hot skillet. The next batch was better, and the first round of girls sat down to eat them with honey instead of syrup.

"We always keep honey here," Clay explained, "because it doesn't spoil. This jar is from a beekeeper in Rockwood. Go easy on the sugar, girls. That's all there is. You should all drink your coffee black anyway, like real men."

"We're not men, Clay, and we don't want to be," Tiffany declared.

"It's just an expression," Elaine said with a chuckle. "Maybe you should put just a little bit of instant coffee in your water, so you don't need much sugar. Could they use a bit of milk in it, Clay?"

"Okay." He got the carton from the old icebox and poured small amounts into the cups the girls held out, then added a bit to his own.

Cleanup after breakfast took some time as they heated water for both washing and rinsing.

"Now what?" Ollie asked.

Elaine looked around the small living room that was filled with girls, waiting for someone to direct them, and Clay, who was poking at the fire with the damper open. "Amuse yourselves for a few minutes, and I'll try to think of something." She had yet to call her parents, so she took her phone to the kitchen for a little privacy. Her mom wasn't surprised that she wasn't on her way, since it was also snowing in central Missouri.

"Don't take any unnecessary chances," her dad said on the extension.

"No problem there. Right now we're stuck on this mountain. I'll let you know when we get to town and I can start for home."

☞

"Are you married, Clay?" Allison asked.

"Of course he's not married," Sara said. "His wife would be with him if he was."

"I'm single," Clay said. "How about you?"

Allison giggled. "I'm not married. Have you thought about getting married?"

Clay scratched the back of his neck, uncomfortable with the topic. "I've just not found the right woman," he said, foreseeing their next question.

"Miss Montana is sure nice," Allison said. "I think she likes you."

Clay cast a sideways glance toward the kitchen where Elaine was talking on the phone. "That's nice. She seems nice." Nice. Was that the only word he knew? "You girls want to play a game?" He strode to the spare bedroom and found the old checker board. That would only occupy two of them at a time.

"Here, girls. We'll have a checkers tournament." He took paper and pencil from the end-table drawer and drew up brackets with all the girls' names and his and Elaine's. "Who knows how to play checkers?"

Holly and Jennifer held up their hands.

"You two teach the others. You'll be the first pairing." Within an hour the tournament was over.

"Now what?" Ollie asked.

"Do you think we'll get home today?" Jennifer asked.

It was after eleven, but there was no sign of the snow letting up. It must have been six inches deep.

Clay turned on his portable radio at the same time that Elaine's phone rang. She answered and handed the phone to Allison.

"Girls, you can all call your parents when Allison gets off the phone." She turned to Clay. "Any news?"

"More snow predicted. Let's face it. You may be here for a while."

"What about food?"

He motioned for her to follow him to the kitchen. He showed her the canned goods in one cupboard, plus staples of beans, rice, spaghetti, flour, and the dwindling supply of sugar stored in big glass jars. He had an onion, eggs, milk, a pound of bacon, and a steak in the ice box. Plus a twenty-pound bag of potatoes. It had been on sale, so he'd grabbed the bag instead of buying a few potatoes and had planned on taking the extras home. The huge tin box held the things he'd put in yesterday—a fresh loaf of bread, a bag of corn chips, a box of vanilla wafers, and the pancake mix that now needed to be stored in an empty glass jar.

"How long do you think it will be before a truck can make it up here to tow the van?" Elaine asked.

"A long time. We should be able to make it off the mountain before then, but I'm not sure how. I drove my pickup, and there's not room for everyone in it, even when it is safe to drive."

"We need wings," Elaine said.

"Exactly!" he exclaimed. "And I know just how to get them. Excuse me."

Clay went to the privacy of his bedroom to call his friend John Talbot. During the tourist season, when the Ozarks were packed with strangers seeking the serenity of fall colors or the beauty of the flowering dogwoods in the spring, he flew helicopter tours. He started out of Eureka Springs and flew over the huge statue of Christ, over the lake area around Branson, and over Boston Mountain.

John answered on the sixth ring, when Clay was almost ready to hang up. He told John his circumstances.

"Be glad to help out," John said, "but not in this snow. And it looks like we're going to get quite a bit more before it ends. As soon as it quits, we'll have you out of there. How many girls?"

"Seven. And a teacher. Nine of us in all."

"I can only carry four at a time. Need three trips. And need parental permission."

"I'll work on that from this end. You just send a prayer heavenward that this snow ends soon."

Chapter 5

H ere's the plan," Clay said over a lunch of peanut butter sandwiches, "which entails several steps. First, we have to call your parents again and have them call my friend John and give their permission for you to take a helicopter ride."

"Helicopter!" Jennifer exclaimed.

"That's the only way we're going to get off this mountain in less than a week," Clay said.

"A week!" Ollie exclaimed. "That's after Christmas!"

"Or at least a few more days. It's a Bell Jet Ranger, the safest single-engine helicopter. Be sure and tell your parents that when you call. There's only room for four passengers at a time, so we'll have to go in groups. But the helicopter can't fly until the storm passes through. Meanwhile, we can take turns clearing off a landing pad on the road."

"We could use a clear path to the outhouse, too," Elaine said. "That snow's getting deeper. We need the dishes done, what few there are. And should we put more wood on the porch?"

"Wouldn't hurt," Clay said.

Elaine divided the girls into work details. The problem was shoes. With only two pairs of extra work shoes, only two girls could be outside at one time. Or one and Elaine. What could she do to entertain the other girls?

"If we're going to be here much longer, we need some Christmas decorations," Tiffany said. "Do you have any up here, Clay?"

"No. I was planning on being back in Rockwood with my family on Christmas Eve."

Elaine thought of her own family. Her mom would have put up a huge tree covered with decorations that she'd collected all her life. Electric candles would glow from every window. Nothing like candles to add Christmas cheer. They had worked wonders for their choir program at Beaver Cove.

"Girls, clean up the kitchen. Clay, would you come outside with me?" She grabbed her coat and led the way to the front porch.

"What's up?"

"Would you mind if the girls decorated your house? We have all that craft stuff in the van and lots of candles. I'd make sure they didn't harm anything, and it would keep them busy."

"Whatever will keep them busy is fine with me. Got the keys?"

She dug in her coat pocket and held them up.

"Okay. Just a minute." He went back inside and returned with an old straw broom.

This time Clay broke a path, and Elaine was careful to step in his footprints as they made their way through the snow to the van. He cleaned off the back with the broom, then unlocked the door and after some tugging, managed to get it open.

Elaine climbed inside and took stock of the mess. Clay climbed into the confined space and pulled the door to without allowing it to shut all the way. They filled cardboard boxes with the spilled contents. Elaine made sure every scrap of paper, every shaker of glitter was in the boxes. Then she found the candles they had used at the performance.

"Ready?" he asked. She nodded, and he pushed the door open and climbed out. She handed him two large boxes and piled a plastic sack on top of those. She climbed out and retrieved one box of supplies, and then he shut the door.

"This should keep them busy for some time," she said.

"A stroke of brilliance," he said, as they struggled through the snow with their burdens.

The girls were at the two front windows, peering out when the two adults clambered up onto the porch and stamped snow off their shoes. Tiffany swung the door open, and they deposited their bounty on the floor.

"Here's the plan," Elaine said.

"We sure have a lot of plans," Sara said.

"Yes, we do," Elaine agreed. "Those of you who aren't on outside duty can make Christmas decorations. I don't know what the senior citizens were making with these things, but I'm sure you can come up with your own ideas to make this place festive."

The girls examined the craft materials, pulling this and that out of the boxes.

"You have to keep things neat," Elaine cautioned.

She could already envision the mess the girls could make, but at least they seemed excited about the project.

The first outside crew consisted of Clay, Elaine, and Tiffany. They made a foot-wide path to the outhouse with two shovels and a hoe that Clay brought from a stone outbuilding.

Next, Elaine sent Jennifer and Megan out to carry wood to the back porch. Clay gave the girls directions, then he headed to the road to survey a helicopter pad.

Elaine and Tiffany stretched their cold, sock-covered feet in front of the stove.

"I wonder when my parents will get electricity back?" Tiffany said.

"I'm sure crews are out working now," Elaine said. "This snow doesn't help travelers, but it's not as heavy on utility wires as ice. We'll find out about electricity tonight when we call your parents for permission for the helicopter ride. Or were they going to a shelter?"

"No. Mom said the fireplace was keeping one room warm, so she and Dad and the boys were staying in there in sleeping bags. I guess I'd be in the same fix if I were there instead of here."

"But you wouldn't have all your friends with you," Sara pointed out. She was sorting craft material on the kitchen table. "Hey, we need a Christmas tree." She hurried to the kitchen window. "You think we could cut down one of those little ones in the woods behind the outhouse?"

"Oh, could we, Miss Montana?" Ollie asked.

"We'll have to ask Clay. I'll go out next shift and talk to him."

"You can stay warm," Ollie said. "I'll ask him when Allison and I take our turns on the helicopter pad."

Why not? Elaine decided. These girls seemed to know him better than she did. Although he had been more than kind to them, she still sensed that he wished they were out of his life. He'd sure come up with a rescue plan quickly enough. She couldn't blame him there. As pleasant as this mountain home might be as a retreat, right now it was crowded and dark. They were saving the kerosene lamps for nighttime, and the heavy cloud cover didn't allow much daylight into the house.

The wood-moving detail returned to the house, and Ollie and Allison donned the shoes and headed outside. From the window, Elaine watched them approach Clay. They talked a moment, he pointed to the back, and then they started shoveling snow off the road.

Snow continued to fall as they worked, and not much time had passed before Clay sent the girls in for the next crew. The shoes were needed for treks to the outhouse, so Elaine took that time to heat some water for coffee to send out to Clay. He had to be cold. His navy coat was nearly white, and his constant movements couldn't keep the snow from accumulating on it. By the time the shoes were on Sara and Holly, Elaine had a steaming cup of coffee ready for them to carry to him.

Again she watched from the window. He glanced her way and held the cup up in a thank you, and she waved a "you're welcome."

"Did you make much progress, girls?" Elaine asked. "It's hard to tell from here."

Ollie stood with her back to the stove, her hands behind her. Allison had peeled off her socks and had hung them on the handle of the stove door.

"Those shoes are wet inside. We need to dry them before the next group goes out. I wonder if Clay has a hair dryer. That would dry them pretty quick."

"Duh," Ollie said. "Where would he plug it in?"

"Oh, yeah," Allison said. "How did people *live* without electricity?"

"In a slower world, I imagine," Elaine said. "What about the Christmas tree?" The girls who stayed inside had been making decorations, as if there were no doubt that Clay would get them a tree.

"He said okay, but it would be awhile before we could get it," Ollie said. "He'll get one before he comes in. I told him to yell and we'd come out and help him. Don't you think he's cute, Miss Montana?"

"He's very nice looking."

"I think he likes you," Ollie said.

Elaine cleared her throat. "I think he likes all of us." Okay, that wasn't really true. She thought he wanted them out of his life, but maybe that was just because they were an additional responsibility that he didn't need, not because of dislike. He'd had to share his house, his food, and his clothes.

"Of course, he does," Ollie said, "but he likes you especially. He looks at you nice."

Elaine waved her remark away and quickly changed the subject. "What are you girls making?"

"Wreaths," Tiffany said. "We're cutting these Styrofoam cups into circles and putting green glitter on them. Hey, we should use the gold glitter so they show up on the tree."

"I'm sticking silver glitter on these craft sticks," Megan said. "They'll look like icicles. Oh, how are we going to hang them?"

Elaine remembered seeing some thin wire on a spool in one of the boxes. She dug through a kitchen drawer, looking for a knife, but found an ice pick, which would work even better for making holes in the top of the sticks.

A hammer and a hard surface would make it easy to poke holes in the sticks, but she couldn't find a hammer. For the hard surface she settled for a log that had been split several times, having two flat sides. With a lot of force, she could put her weight on the ice pick and twist it around a bit until it made the hole. After the first four were done, she decided to find something to use as a hammer.

Rocks were out of the question. They were buried under an inch of ice and covered with six inches of snow. With the eye of a scavenger, she walked through the house. There was nothing useable in the spare bedroom where the girls stored their pallets. She hesitated before going into Clay's bedroom, but once she spied an old iron doorstop next to the door, she charged in. The doorstop was shaped like a frog with a flat side on the bottom, and it was certainly heavy enough. It was a little awkward to grasp, but she could manage.

She glanced around the room. Clay's bed was bare except for one quilt. He had obviously stripped off the other quilts so the girls could use them. He must have frozen last night. Not much heat from the stove reached back here.

He might not have liked their group descending on him, but he was sharing everything he had with them. What a generous soul.

Beside the bed on a small table were a black Bible and a drinking glass. On the wall above the bed was a picture of a small boy and an old man. She wondered if it were Clay.

Against one wall was a washstand with a towel and an empty washbasin. An old chest of drawers stood against another wall. That must have been where he'd found all those clothes. On the floor at the end of the bed was a backpack, next to it a suitcase. Odd he would have both. Perhaps he had hoped to hike in the woods that covered the mountain.

She felt she was getting a glimpse of Clay's character. She wanted to know more about him, but so far they really hadn't talked. They'd been more concerned with feeding the girls and keeping them safe and warm.

"Miss Montana," someone called from the other room.

"Coming. I found a hammer," she said as she hastened back into the living room.

For the next half hour, Elaine sat on the floor in front of the fire and pounded holes in craft sticks. She glanced up when she heard the stomping of feet on the front porch. Time for a shift change, and it was her turn to go back out.

Holly and Sara scurried in. Clay stood on the porch. "Would you bring the water buckets out back, please?" he asked before he shut the door.

Elaine hurried to the kitchen and poured the last of the water into the large pot on the stove. Then she carried the two empty buckets to the back porch, where Clay waited.

"Do you want the next shift outside?"

He shook his head, which dislodged some snow from his hood. "The snow's coming down faster than we can move it. Let's take a break and start again later. I'll leave the water here, then get that tree."

The girls chattered in the living room, while through the kitchen window Elaine watched him draw water from the well. As soon as he'd set both buckets by the door, she opened it and carried them to the kitchen.

"Miss Montana," Holly said. "Here are the shoes."

"Clay's taking a break for now. No more shifts."

"I know, but I think he wanted you to help him pick out the Christmas tree," Holly said and held out the shoes.

"Oh. He didn't mention it."

"We talked about it when we were shoveling," Sara said. "Get us a pretty one."

"A big one," Ollie said. "Well, maybe middle-sized. We don't have a lot of decorations."

"You're sure he wanted me to help?" Elaine asked. It wasn't that she was unwilling to help him, but it was odd that he hadn't mentioned it when he left the water.

"We're sure," Holly said with a big smile.

Chapter 6

They wanted a Christmas tree. He guessed he couldn't blame them. When he'd been their age, he'd wanted the tree, the parties, the whole holiday thing. And as much as their being there was an inconvenience for him, it certainly wasn't how these girls had planned on spending the last few days before Christmas, either. Actually, they were being good sports about it. Not one of them had complained about the physical labor he'd demanded from them.

He stomped his way to the outbuilding and looked around for something that would hold the tree. There had been some old buckets around at one time. Now what had he done with them when they'd sprung leaks and could no longer hold water?

He found one against a wall, just to the side of the tools, which hung neatly along one wall. Now he needed dirt to hold up the tree. With the ground covered with ice and snow, the only place to easily get it was from the hard dirt floor of the building. He took the ax from its hanger and dug into the earth that had been pounded into a hard surface by generations of

Stevenson feet. He scooped the dirt into the bucket ready for the tree. He thought he heard his name, so he walked out of the building and back into the snow.

"Oh, there you are," Elaine said from the shelter of the porch.

He watched her step gingerly off the porch and follow the outhouse path that needed to be cleared of the new snow. He'd do that again before he took the tree inside.

"Are you ready to pick the tree?" she asked.

He nodded and held up the ax as she made her way to his side.

"Well, I'll be glad to give you my opinion. The girls want a big one, but I think a small one will do fine. Do we need to go far into the woods or will one on the edge do?"

She was going to help him with the tree?

"There are plenty of dwarf pines on the edge that will never make it to maturity in the shade of the big ones." He stomped toward the woods, and she followed in his tracks.

He slowed along the edge of the yard, eyeing the little trees. Well, if she wanted to help, he would welcome her opinion. He didn't want to disappoint the girls, but most of the scrub pines weren't full limbed and would look pretty scrawny as a Christmas tree.

"See any good ones?" he asked.

"Maybe farther in the woods?" she suggested.

He doubted that, but he veered into the woods on the path. It wasn't much of a path now that it was snow covered, but at least it was a gap in the thick covering of pines.

"Oh, there *is* a place," he said, "another hundred yards." Yes, there was the clearing ahead where the snow was deeper, but on the edge were several small trees. It was one of his thinking spots, and the peacefulness he usually found there surrounded him, even with her along.

"Oh, Clay, this one is perfect," Elaine said, knocking snow off one tree.

It was a three-foot tree, nicely proportioned and fairly full.

"Stand back," he said. She walked to the other side of the clearing, and he made a notch on one side, then swung the ax several times on the other side until the tree fell. With another swing he severed the last fibers and freed the tree from its roots.

"They'll love it," Elaine said. She held out her arms as if she would carry it.

"I'll get the trunk, you carry the top, and we won't have to drag it. There's enough snow on it as it is. Take awhile to dry off."

She took her end, and they started out of the woods.

"You know these woods well, don't you? Did you ever chop a Christmas tree here before?"

"Many times. Grandpa and I traipsed all over this mountain. He loved this place as much as I do. He knew every clearing and every outcropping of rock. It wasn't a place to farm, but it was a place to live. When it's clear," he said, waving his hand at the snow as they left the woods and entered the yard, "you can see for miles to the south. It's awesome."

"I've driven on your road several times," Elaine said, "just for the view. It's breathtaking from the highway, but nothing compares to this side of the mountain."

He was glad she shared his idea about the beauty of this place. For some reason, that was important to him.

At the outbuilding, he had Elaine get the bucket of dirt, and he shifted the weight of the tree to carry it alone to the house. He had intended to shovel the path to the outhouse, but it and one to the well had recently been cleared.

Inside, the girls exclaimed over the tree and debated on where it should be put once Clay had it firmly standing in the bucket.

"By the window, of course," Tiffany said. Her socks were hanging on the stove handle, so Clay surmised that she had been the one to clear the paths. "That way if anyone goes by, they can see it."

"Who's going to go by here?" Jennifer asked.

"Well, when the helicopter comes, the pilot can see it," Tiffany said.

"Good plan," Clay said. He moved a small table in front of the window and set the tree on it.

"Too bad we don't have Christmas tree lights," Allison said.

"Where would we plug them in?" Ollie asked.

"Oh, yeah. I keep forgetting."

"We can set candles around it, but not close," Elaine said. "We don't want a fire hazard."

"Last night's smoky affair was enough," Clay said

with a chuckle. "I think we need to keep you away from fires." He reached out and patted Elaine on the shoulder as a way of showing he was teasing.

The girls exchanged glances, and he withdrew his hand. He hadn't meant anything by the gesture, although it felt rather nice. But he knew he'd better watch his step around these girls. They didn't miss a thing.

His phone rang, and he reached for it. Not a moment later, Elaine's phone rang.

John was on the line. He'd checked with the weather service, and from what was predicted, he thought the snow would continue for another day. The front had stalled over them, and another foot of snow could drop before it quit, but by late Sunday afternoon or night it should stop. That meant it would probably be Christmas morning before he could get the helicopter in the air.

"Clay, what's the pilot's number?" Elaine had given the phone to Jennifer and handed a paper and pen to Clay. He wrote down the number.

"Wait," he said. "John's on the line. Hand me that phone and we can get one call out of the way." He spoke briefly to Jennifer's dad and to John, then held the phones together so the two men could talk.

"All done?" he asked John, then handed the phone back to Jennifer and punched off his phone.

"That was weird," Holly said. "Two phones talking to each other."

"It's a weird holiday," Sara said. "Well, can we decorate the tree now, Miss Montana? We have quite a few things made."

"Why don't we wait until after supper? It's time we should be starting it."

"What are we having?" Allison asked. "Tacos? Pizza?"

"Potato soup," Elaine said. "One of my specialties."

At least she was putting a positive spin on the meal situation, Clay thought, as Elaine assigned girls to KP duty. And they had plenty of potatoes.

❦

They wouldn't have any crackers, and the cheese, diced tomatoes, and green onions she added to her special recipe would be missing in this potato soup. At least she planned to use a cup of the milk instead of using just water. And they had lots of potatoes, so the girls could have their fill.

Jennifer and Sara were peeling potatoes, while one at a time the others went from the kitchen craft table to the living room so they could call home.

"Anybody make a star for the top?" Elaine asked.

"We always use an angel on our tree," Holly said.

"Why don't I make the star?" Clay asked. He'd wandered into the kitchen after stoking the fire in the living room.

The crew at the kitchen craft table made room for him.

"Do you use a star on your tree?" Megan asked.

"Yes. A shining gold star. Hand me those scissors, please."

Elaine chopped onion while she listened to the conversation at the table. Did he put up a tree at his own home, or was he talking about his family's tree? Holly asked the question for her.

"Do you put a tree up at your own house?"

"Yes, because I like the festive look of it. But my mom also puts a gold star on the top of her tree."

"Every family has its own traditions," Elaine couldn't help but add.

"Your mom? Don't you have a dad?" Holly asked. She was picking up on the little nuances of his conversation, and again Elaine listened intently.

"My dad died of cancer when I was fourteen. My grandpa, who owned this place, sort of took his place. He used to bring me out here a lot. We called it camping, even though we stayed in the house, because, as you've noticed, the amenities are lacking. But there are a lot of things about this place that are more important than electricity or plumbing."

"Like?" Holly prompted.

"Peace. Solitude. Oneness with nature. Closeness with God."

"You are higher up here," Holly said, "so you'd have to be closer." The others laughed.

It was pleasant in the kitchen with the girls working at the table and at the counter. There was a tangible companionship among the group—all working together to keep spirits up. Elaine glanced out the window. Snow still filled the air, but in here they were safe and warm. For the hundredth time she thanked God that Clay had rescued them.

While he was intent on gluing craft sticks into the shape of a star, Elaine studied him. He was cute, as one of the girls had mentioned. His wavy brown hair was cut rather short, befitting the man who ran an industry as he did. She remembered that Stevenson Wood Products was located on the street behind McDonald's. She'd thought it odd that a factory like that had not been in the industrial park, but from the old brick in the building, she had gathered it had been there long before the fast-food restaurant had opened in town. When she'd mused about that, long ago while on a quest for a double cheeseburger, she'd had no idea that she would someday know the president of the company—and stay in his mountain house.

With the soup bubbling on the stove, Elaine joined the others at the table. She glanced in the living room and saw Tiffany on the phone. She thought she was the last of the girls to call her folks. She didn't even want to think about the size of her cell phone bill for the month. Oh, well, the girls were her responsibility. And she'd always thought of that phone as an emergency tool. It had sure come in handy on this outing.

"Did anyone use the balls?" Elaine asked.

"What balls?" Holly asked.

"I remember some Styrofoam balls in a little sack. I picked them up in the van." She rummaged through a box that had been put on the floor and found the sack. "Ornaments," she said. It took little talent to smear glue on the balls and roll them in glitter. She made blue, red, gold, and silver ones. For hangers she twisted thin wire and stuck them in the balls.

"Okay, what do you think of this?" Clay asked. He held up a gold glittered star.

"Beautiful," several girls exclaimed.

"When I was young, we had a lighting ceremony,"

Elaine said. "After we decorated the tree, we'd plug in the lights at the exact time that my dad would put the star at the top. Then we'd have hot chocolate and cookies."

"Clay can put the star on top after we light the candles in the window," Tiffany suggested. "We don't have any hot chocolate or cookies, do we?"

"Maybe we can improvise," Clay said.

"What time do you want supper?" Elaine asked. "Do you want us to go out and shovel the pad again?"

He shook his head. "I think we'll have plenty of time for that tomorrow."

"Well, then, girls, let's finish up here and clear off the table."

Within a few minutes, the kitchen table was set with six bowls that were in the cupboard and three cups that would serve just as well. Elaine dipped up the soup, Clay offered a simple grace, and they all dug into their potato soup.

"Delicious," Clay said. "You're a good cook, Elaine."

"Thank you, Clay."

Elaine noticed the girls exchanging glances. It was a simple compliment. Why were they acting so junior highish? Probably because they were in junior high, she thought with a silent chuckle.

Dishes were quickly washed, rinsed, and dried so the decorating could commence. Clay shoveled the outhouse path again and brought in more water, and the girls took turns wearing the shoes, dried now from being underneath the pot-bellied stove. Finally it was time to decorate the tree.

Clay moved over beside Elaine. "Shall we have coffee and vanilla wafers? It's the best we can do."

"I'll put on the water," she said. That was exactly what she wanted, but it was not her place to offer his food to the girls.

The girls sang carols as they decorated in the glow of two kerosene lamps. They sang not in their angel voices of the concert, but more in the raucous way they'd sung in the van.

Clay set the candles on the windowsill, away from the tree. When all the ornaments had been hung, the girls stepped back and admired their work.

"It's so glittery," Ollie exclaimed. "It's beautiful."

Elaine thought so, too. The lamplight caught the glitter on each ornament and made each one twinkle. She dipped up very weak coffee and brought the sugar jar to the living room. Clay put the vanilla wafers in a bowl.

"Are we ready for the lighting ceremony?" Megan asked.

They decided that Elaine would light the first candle with a wooden kitchen match, then each girl would light a candle with Elaine's. When the last candle had been lit, Clay placed the star on the top, while the girls oohed and ahhed.

They toasted each other with their sweet week coffee, except for Holly, who decided she'd drink her coffee black. The vanilla wafers tasted like the finest homemade cookies to Elaine. Again, it was a moment to savor. A moment of contentment.

"You know what's missing?" Tiffany asked.

"What?" several said.

"Gifts."

"No," Clay said. "We do not need gifts!"

Chapter 7

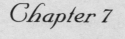

The companionable mood quickly took a nose-dive. What was the matter with Clay? Why had he changed so suddenly from the man who was being so kind to them to the man who barked, "No gifts"?

"What's wrong with Christmas presents?" Ollie asked, although Elaine would have preferred that the matter be dropped.

"Christmas is not about gifts," he said in a lecturing tone. "It's not about what you can get. I'm so tired of the commercialization of Christmas. Stores shove Christmas merchandise down our throats before October, maybe even September."

"The girls aren't going to buy gifts," Elaine said calmly.

"That's right, they're not," he said adamantly.

"Do you give gifts to your family?" Ollie asked.

Why wouldn't that girl drop the subject?

"Yes, but only so they won't be disappointed."

"These are great vanilla wafers," Elaine said, to change the subject from one that obviously distressed

Clay. She vowed to get to the bottom of it, but not in front of the girls. Maybe she could take a shift outside with him and talk then.

"Yeah, these cookies are really good," Tiffany said.

"I think it's time we turn in," Elaine said. "Let's get our pallets put together." It was only a little after eight, but the outside work had tired them, and she knew they would whisper even after the lights were out.

They left the candles lit while they rearranged furniture, dragged the mattress to the kitchen, and laid the coats out for padding for the other pallets.

Clay brought in wood. "Don't even think of feeding the fire," he told Elaine in a teasing voice, and the girls laughed. At least he was in a better mood, and it lightened all their spirits.

With the girls settled in place, Elaine blew out the lamps and candles, except for one she used to light the way to her chair. She made sure she had matches on the table beside her recliner. After the blackness of last night, she didn't intend to be without a source of light if it was needed. But she'd do as Clay asked and let him get up to feed the fire.

"Girls, shall we say our evening prayer?" They quieted down, and Elaine started, "Father, thank You for the girls being such willing workers."

"Thank You for our Christmas tree," Tiffany said.

"Thank You for the phones," Allison added.

"Thank You for Clay knowing the helicopter guy," Ollie said.

"Thank You for Clay sharing his food with us," Jennifer said.

"Thank You for the warm fires," Sara continued.

"Thank You for the black coffee," Holly said, eliciting some giggles.

"Thank You for these dry socks," Megan said.

Elaine thought she heard Clay in the other room, but she couldn't make out his words. "Amen," she said, and the word was echoed around the room.

It was probably another half hour before the girls stopped whispering among themselves, yet Elaine lay awake for longer. She couldn't figure out Clay. He was a successful businessman, so money was not a worry to him. He loved his family—that was apparent from the way he had teased his sister on the phone and the way he talked about his grandpa. He was generous with everything he had in this house, so why was he so opposed to Christmas presents?

And there was one more thing. She was attracted to him, and that surprised her. He was different from the guys she usually dated. He wasn't into the arts, for one thing, and most of the men she saw socially were musicians or interested in the theater. Clay was a businessman and a practical guy.

He had a commanding air, and it wasn't just because this was his house and he was in charge. She suspected he would have that authority in most aspects of his life, probably because of his company. A man couldn't be in charge of a big work force without having a commanding air. Certainly she and the girls had done everything he'd asked, but this was his place and he knew all about basic operations of things, like the lanterns and the stove.

She was intrigued by him. He sought solitude, but he didn't seem lonely. In his day-to-day life he would be surrounded by people, so wouldn't it be normal to seek time alone? Didn't she do that on occasion? She was surrounded by students all day. On the weekends, she took long drives by herself. That was how she knew about this road that cut off from the highway.

Maybe that was what intrigued her about Clay. He had some of the same needs she had, not anti-social needs, just minor eccentricities.

He was a religious man. His Bible was beside his bed, and he had said he liked being here on the mountain because he felt closer to God.

She must have dozed, because the creak of the wood stove being opened woke her. It was a repeat of the night before, with Clay stoking the fire.

Determined to get to the bottom of the no-gifts rule, she reached over and lit the candle. "Can we talk?" she whispered. From the flicker of light over the girls, they appeared to be deeply asleep. She doubted anything would wake them.

"Just a minute." He added wood to the cookstove, then returned to squat beside her recliner on the side away from the girls' pallets. "I'm sorry I snapped at you all earlier."

"That's okay. The question is why?"

"I knew you'd ask, and I've been trying to come up with a good answer. It's not simple."

"I've got all night," Elaine said in a soft voice.

❦

Clay stood up and went through the wide doorway

into the kitchen. As quietly as he could, he lifted a chair from where it had been pushed against the wall and carried it back to the living room. He might as well be comfortable while they talked; he didn't see how this could be a short conversation.

"It's not a simple answer because I'm not sure why," he said.

"How long have you been opposed to giving Christmas gifts?"

"Not exactly opposed, just disapproving." How could he explain this? "It started when I was eleven. I wanted a bike for Christmas. Not just any bike, a blue dirt bike. I even knew the exact model number."

"And you didn't get it?"

"No. I got a different model, but that wasn't what I wanted. I wanted one like Josh Evans had."

"You were disappointed."

She seemed to be one step ahead of him. "Yes. I was sorely disappointed, and I didn't keep it to myself. I told my folks, and I was a brat about it. They put the bike in the garage and said I should receive a gift in the spirit it was given. When I was ready to apologize, I could have the bike."

"You never apologized, did you?"

"That bike is still in my mom's garage. I was too stubborn to admit I was wrong. Of course, I knew that Christmas was a celebration of the birth of Jesus, but as a kid, getting gifts overshadowed that for me. I see kids today being as greedy as I was, and that greed is fed by the commercialization of Christmas."

"So, what do you give your family as gifts?"

"I work with wood. Each year I give the same gift—a finished board with a Bible verse burned into it. I study on it. I pick the right verse for each family. And for the kids, I buy books. I try to pick each book to match the likes of the child. I don't get whatever the toy fad is for that year. The kids don't give me a wish list, and they know what to expect from me."

"And they aren't disappointed."

"Exactly." So she understood his feelings on the subject. This little talk had turned out easier than he'd anticipated.

"It sounds to me as if you give the perfect gifts," Elaine said. "Now, about the girls. They're all around fourteen, and they are very smart girls. They know the true meaning of Christmas, but they also know this season is for sharing love and friendship. Do you really object if they want to make gifts for each other?" In her earnestness, she reached out and touched his hand.

He pondered her question as best he could while her hand rested atop his. "I don't object. With only craft stuff to choose from, they can't get overwhelmed by giving the best gift or expecting more." He chuckled softly. "And it will keep them busy. They'll be listening for the chopper all day, but it may be Monday before we're rescued." He told her John's weather prediction.

"Well," she said and withdrew her hand, "they should still be home for Christmas. Their parents can call John whenever they want an update on the airlift. What a Christmas adventure. I never dreamed it would be like this."

"What were your plans?"

"Going home to my folks in Missouri for a few days."

"You may not make it on Christmas. We don't know how the roads are at home. If this stuff is coming down here, it's probably coming down in town."

"I know. I'll miss Christmas dinner, but I can go home later in the week. We don't start school again until after New Year's." She yawned. "Well, it's getting late. We'd better get some sleep."

"You're right," he said. "Good night." He returned to his bedroom and wrapped up in the quilt. So they would make gifts for each other. He wondered what he could give to each of the girls. He didn't know them very well, and yet each one already had a distinct personality.

Elaine Montana certainly had quite an effect on him. He'd like to learn more about her. Maybe he could pump the girls for some information. He wasn't likely to have any more time alone with her.

When Clay added wood to the fire around four, it was still snowing. He shined his flashlight out his bedroom window, but he couldn't judge the depth.

☙

"Look outside," Tiffany said in a loud voice that woke Elaine. "It's still snowing."

Elaine glanced at her watch. Not quite eight. They had slept much longer than she'd thought possible. She sat up in the recliner, stiff from her odd bed. The girls were already putting on the shoes for the outhouse. How she wished she could have a hot shower and wash her hair. Well, maybe tomorrow she'd be in her own apartment and could indulge herself. For now, she'd make do with washing her face and rubbing her teeth with Clay's toothpaste.

"Hey, Clay's already shoveling the path," Holly said. "Look at that snow. It's got to be two feet deep."

"That's from the path, too," Tiffany said. "I wonder if he has a yardstick."

Clay stomped on the back porch and came in. "That front must be sitting right on top of us," he said. "Over a foot so far."

"You think we'll get to go home today?" Jennifer asked.

Clay glanced at Elaine. "It will probably be tomorrow—in time for Christmas dinner," she said.

"Speaking of food," Sara said. "Do we have anything for breakfast?"

Elaine didn't answer, waiting for Clay to speak. "We'll find something," he said and moved over beside Elaine. "We need to plan on four more meals. This morning we can have bacon and eggs, and there are always potatoes."

Elaine looked in the icebox. "We should save a couple of eggs for tomorrow's pancakes. I can fix shepherd's pie for supper with this steak. Weren't there beans in the pantry? We could put those on to cook for lunch."

"We can have a breakfast feast," he told the girls. "Bacon, eggs, and hash browns."

By the time the girls finished with morning cleanup, put away their beds, and the cooking was done, over an hour had passed before they sat down to their meal.

"Where's that other kitchen chair?" Tiffany asked.

"Oh, it's in the living room," Elaine said.

"Who put it in there?" Megan asked. "I stacked them all over here last night."

Elaine glanced at Clay, and Megan turned to him. "You put that chair beside Miss Montana's recliner? In the night?"

"We were talking," he said, sounding like a teenager caught out after curfew, "about gifts. And we decided you can make gifts for each other if you want."

At once, the girls broke into noisy chatter, and it didn't end with breakfast but continued through cleanup and assignments of shoveling duty. Elaine put beans on to boil in a large pot, and then she, too, became caught up in the excitement of making presents.

"No one can come over here," Ollie said from one corner of the living room. She had taken several craft items from the boxes and sat with her back to the others.

"Same here," Holly said. She staked off her territory in the kitchen.

A contented silence filled the house as the girls worked on their projects. Every half hour, the changing of the shoes meant a new shoveling crew and two new girls to work on their secret gifts.

At noon, Clay declared that the shoveling was over until late afternoon. They had cleared a lot of snow, but more came down to take its place.

While the group ate beans around the kitchen table, Elaine said, "This is Christmas Eve. And it's Sunday. We didn't have a morning service, but I think we should have a Christmas Eve service."

The idea met with enthusiasm, and a debate ensued over what would be included in the service. By the meal's end, the program had been set, with Clay reading the Christmas story from the Bible and the girls singing the program they had given on Friday night in Beaver Cove.

"What about you, Miss Montana? What will you do?" Allison asked.

"I'll be the audience."

Chapter 8

S houldn't we wear our dresses and choir robes?"
Sara asked.

"Maybe the robes," Elaine said. She was playing Sara in the losers' bracket of another checkers tournament that Clay had set up. Some of the girls were still working on their presents, and Elaine wanted out of this game so she could work on hers.

"I wish I could take a bath and wash my hair," Sara said.

"I know. But heating water for all of us to bathe, plus putting back on dirty clothes, just doesn't seem worth the effort. By this time tomorrow, you'll be clean again."

"I hope. Hey, the snow's letting up. Do you think he'll come today?"

"Maybe, but I doubt it." No way was Elaine going to build up Sara's hopes. Counting on tomorrow was enough.

"King me," Sara said, as another checker made its way to Elaine's end of the board. A short while later Sara won the game, and Elaine escaped to let Megan play.

Clay had gone outside to move wood to the porch.

He hadn't requested a work crew, so Elaine figured he needed time alone. But she wanted to talk to him, and she donned the shoes and headed outside.

"Need help?"

"I'm about finished," he said, knocking snow off some logs. "We should only need it until tomorrow morning."

"Okay. I was wondering if I could use the shovel. I wanted to find some small stones from this place, if that's all right with you. They're for my gifts."

He stacked a load of wood on the porch. "There's a rock pile behind that shed. Wouldn't take too much digging to find some."

"Thanks." She took a shovel and cleared a narrow path to the outbuilding. "Where?" she called back.

"East corner."

She dug until she hit rock, then she brushed snow off with her gloved hands. It took more pounding to break through the ice. These weren't exactly what she had in mind. The stones were pretty good sized. She sorted through the pile until she found some smaller ones. Perfect. She stuffed some in her pants pockets, in her coat pockets, and in her shirt pocket. Now to get a little privacy so she could make her gifts.

"Did you find what you needed?" Clay asked. She'd been so intent on finding her rocks, that she hadn't heard him make his way to the shed.

"Exactly what I needed." They stood just inches apart, looking into each others eyes.

"I want to thank you for listening to me last night. I intend to get that bike this Christmas."

Elaine smiled. "So you're going to tell your mom you're sorry you were a brat. How many years ago was that?"

"Over twenty years. I haven't always held this grudge, you know. I'd forgotten about the bike until you made me think of why I'd become such a Scrooge at Christmas."

So, he was at least thirty-one. She'd thought as much, but she wasn't a good judge of age.

"You're no Scrooge. You're one of the most generous men I've ever met. You've given us everything you have, including your solitude, which I know you value."

"Miss Montana," Ollie called.

Elaine and Clay stepped from behind the outbuilding. Ollie stood in the open doorway. "Telephone."

"I'll be right there," Elaine said.

Ollie's eyes were twice their normal size, and she squealed and slammed the kitchen door.

"Oh, no. I feel like we've been caught doing something wrong," Elaine said.

Clay took her hand and pulled her back behind the shed. Before she understood what was about to happen, he kissed her. Just a quick peck on the lips, but it was a kiss.

"I hate to be convicted of something I haven't done, and I'd never convince them that I haven't wanted to kiss you for some time."

Elaine laughed self-consciously, but she didn't admit that the same thought had crossed her mind lately. "I'd better get the phone."

Clay carried the shovel back to the helicopter pad

to clean it once again, now that the snow was letting up, while Elaine tromped to the house. Inside, the girls stood grinning at her.

"My telephone?" Elaine asked, as she shrugged out of her coat.

Ollie handed it to her. Who else would it be but her mother? "Yes, Mom, still here, but we hope to be rescued tomorrow." She walked into the living room for some privacy and explained the situation.

"Okay, girls," Elaine said when she'd hung up, "we need to peel some potatoes for the shepherd's pie. Allison and Holly, your turn." She took the steak from the icebox and cut it into slivers. It would cook fast and go farther if it were small. Once the potatoes were boiling, Elaine grabbed her coat and escaped to the spare bedroom.

She sorted her stones and wiped them on a tissue from her coat pocket. Her plan was simply to give the girls something to remind them of this old place. She'd like to paint a gold star on the stones, symbolic of Christmas and of Clay making the star for the top of the tree. She'd seen a gold ink pen in the craft boxes and hoped the girls hadn't used it up. After supper, the rocks would be dry enough for her to draw on them.

As soon as the potatoes were done, Elaine browned the meat slivers, added a can of corn to the skillet, and topped them with mashed potatoes. Normally she would have poured gravy between the corn and potato layers, but she didn't have any broth to make it with. It would be a dry casserole, but it would be edible.

The girls set the table with plates and candles for the

festive Christmas Eve feast. Once they had said grace, Elaine explained that another of her family traditions was to have shepherd's pie every Christmas Eve.

"I'm sure the shepherds didn't eat this, but we always pretend that they did. And we always eat in candlelight because it flickers like the light from their campfire."

"You have some good traditions, Miss Montana," Holly said.

"I imagine your family has good ones, too." They went around the table, talking about how each family celebrated the holidays.

"You know what we need?" Tiffany asked.

"What?" several asked.

"Mistletoe."

"Maybe we don't need it," Ollie said and grinned at Clay and Elaine.

Elaine ignored her. "Is that a tradition at your house, Tiffany?"

"Yes. We hang it in the kitchen doorway, and once you're under it, you can't move away until someone kisses you. It started with Mom and Dad kissing us, but maybe it's time to move on to others," she said with a laugh.

The others joined her laughter.

Elaine loved the sound of it—from Tiffany's high-pitched giggle to Megan's more throaty laugh.

Elaine let the girls do the dishes while she worked on her Christmas presents. It didn't take long to draw the stars, and she was pleased with the outcome.

With coffee water set on the stove, program preparations began in earnest. Candles were lit in front of the tree, the girls donned their choir robes over Clay's old clothes, and Clay carried his Bible in from his bedroom.

The girls stood and sang several carols in their sweet angel voices. Then they sat down on the floor, and Clay read the Christmas story. When he finished, they sang three more carols, ending with "Oh, Holy Night."

Elaine didn't think she'd ever heard a more beautiful rendition. The girls' voices blended as one, every note clear and bright. Clay seemed as enthralled by their performance as she was. They both clapped and clapped while the girls bowed.

The girls drank coffee and ate the bag of corn chips from Clay's big tin box. This time, three of the girls drank it black, since the sugar supply was almost gone.

The pile of gifts under the tree had been steadily growing all day long. Elaine took pages of a newspaper Clay had brought with him and wrapped her star stones. She slipped her presents under the tree, too.

She let the girls stay up longer this night, and then prepared for the outhouse treks. Allison was the first one to wear the shoes outside.

"It's stopped snowing!" she yelled from the porch.

The girls rushed to the doorway. "We'll be rescued. Will he come at night?"

"Too dangerous. It will be morning," Clay said from the living room, "but we'll need to be ready."

Evening prayers were identical thanks from each girl for the birth of Jesus and the snow stopping. Even though Elaine encouraged the girls to get right to sleep, talk was not even in loud whispers but in normal voices. Excitement ran high, but finally the soft sounds of even breathing filled the house.

Elaine half-hoped Clay would stop by her chair for another midnight talk while he was stoking the fires, but even though she awoke when he added wood, he went right back to his bedroom.

At first light, the girls were awake. The morning sun rays shone through the windows, and outside the world glistened white, nearly blinding in its brightness.

"When will the helicopter come?" the girls asked over and over.

The morning cleanup rituals were performed and the pallets were put away. With black coffee all around, since there was no more sugar, the group sat down in the living room to open Christmas presents.

"The gifts under this tree reflect the friendship and love we have for each other," Elaine said. "Like the three wise men who brought gifts to the baby Jesus to honor Him, we have made presents to honor our friendship for one another."

Each girl took a turn passing out the presents she had made. The girls exclaimed over tissue flowers, Styrofoam brooches, craft stick boxes, glittered pictures, craft stick crosses, glittered clothespin note holders, and glittered Styrofoam pencil holders, complete with one used pencil each. Elaine's paperweight star stones were a hit. They were thanking each other for their wonderful gifts, when Clay excused himself, went into his room, and returned with sheets of paper.

He handed one to each girl. Elaine read hers. " 'Love is patient, love is kind. . . . It always protects, always trusts, always hopes, always perseveres,' 1 Corinthians 13:4-7."

Love. It was the best Christmas gift. Oh, she knew he wasn't professing love to her. They'd known each other for not three full days, but there was a hint here of things to come. She met his gaze and smiled.

"Thank you, Clay. I will treasure this."

As others were expressing gratitude for their verses, Tiffany said, "Listen. Listen!"

The unmistakable sound of whirling blades got louder and louder.

The girls shouted and yelled and hugged each other.

"Let's get organized, girls. Tiffany, Allison, Ollie, and Jennifer—get your clothes and put on your shoes." Elaine was sure they would forget something, but she planned to go through the place carefully before she took her turn in the helicopter.

The first load of girls hugged Clay and thanked him before they climbed on board. The other girls waved from the window as the rotary blades raised a whirlwind of snow, making it unwise to stand on the porch.

"Let's get the rest of you ready," Elaine said. "First get your clothes together, so you're ready to load, then report for kitchen duty."

She washed all the cups they'd dirtied, while the girls put on their shoes. They were a sight with their rolled up pants legs and heels, but their beaming faces told of their great excitement.

Within a half hour, John was back for the next load. Elaine herded the final three girls aboard.

"Thanks, Clay, for teaching us to drink black coffee like real men," Holly said and laughed. "Aren't you coming with us, Miss Montana?"

"No. I'm going to get all the supplies packed and take down the Christmas tree. We'll leave this place like we found it. I'll come with the next load."

Elaine and Clay headed back inside before the whirlwind of snow began.

"You could have gone," he said, "but I'm glad you stayed."

"I know," she said as she moved toward the spare bedroom. She gathered her clothes and all the choir robes and stuffed them in a plastic bag. Nothing else was amiss in the room.

In the kitchen, she looked in the icebox. "Want some milk?" She emptied the carton into a glass and handed it to Clay, who took a drink and then handed it back to her.

"We'll call this breakfast," he said.

She put her lips where his had been. Sharing this glass seemed such an intimate gesture.

"One potato left," she said. Those and the two eggs they'd been saving for this morning's pancakes were all that remained of Clay's holiday supplies.

She washed their shared glass and dried it. Clay emptied the water buckets and stirred the fire in the cook-stove so it would quickly burn out. The craft supplies were packed neatly in boxes, but Elaine decided not to lug those on the helicopter. When the wrecker could make it up the mountain for the van, she'd stop by the cabin and get them.

With the kitchen in good shape, they moved to the living room, and Elaine started taking ornaments off the tree. "Shall I toss the decorations?"

"Let's save them. We might want a tree up here next year."

We? Had he included her in next year's plan? Elaine carefully placed the ornaments in a grocery sack, and Clay set the bare tree on the back porch.

"I'll take it to the woods when I'm here next time."

"And I'll return all your clothes—freshly laundered—when we come get the van."

Elaine heard the helicopter approaching.

"I guess it's time to go."

Clay carried his suitcase and backpack to the living room. Elaine had her plastic bag.

"Got your phone?" he asked.

"In my purse."

"Got your purse?" he said and chuckled. She laughed, remembering their trek in the freezing rain to fetch her purse from the van.

Clay stirred the fire in the pot-bellied stove.

They carried their belongings to the helicopter and then returned for one last look around.

"I think we've got everything," Elaine said, feeling reluctant to leave.

"I believe so," Clay said.

"I can't thank you enough for all you've done," she said. "I don't know how we would have survived without you."

"And I don't know how I would have survived without you," he said. "I came here knowing I was missing something but not knowing exactly what it was. You were what was missing." He drew her into his arms. "You have made this Christmas the most memorable of my life—so far. And it's not over yet. Will you come with me to my family's Christmas dinner?"

She smiled and nodded her acceptance. He kissed her, and then with his arm around her shoulder, he escorted her to the helicopter.

VEDA BOYD JONES

Veda enjoys the challenge of writing for diverse audiences. She is the author of twenty-four books: from a tiny picture book for beginning readers to biographies and historical novels for middle-graders to romances for the **Heartsong Presents** line. In this Christmas story, Veda included some of her family's Christmas traditions. "My husband puts the star on the top of the Christmas tree while the boys plug in the lights for our Christmas lighting ceremony. We also have shepherd's pie on Christmas Eve, even though we know the shepherd's didn't have that for supper on that special night two thousand years ago. We imagine them staring up at the Star of Bethlehem, and it reminds us of the true meaning of Christmas."

The Gift Shoppe

by Darlene Mindrup

Chapter 1

The bell over the shop door jangled and a gust of freezing air blew in as a customer entered. Amy Latimer looked up from arranging a display. Her smile widened into a full grin as she recognized her customer.

"Well, hello, Michael. What brings you out on such a cold day?"

Dark brown eyes flicked downward to where Amy was on her knees, and her smile was returned in full.

"Hi, Amy. I. . .I needed to buy a gift for someone, and I wasn't sure what to get. I remembered that you worked here and thought if anyone could help me, it would be you."

When Amy's emerald green eyes met his, she was momentarily startled by the intensity of his expression. Only for an instant was that unreadable emotion in his eyes before they once again became the blank, but friendly, look of a customer.

She took the hand he extended to her as he helped her to her feet. Although the temperatures outside were barely above freezing, she couldn't help but notice the warmth of his fingers as they closed around hers. Her skin tingled from the brief contact.

He was an attractive man, and although she didn't know him well, since he had only recently begun attending her church, she had found her eyes often drawn to him in their singles' class. His responses to the teacher's questions showed an obvious insight into the Scriptures that Amy had to admire. Envy might be a closer word, but then envy was a sin and she hoped she hadn't gone that far yet.

Lately, her activities left little time for Bible study, but she did manage her daily devotions. Michael, on the other hand, seemed to live and breathe the Scriptures he so often quoted. He would make a wonderful minister of the gospel.

Snow dusted his black hair and for a moment she was tempted to brush it away. The warmth of his expression belied the cold crystals clinging to him. His eyes were friendly and inviting, almost as though he could read her thoughts.

Frowning at her reflections, she quickly retreated behind the safe confines of the counter. Michael followed and stood just across from her, his twinkling brown eyes smiling into hers. Unable to hold his gaze, Amy fidgeted with items next to the cash register.

"You say it's for someone special?"

His eyes suddenly lit with laughter, and his lips twitched with restrained humor. "I didn't say that, but yes, I guess you could say she's special."

Amy felt a slight twinge at the reference to gender. So there was a special girl. She had often wondered, though she had never noticed Michael with a particular girl. She immediately began wondering who the girl might be, her mind submitting and then rejecting the females of their mutual acquaintance.

"It's a New Year's gift," he told her, his hooded eyes moving slowly over her telling countenance. "What can you suggest?"

Flustered, she shrugged her shoulders. "Well, I. . .I don't know. Could you give me a little more information?"

"I'm not sure what to tell you. Maybe you could suggest something that *you* might like."

"Well, I could," she hesitated, "but she might not like the same things I do."

He smiled. "Actually, she's very much like you. If a guy you barely knew wanted to buy you a gift, what would you find appropriate?"

She refrained from telling him that the likelihood of that happening was next to nil. She thought about it a minute and then told him, "I think maybe a scented candle might be nice. One could hardly consider a candle offensive. And it would be a good way to ring in the New Year, a light to shine through the coming months."

Although his lips twitched slightly, his eyes were serious. "I think you must be a romantic, Amy. That's a good idea. Will you help me choose one?"

Thinking it an odd request, Amy realized her duties and moved from behind the counter to show him the candles. He was standing close behind her, the scent from his aftershave drifting tantalizingly around her. She felt suddenly clumsy, her hands shaking so badly she almost dropped a candle she was holding.

When she turned, she found herself mere inches from Michael's black wool overcoat. Her eyes barely reached the top button of the garment. Feeling at a slight disadvantage, she moved quickly out of his way.

"Which scent do *you* prefer?" he wanted to know.

"Well, I. . .I like them all."

"Surely you have a favorite?"

Growing irritated at her body's strange reaction to his presence, not to mention this odd conversation, Amy almost snapped back an answer. Taking a deep breath, she silently counted to ten like she had been taught to do as a child. She hadn't inherited her grandmother's flaming red hair for nothing.

When her gaze finally connected with Michael's, she found his look contained nothing more than honest curiosity.

"Cinnamon spice is my favorite," she told him.

He lifted the lid on the candle jar, sniffing its fragrance. "Mmm, I can see why." His laughter was infectious. "This reminds me of my mother's snickerdoodles."

Amy grinned. "Are you a snickerdoodleoholic, too?"

He tried to look guilty but only succeeded in looking pathetic.

"Guilty, I'm afraid. Most people prefer chocolate chip, but there's just something about a nice, warm snickerdoodle."

Chuckling, Amy handed him another jar. "Try this one."

He took the jar and inhaled its fragrance. His surprised eyes met hers. "Apple pie?"

"Mmm-hmm. I don't think there's a fragrance they

haven't thought of."

His eyes began to gleam. "Now I get it. The way to a man's heart is through his stomach. Light a candle, invite a fella over, and *wham* he's hooked."

Placing her hands on her hips, Amy cocked her head to the side, throwing him a mock glare. She was enjoying this banter. "Now don't go telling everyone you know."

He placed a hand on her shoulder and closed one eye in a slow wink. Amy felt her heart stop for a brief second, then continue at a thundering pace.

"Your secret is safe with me."

After several moments of indecision, he finally decided on the cinnamon spice. Amy wrapped it for him, her fingers fumbling under his watchful gaze. Flipping her long red hair behind her shoulders, she watched him walk to the door.

For a moment his dark eyes met hers again, the pupils dilating until they reminded her of a shimmering onyx stone. He opened his mouth as though to speak but snapped his lips together, suddenly opened the door, and left. The bell jangled as the door closed behind him, shutting Amy in with her thoughts.

Slowly releasing her breath, she returned to the display shelf and began to rearrange the candles to fill in the bare spot Michael had left. Her fingers slid slowly over a display of cinnamon scented candles. Never again would she be able to smell this fragrance without thinking of him.

❦

Michael strolled down the street oblivious to the cold.

His lips quivered slightly as his thoughts drifted back over his encounter with Amy.

Others in the church had warned him the woman had absolutely no confidence in herself. The way she dressed spoke clearly of that fact. Still, ever since arriving in this town and attending the same church, she had intrigued him.

Amy had two qualities he found rare among the women of his acquaintance—sweetness and shyness. Perhaps those two things might put others off, but not him. If anything, he found them refreshing.

Although Amy had several friends, he could not ascertain whether any of them were really close to her. There was something so infinitely lonely about her that he felt compelled to try and be her friend. He didn't bother to analyze such feelings; he just proceeded to put them into practice.

Since he had been warned by the others to tread lightly when seeking her friendship, he tried to think of a way to make her feel comfortable with him. The idea of buying gifts for some unnamed girl had seemed to be just the thing. That way she wouldn't feel as though he were trying to pay her any personal attention. She would feel safe.

Her amiable sense of humor was a bonus. He would enjoy getting to know her better, but he had to remember to be wary. All he was looking for was a friend. He must be careful not to give her the wrong idea.

He crossed the street, slid behind the steering wheel of his car, and dropped the candle on the front passenger seat. Quickly leaving the parking area behind, he braked at the first traffic light. When the light turned green, it reminded him so much of Amy's remarkable eyes that he just sat there thinking about them until an angry blast from behind reminded him to get going.

Shaking his head wryly, he soon left Farmington far behind.

Chapter 2

A sharp wind rattled the large glass window that overlooked the street in front of Amy's shop. Bare limbed trees lined each side of the road, bending and swaying in time to the gusting wind. Amy had just rearranged her last window display when she glanced up and saw Michael striding across the street in her direction. His dark hair fluttered across his forehead, and he brushed it back impatiently. Her heart gave an odd little jump before settling down again to its normal rhythm.

The bell jangled as the door opened, and Michael came in rubbing his hands together against February's biting cold. He smiled when he saw her.

"Hi, Amy."

Each time she saw him, she couldn't help but notice how attractive he was. He had the kind of deep voice that would cause most women's hearts to flutter, but his shining dark eyes attracted her most. They were so full of life that they made her want to reach out and snatch some of that vitality for herself.

"Hi, yourself," she answered him, carefully adjusting

a glass dish of Valentine's Day candy on the window display shelf. "You must like being out in the cold."

He grinned. "Well, at least it's not snowing."

Amy laughed, remembering that after last Sunday's sermon Michael had told her he didn't mind the cold, but he could do without the snow. She had wondered then why he had chosen to live in a northern climate like Ohio. As far as she knew, he had no relatives in the vicinity. Being shy, she had refrained from asking, thinking the question rather personal.

He unwrapped his burgundy wool scarf from his neck, dropped it and his coat on the counter, and moved toward the spot where Amy stood fidgeting with the Valentine's Day display. He reached around her, bringing him into such close proximity that Amy could smell a mixture of cologne and cold. It was an enticing fragrance, and she found her nose twitching in appreciation. His shoulder brushed hers when he lifted a mug filled with chocolate kisses, and Amy's stomach tightened strangely.

"This is cute," he told her, "but maybe not quite right for a friend. It might seem suggestive, don't you think?"

His mischievous gaze met hers, and Amy found herself holding her breath. Was it possible that he was aware of the curious effect he had on her? Quickly she moved away from him, an unconscious frown creasing her forehead.

"You. . .you need another gift for your. . .your friend?" Amy asked him.

Although a smile was on his face, Michael's eyes were serious. He hadn't missed her reaction to his nearness.

He nodded but made no comment, his narrow-eyed look never leaving her face.

"What did you have in mind?"

"I don't know. You did such a good job choosing the last one, I thought you might help me with this one." His voice was velvet soft, and Amy shivered slightly. How could any one man be so devastatingly handsome?

"Well," she finally managed. "It *is* almost Valentine's Day. Is that what you had in mind?"

He pursed his lips slightly, his gaze continuing to roam over her face. There was something almost probing in his look.

Shoving her hands into the pockets of her denim jumper, Amy squirmed under his assessment. What did he see when he looked at her? She knew she had no physical beauty to speak of, and lately her clothing had become rather shabby. Thinking about Michael had made her realize this, but she wasn't quite certain why her clothes should suddenly matter. Someone like Michael was definitely out of her reach even if she *had* been searching for a relationship.

"Yeah," he agreed softly, watching the changing expressions on her face. "That's what I had in mind."

His gaze caught and held hers. Swallowing hard, she asked him hesitantly, "Well, did she like the candle?" She had to quell the desire to hope the woman hadn't. What was the matter with her anyway? She tried to rein in her unruly and unkind thoughts.

"She thought it was perfect," he told her, the twinkle back in his eye.

It figured.

"And would you like something a little more romantic this time?" She dropped her gaze to the glass shelf beside her, afraid that he would see the envious thoughts flashing through her mind. She picked up a glass figurine of a dove and nervously began twirling it in her fingers.

He hesitated. "No," he decided. "I don't think so. We're just friends, really."

Amy's breath came out in a soft sigh. She hadn't even realized she had been holding it. Her curiosity about this unknown woman was going to get the best of her if she didn't watch out. Michael's friendships had nothing to do with her, really, so why was she being so nosy?

Moving to an aisle display, Amy lifted a CD of popular Christian music. "This is a great CD. I mean if she likes. . .she *is* a Christian, isn't she?"

"Most definitely," he confirmed, his eyes still glimmering. "And I think that's a great idea. Music for the soul, you know."

Amy grinned, beginning to enjoy this game of analogies. It would seem Michael was a romantic too, and she felt a sudden kinship with him.

He laid the CD on the counter and pulled his wallet out of his pocket. "Do you like music, Amy?" he asked, his attention focused on the bills he was slowly pulling from his billfold.

"Some," she answered wrinkling her nose. "I'm more into the classics. You know, Tchaikovsky, Mozart, Brahms. Rock has never been my thing."

Clutching the money in his fist, his enigmatic eyes met hers.

"The symphony in Columbus is doing a concert of Mendelssohn's work. Would you like to go?"

A paralyzing fear shot through Amy at his suggestion. The idea of being alone with a man left her shaken. She chided herself for her timidity, but she just couldn't stop her feelings. In her lifetime, she had dated little, and her last encounter was so disastrous it had left her ego shattered. Admiring Michael was one thing, but being alone with him was quite something else. Biting her lip, she answered him doubtfully. "I. . .I don't know, Michael."

For just a moment his eyes darkened with some unnamed emotion. Taking a deep breath, he gave her a halfhearted smile. "I was thinking it might be a fun outing for the singles' group. . .but if you're not sure. . ."

The obvious relief on her face brought a slight twitch to his lips.

"I didn't know. . .that is, I thought. . ." She stopped, frowning heavily. "What I mean is, I think the singles would love it."

He stood watching her for what seemed an eternity. Finally, he handed her the bills he was still holding.

"Good. I'll make the arrangements."

Amy handed him his bag, only remembering then that the CD was for some special girl. She should have realized he was asking on behalf of the singles' group and not for himself. She felt like an idiot and decided that Michael must think she *was* one.

She hesitated then returned his brief smile, watching as he crossed the room and carefully shut the door behind him. Hurrying to the front window, she continued to observe him until he disappeared down the street and finally out of sight. Sighing, she turned back to her work.

❦

Michael felt Amy watch him as he walked down the street. He frowned, remembering the panic that had filled her eyes at his invitation. Something must have happened to her to cause such a reaction from so simple a suggestion. He would love to know what that something was.

Probably a man was involved somewhere. His eyes darkened with anger. Just thinking about someone hurting such a shy, sweet girl caused his hands to clutch into fists at his side, wrinkling the brown paper bag with the CD.

Although his invitation had been spur of the moment, her reaction had dented his ego some. Obviously, she felt much better in a group, at least where men were concerned.

Maybe that would be a better idea anyway. This was still too soon for a date, and perhaps he had moved too fast. She was slowly opening up to him, and he didn't want her to suddenly retreat back into her shell.

His mind boggled over the fact that such a timid person could own her own shop. He had seen her with other customers, and she seemed to be a different person. Her eyes sparkled, and she forgot to be reserved. He was certain that was how she was meant to be, and he was suddenly challenged to see if he could help her be that way all the time.

Chapter 3

A blustery wind rattled the shop windows as Amy settled herself into the wrought-iron chair next to a diminutive matching table in the corner of the room. Only last year she had decided that it would be a good idea to have this little nook for her customers to rest in after a hectic day of shopping. Since her shop was so small, there was only room for the one table and four chairs.

Being a romantic at heart, the decorations in her store took on the flavor of a more Victorian era. The cushions on the chairs matched the mauve and ivory coloring of the sheer lace curtains bordering the plate glass street window. Touches of ivory lace were everywhere, from the mats on the table to the doilies that dotted her shelves.

Farmington being a small community, many people found their way to the little shop at the end of the day to have a hot cup of flavored coffee or cocoa. In the summer, soda drinks were more popular; but summer or winter, it was the friendly atmosphere and companionship that brought in people.

Although her shop was small, it was well frequented. Still, Amy knew she would have few customers today. The wind had reached almost gale force and not many people would brave this weather when they could be snuggled at home, safe from the elements.

Lifting her feet to the chair across from her, she propped them on the edge and grinned at the snuggly bunny slippers she had slipped on earlier. She kept a pair of the fuzzy slippers at the shop for the times she stayed late to do inventory. They weren't very professional, but professional or not, she felt decidedly cozy. Besides, she wasn't expecting anyone due to the ferocious weather. The only reason she had opened the shop in the first place was to keep from being bored and alone at her apartment. Although she had plenty she could do at the apartment, her heart just wasn't in the household chores. Lately, the store had come to seem more like home anyway.

She had just lifted her own cup of Dutch hot cocoa when the bell jangled and the door slammed inward with a brutal gust of wind. Amy slowly set her cup back on the table, staring in surprise as Michael struggled to close the door behind him. His eyes swiftly searched the shop, stopping when he spotted her.

"Hi!" he greeted, cheerfully rubbing his hands through his dark hair to straighten it into some semblance of order.

"What on earth are you doing out in this kind of weather?" she asked, unable to keep the amazement from her voice. She wasn't certain if her rapidly beating heart was due to the surprise or the mere sight of

Michael standing there so tall and self-possessed. She pulled her feet from the chair and quickly tucked them out of sight beneath her chair.

Unbuttoning his coat, Michael crossed the shop until he reached her side. Dropping his coat onto an empty chair, he slid into the seat across from her.

"It's St. Paddy's Day," he told her, as though that explained everything. He was certainly dressed for the part; his forest green cable knit sweater and slacks coordinated nicely with his dark features.

Her own shamrock green pantsuit did nothing for her complexion, and she was well aware of it. Each time she saw Michael she worried about the contents of her meager wardrobe, thinking that she really should do something about buying some newer items. Each time, she talked herself out of it. Why should she try to look nice for a man who had someone special in his life? Besides, what was there about her to attract such a man?

Feeling at a disadvantage, she became instantly defensive. One perfectly shaped red eyebrow winged its way upward. "And?"

He looked at her as though she were slow-witted. "I need a gift for my friend."

Amy settled back against the chair. "Is this going to be a monthly thing or just holidays?"

His slow smile caused butterflies to flit in her stomach. When his dark eyes met hers, she had to force herself to concentrate on his next words.

"Well, I thought a gift a month, you know, a special gift, would be kind of. . .well. . ."

"Romantic?" she supplied, feeling her heart sink.

"Well, yeah. I guess."

Watching the emotions crowding her face, his own look became guarded. For the first time, he seemed rather at a loss.

Thinking she understood, Amy reached across the table and enfolded his cold hand briefly within both her own. She gave it a reassuring squeeze. "Michael, I think it's a very thoughtful thing to do."

When she would have removed her hands, he turned his palm upward, capturing her fingers within his own. He held onto her hands a moment longer before slowly releasing them. Amy frowned, her confused green gaze meshing with his enigmatic brown one.

There were times when she almost thought Michael flirted with her; but if he had someone special, Amy was certainly not interested. He didn't strike her as the kind of man who was a perpetual flirt. There was something so infinitely honest about Michael that it was just too hard to imagine such a thing.

Maybe he didn't realize how his actions seemed, or maybe she was just reading too much into them. After all, a man as handsome as he could have his pick of women. The single women at church flocked around him like bees around honey. More than likely, he was just being friendly and she had misconstrued his intentions.

She got up from her seat. "Well, let's see. What can we come up with this time? Is she Irish?"

"She told me she has Irish blood."

Amy smiled. "So do I! That makes St. Patrick's Day one of my favorite holidays."

When Amy turned, the look on his face puzzled

her. It was there but a moment, and then a shutter seemed to come down over his features.

"So, what would appeal to *you* then?" he asked.

"Gold?" she teased.

His lips twitched, his eyes taking on that teasing sparkle she was growing to know. "How about this cute mug with the *gold* coins?"

"Mmm. Chocolate coins," she told him, wiggling her eyebrows up and down. "Even better than gold."

He chuckled. "Boy are *you* easy to please."

Michael put the mug on the counter as he pulled his wallet from his back pocket. To Amy's surprise, he reached across the counter, wrapped one large hand behind her neck, and pulled her forward until he could softly kiss her cheek. As he released her, his fingers grazed her face where his lips had rested just seconds before.

When his gaze locked with hers, the impish twinkle in his eyes caused Amy to catch her breath.

"The mug," he told her, tongue in cheek. "It says, *'Kiss me, I'm Irish.'*"

Amy watched him walk away, and as the door closed behind him one thought spun through her head: *What a lucky Irish girl!*

She was surprised when the door opened again and Michael peeked his head back inside. His eyes, dancing with laughter, focused on her feet.

"By the way—I love the shoes."

Grinning, he ducked out the door and was gone.

❦

Michael hadn't gone far when the smile suddenly left

his face. Standing in Amy's shop watching her move about, he had come to a surprising conclusion. He was attracted to her.

She had actually never done anything to induce his attention, so why was he interested in her? Maybe that was it. For a long time women had chased him, and although he wasn't conceited, he was intrigued that this one woman seemed immune to his charms.

He must have been insane to kiss her like that. Probably she would turn tail and run the next time she saw him. He hoped he hadn't messed up their friendship with that rash action, because he enjoyed her friendship. She was an undemanding sort of person, and although he had never really spent any time alone with her yet, he determined that he was going to. He would find a way.

Her skin had been smooth beneath his lips and fingers, and her hair had smelled like honeysuckle. He stopped in his tracks, tempted to turn back and repeat the experience, only this time more thoroughly.

He grinned. Talk about impulsive! That would certainly put an end to their slow blooming friendship.

Forcing himself to move, he continued on his way, thanking the good Lord Amy wouldn't be able to avoid him totally; after all, they attended the same church. He closed his eyes and sent up a prayer for divine intervention.

Chapter 4

The German cuckoo clock on the back wall chimed five times, letting Amy know it would soon be closing time. She had just rearranged her window display for the fourth time before she realized what she was doing. Aggravated with herself, she began to chide herself out loud.

"You know you're just wanting to watch the street to see if Michael comes. Sometimes you can be such a dummy. He already has a girl, you know." Her shop closed in just one hour. Michael had never been this late buying his gifts before.

Still, her vigil was rewarded several moments later when she saw the object of her imaginings coming toward the shop. Somehow she had known he would come today. After all, Easter was only two days away.

At first, she thought she had solved the riddle of Michael's "secret" friend when she had seen him sitting with Debra Amis from the singles' group, but that had only happened one Sunday. Then there had been Cynthia Walker. He had spent most of last Friday's hayride sitting and talking to her, but on the way home he had dropped down beside Amy, and they had joked and laughed all the way back to the church.

He didn't really spend much time with *any* one woman, and Amy began to wonder if perhaps this girl lived in Houston, where Michael had lived before he moved to Ohio. So far, Amy didn't possess the fortitude necessary to ask such a personal question.

One thing she had learned about him was the fact that he had been transferred to Ohio from Houston when his company opened a new business just outside of Farmington. After quite some time, he had admitted to her he was the president of Comlink, the largest builder of computer chips in the country.

Now, as Michael came through the door, she found her insides doing that peculiar little flip he seemed to inspire. She was beginning to think she had a major crush on the guy, and the knowledge unsettled her. She had thought herself above such juvenile antics.

"Hi!" she greeted him.

The smile from his lips reached all the way to those incredible dark brown eyes. "Hi, yourself. It's almost Easter."

She knew exactly what he was implying. "I have a few things you might like. For your. . .your *friend.*"

"Bunny slippers?"

She cocked her head to the side, frowning at him. Still, she couldn't resist the grin that tugged at her lips. "Sorry. I'm all out. I have some other things you might be interested in, though."

"Great," he told her, face solemn, eyes sparkling. "Just lead the way."

"I love Easter," she told him as she moved among the shelves, showing him first one item then another. "I have to admit. I'm a big fan of bunnies and fuzzy little chicks."

"I noticed." He grinned, looking at her feet as she self-consciously scuffed her pumps. "I take it bunny slippers don't go with. . ." He paused, his gaze raking over her figure. "With blue."

"Very funny. I meant that I love bunnies at Easter."

"Surely, Amy, you realize there's more to Easter than that," he told her, suddenly serious.

When she looked into his eyes, she could almost see the tortured figure of Jesus hanging on a cross. His expression was so solemn that she hastened to reassure him.

"Oh, I agree. It's one of two times in the year when people recognize Jesus, even though they don't acknowledge Him any other time. It's great that at least we have *those* opportunities. I just wish people could see Jesus *every* day of the year." She wrinkled her nose at him. "Do you see what I mean?"

For once his eyes lacked their normal mischievous sparkle. He took the porcelain bunny from her and inspected it. The ornament seemed so fragile, lost within the strength of his large hands.

After a moment, his dark brown gaze clashed with her vivid green. "Do *you* like this?"

Amy almost said no, but that would be a lie. For some reason she was reluctant to see her favorite ornament go to Michael's unknown girl.

"I love it," she told him honestly.

"That's good enough for me. I'll take it."

She led the way to the counter and rang up his purchase. "You're beginning to be one of my best customers," she told him, only half joking.

The sparkle was back in his eyes. "Lady, you ain't seen nothing yet."

Amy took the bunny and wrapped it for him. Michael's voice was casual, but his eyes seemed rather pensive when they met hers. "Will I see you tonight?"

"You bet." She returned his smile, handing him his package. Watching him leave, she realized she was looking forward to tonight's singles' group get-together more than ever.

❦

"Amy! Over here."

Amy made her way across the church cafeteria to the wildly waving blond behind the counter.

"Hi, Glenda. What's up?"

Although the counter was at least two feet wide, Amy's petite friend managed to reach across it and latch onto Amy's arm.

"You've got to help me out! Debra came down with the flu, and I haven't been able to find anyone to fill in." She looked so harassed, Amy hastily assured her she would help.

"What do I need to do?"

Glenda handed her an oversize apron that easily covered Amy's plump person. Tying the strings behind her back, Amy frowned as she read the message on the front.

"Don't you have anything else?"

Noticing the direction of Amy's regard, Glenda

quickly read the message on the front. *Kiss the Cook.* She tried to hide a giggle.

"Sorry. That's all we have."

Amy pursed her lips, one eyebrow cocking upward. "You don't look sorry at all."

Glenda placed her hands on her hips and allowed her grin full rein. "You could do with a little. . ."

"Don't say it!" Amy hastily interrupted her. "And shame on you for even thinking it."

Standing with her head thrown back, her look one of challenge, Glenda told her, "I've been praying for you, my friend."

Surprised, Amy stopped arranging the paper goods on the table.

"What have you been praying?"

Glenda took the plastic forks from her and motioned her to the simmering pot on the stove. Amy lifted the lid and took an appreciative whiff.

"Yum! Sloppy joes. I love the way Irma adds cans of tomato soup to give it extra flavor."

"Forget the sloppy joes," Glenda told her impatiently, returning to their earlier conversation. "I've been praying that a charming handsome man will come whisk you off your feet, carry you away, and marry you."

"Will any man do?"

The deep voice made Glenda squeal, dropping the napkins she was clutching in her hands. Amy jumped at the same time, splashing sloppy joe mix on her apron. Two pairs of incensed eyes focused an accusing glare on the man standing at the counter that separated the dining area from the kitchen.

"Michael Compton, you nearly gave me heart failure!" Glenda scolded good-naturedly. "How long have you been eavesdropping?"

Michael's eyes met Amy's for a brief instant before, flushing scarlet, she turned back to stirring the pot without commenting on Michael's interruption.

"I wasn't eavesdropping. Gary asked me to come and tell you that the cookies have arrived."

Throwing the napkins on the table, Glenda hurried past Michael, her expression one of relief.

"It's about time," she told them over her shoulder. "I thought we weren't going to have any dessert."

Michael reached over and straightened the napkins, watching Amy as she steadfastly refused to look his way. The color in her cheeks rivaled the sloppy joes' red pot.

"How about it, Amy?" he asked softly.

Flustered, she had a hard time meeting his look. "How about what?"

"Will any man do?"

Shrugging, she turned back to the stove. "Beggars can't be choosers."

She heard the kitchen door open, and in the next instant Michael was beside her, pulling the wooden spoon from her nervous fingers. He took her by the shoulders and turned her to meet his look. Reluctantly, she did so, surprised at the anger flickering in his eyes.

"That's a foolish thing to say," he told her, his deep voice laced with outrage.

She knew he was right. Why she had said such a thing, she didn't know, but the words couldn't be unsaid now. Trying for a smile, she told him, "I was just kidding."

His eyes remained serious. "That's not something to kid about." Shaking his head, he told her, "Sometimes, I don't know about you. Just when I think you're making progress, you surprise me with something else I wasn't expecting."

Forgetting everything else, Amy turned surprised eyes on him. "What do you mean making progress?"

"I'll tell you sometime."

His husky voice did funny things to her insides. Pushing away from him, she picked up the spoon again and began vigorously stirring the contents of the pot.

Michael bent his head until his face was almost touching her shoulder. "Smells good."

Amy clutched the spoon so tightly she was certain it would break. When she turned her head slightly, their faces were mere inches apart. Amy swallowed hard.

"I like the apron, too," Michael told her impishly.

Amy quickly moved away from him. "Don't you dare," she opposed him, remembering his reaction to the Irish mug. It had been over a month, and she still couldn't get the feel of his warm lips out of her mind.

"Dare?" he questioned, his eyes challenging. He took a step forward, and Amy hastily took one in retreat.

"What's going on in here?" Glenda demanded from the open doorway. Glancing from one to the other, her blond brows lifted slightly. "Michael, stop harassing the cook," she told him, placing the box of cookies on the counter next to the hamburger buns. Turning to Michael, she propped her hands on her hips. The gesture was so familiar, Amy had to suppress a smile.

Michael grinned at her innocently. "I was just telling her how much I liked her apron."

Blinking her eyes, it took Glenda a moment to catch his meaning. When it dawned on her what he was talking about, she studied Michael's face, her questioning blue eyes locking with his brown ones. There was a message hidden in their depths that Glenda seemed to have no problem deciphering. Sudden comprehension filled her features, and an understanding look passed between the two. Amy felt decidedly left out by their silent interchange.

Michael pulled his gaze from Glenda's. "I'll leave you two to your kitchen," he told them, his look fleetingly resting on Amy. "And I'll talk to *you* later. We have some unfinished business to attend to."

The promise in his words set Amy's heart quick stepping. She silently watched him disappear through the doorway.

Glenda leaned over the counter that separated the kitchen area from the dining area and watched Michael cross the room to a group playing table tennis. He laughed with them a moment before he opened the door and left the room. Her eyes narrowed to slits, and she smiled like a cat that has just discovered a fresh pot of cream.

"Yes, Michael Compton," she said so softly that Amy barely heard her. "You'll do just fine."

❦

Michael slammed out of the cafeteria, trying to control his rising irritation. Never had he encountered a woman so lacking in conceit. Amy wasn't picking up

on the signals he was trying to send. Glenda understood, so why couldn't Amy? Perhaps the time had
come to grow a little bolder.

Beggars can't be choosers, she had said! He had
needed a lot of self-control to keep from shaking her
until her teeth rattled.

When he had first gotten to know her, her warm and
witty personality had been so obvious. Now, she seemed
to recoil inward whenever he was around. What had he
done to cause such a reaction? He wanted so much to
return to their earlier friendly footing.

The trouble was, he was beginning to want more
than that. He wanted to take Amy on a real date, not just
a group thing. He wanted to get to know the real Amy.

Her thirst for spiritual knowledge had been one of
the first things that had caught his attention. Shame-
lessly, he had used that desire as a means to spend time
alone with her. When they studied together, she forgot
to be reticent. He loved studying the Bible with her. It
was the one thing that she was willing to do alone with
him, and he looked forward to those times.

Amy's questions had inspired him to delve deeper.
Her thought-provoking questions had him scrambling
for the information she wanted. Some of her questions
were beyond his ability to explain. Actually, they were
things that had caused controversy in the church for
years. That's why he took so much time to study
God's Word himself. He didn't want to depend on
others to give him the information he needed. He
chose, instead, to go right to the source.

As he and Amy grew closer to God, they were in

turn growing closer together. Was she aware of it, too? Was she aware, as he was, that the more time they spent together, the more her fear of him was gradually diminishing?

He seated himself on a bench outside the church and watched the stars shimmering in the sky. His feelings for Amy were slowly evolving into something for which he wasn't sure he was quite ready. Leaning his head back against the building, he looked up at the constellations in the night sky. Somewhere beyond that great expanse was the One who could help him truly understand. Closing his eyes, he lifted a silent petition heavenward.

Chapter 5

The snow on the television told Amy that she had slept far longer than she intended. She dragged the remote across the coffee table and switched off the television. Then she huddled under her crocheted afghan, shivering uncontrollably.

The pounding in her head intensified, and she moaned as she dropped her head back to the pillow on the sofa. After a moment, she realized the pounding was at her door, as well as in her head.

Staggering, she made her way across the room, glancing through the peephole. Surprised, she opened the door. "Michael, what are you doing here?" she croaked.

Worried brown eyes scanned the length of her body, taking in her disheveled appearance and wan face. Her clothes were wrinkled from sleeping on the sofa. "You're sick!" he stated unequivocally.

At her confused expression a look of compassion stole across his features. "I came to the shop today to purchase my gift, but you weren't there. And then when you didn't show up for our devotion time at church, I really became worried." His narrowed gaze focused on her weary face. "You didn't answer your phone. I thought maybe you were out, but I didn't think you would stay out this late."

"I. . .I didn't hear it. I was asleep." Amy glanced at her wristwatch. Her eyes widened. "It's after two in the morning!"

"I know." The two words were laced with irritation. Lifting his hand, Michael placed it against her fevered brow. The coolness of his hand against her hot skin was soothing. "You're burning up!" he growled. "We need to get you to a doctor."

"I've already been," she told him, pushing his hand away. "It's just the flu, and I have to let it run its course."

"You should be in bed." He took her by the arm and moving her away from the chill night air. His gaze took in the medicine bottles, empty glass, and tray. "How long have you been like this?"

"I started feeling ill yesterday afternoon," she told him, dropping to the sofa, her shaking body unable to support her. "You shouldn't be here—you could get sick."

"I'm not worried. It's *you* I'm concerned about."

Amy gave him a halfhearted grin. "No one to help you choose your gift today, huh? I'm sorry. I wondered what you would choose, since the only holidays this month are Memorial Day and Mother's Day."

He seated himself beside her, a smile lurking in his eyes. "Well, I was thinking about flowers. You know, April showers bring May flowers?"

She smiled. "Most girls love flowers."

"So I heard."

Amy coughed, and Michael rose from the couch. "Let me get you something to drink. What would you like?"

Part of her wanted him to stay, but the more sane part knew he shouldn't. She would never forgive herself if Michael got the flu because of her.

"You really shouldn't be here," she told him again, though her voice lacked conviction. It would be so nice to have someone take care of her. Her mother was over two thousand miles away, visiting an aunt in California, and Amy missed her mother's tender care. Although she lived on her own, she was comforted knowing her mother was usually just a phone call away. Every time she had gotten sick in the past, her mother came running. This time, she knew she was being a big baby, but she couldn't help feeling sorry for herself. Her body ached, her head ached, and she felt just plain miserable.

"So make me leave," Michael challenged her, his lips tilting up into a grin. He squatted before her, his fingers grazing her cheek softly. His brown eyes studied her dull green ones for what seemed an eternity. "You're sick. Let me help you."

Too sick to think clearly, Amy lifted her own hand and covered his where it rested against her cheek. She leaned her head against his hand, smiling.

"I'd love a cola."

He quickly rose to his feet, stepping away from her. "I'll get you one."

He returned a few moments later with a glass brimming with fizzing cola, the ice cubes clinking against the glass when he handed it to her. Taking a long drink, Amy sighed with relief as the cola slid down her parched throat.

Michael seated himself again, though Amy noticed he was careful to keep a distance between them. He seemed unusually nervous, and for the first time that she could remember, he didn't look her in the eye.

He lifted the remote from the crease in the couch and placed it on the coffee table. "What were you watching?"

Amy frowned. "I don't remember. I just left it on for the noise. It made me feel less lonesome."

He glanced quickly at her, then just as quickly away. "You should have called someone. Everyone was worried about you."

"I really didn't think about it," she told him peevishly. "I just wanted to sleep."

Michael's look fixed pointedly on the sofa before settling on her. One dark eyebrow shot upward.

"I know," she told him testily. "I just sat down for a minute."

"Have you eaten anything?"

Amy shook her head. "No. I wasn't hungry."

"Do you have any chicken noodle soup?"

Again she shook her head.

"How about if I run to the store and get you some?"

She noticed him twisting his watch; for some reason he was agitated. Her heart melted at the realization he really did care about her. Somehow, mostly because of the time they shared at church, meeting to discuss the Bible, he had become one of her closest friends.

"You don't need to do that," she told him, her voice

growing raspier by the minute.

He looked at her then. "I want to."

The concern on his face touched her. "Okay. That really sounds pretty good."

He jumped up, pulling his keys from his jeans pocket. "I'll be right back."

While he was gone, Amy took the opportunity to have a quick shower. Careful to tuck her hair into a shower cap so it wouldn't get wet, she hummed to herself as the warm water cascaded over her shivering body. Odd how a person could be so hot and yet still have the shivers.

She decided to put on her favorite worn sweats. Probably adding the extra heat to her already fevered body wasn't such a good idea, but frankly she just didn't care. Her skin might be hot, but she still felt as though she were freezing. Pulling on her bunny slippers, she wiggled her toes and grinned.

She padded her way into the small kitchen and found the bottle of aspirin she had left lying on the counter. Dropping two into her palm, she returned to the living room and crawled back onto the couch.

Sighing, she put her head against the back. Even that small amount of exertion had exhausted her. Reaching for the cola, she swallowed the tablets and listened for Michael's return.

She hadn't long to wait. He closed the door behind him and handed her the apartment keys, then picked up the tray from the coffee table and headed for the kitchen.

"I'll have this fixed in a jiffy," he told her.

Several moments later he returned carrying the tray laden with a bowl of soup and a cold glass of orange juice. Carefully seating himself, he silently watched her consume her light meal.

When she placed the tray back on the table he asked her, "Feel better?"

She smiled. "Actually, I do. Thanks a lot."

"No problem." He leaned back against the sofa, his features softened by his smile.

Returning to their earlier conversation, Amy told him, "I guess it would be kind of hard to buy a *Mother's* Day gift." She knew she was fishing, and so, apparently, did Michael. His smile broadened.

"Oh, I don't know. Someday I'm sure she'll be a mother. At least I *hope* she will be."

This was the death knell to all of Amy's hopes. Motherhood definitely meant marriage. Her defenses were weakened by her sickness and suddenly her eyes filled with tears. As the tears ran down her hot cheeks, Michael's eyes widened in alarm.

"Amy?"

She sniffed, and immediately he closed the distance between them and wrapped her in his arms. "Don't cry, Amy. What's wrong? Do you hurt? What can I do?"

Her mouth never uttered the words, but her mind seemed to shout them. *Love me. Love me like I love you. Please don't marry that other girl!*

❧

When Michael climbed behind the wheel of his car, he was still shaking. Seeing Amy cry had brought out every protective instinct in him. His first impulse had been to take her in his arms and hold her close. Boy, had that been a mistake! Groaning, he laid his head on his hands where they were gripping the steering wheel.

His heart was only now beginning to slow its erratic pace. Only the fact that he was alone with Amy and she was vulnerable from her illness had kept him from kissing her.

Things were moving much too fast. He needed to slow down and get his bearings. The only trouble was, he was afraid it was far too late.

Chapter 6

The sun beat down and Amy reveled in the warmth after the cold winter and cool spring. She readjusted the sidewalk sale sign on the table in front of her store. Every June she tried to clear out old inventory by having a sale just in time for Father's Day.

As it had every day for the past three weeks, her mind replayed the scene in her home that fateful night before Mother's Day. Michael had been so tender, so loving as he held her close and soothed away her tears.

His gaze had been focused on her face while he used his thumb to wipe away the tears trickling down her cheek. For an instant his eyes had darkened, and his breathing had become labored. When his lips parted slightly, she had thought for sure he was going to kiss her. Ludicrous, she knew, but oh how she had wanted him to.

In the next instant, he was on his feet, his face pale. Making his excuses, he had quickly exited, insisting she promise to lock the door behind him and go to bed. She had been left staring at the closed door. Having just discovered that moment that she loved him left her feeling more defenseless than before.

Since then, at church he had taken pains to avoid being alone with her as much as possible. She had been hurt by his seeming indifference, but she had been more confused. She still couldn't figure out what had happened to turn him from the eager companion he had been, to the detached stranger he now was.

Then, at last night's devotional meeting, no other seat had been available so he had gingerly seated himself beside her. He acted almost as though he thought she might pounce on him!

Amy was determined he understand that she hadn't read anything into his compassion the night she was sick. Since then, she had been rather cool with him, and last night she had avoided eye contact and spoke to him only when necessary. Still, she could not banish the images of that night from her mind. The strain that had suddenly developed between them made her more unsure of herself than ever.

"Hi."

Amy jumped, dropping the porcelain figurine she was holding. It smashed on the sidewalk.

"Oh, now look what you've made me do!"

Michael bent down and began to pick up the pieces. "Sorry. Guess you can add this to my other purchase." His gaze lifted to her face, his eyes studying her.

Amy knelt beside him, face crimson from embarrassment. "That's not necessary," she told him, taking the pieces from his hand. She rose to her feet and finally met his fixed look.

"You wanted something for your friend?" She had decided she would no longer pry into his business. In fact, her desire to know something about Michael's girl had disappeared altogether.

"Mmm," he answered, still watching her closely. He opened his mouth to say something, but Amy interrupted.

"For Father's Day?" she questioned, one brow lifted dubiously.

"I was thinking more along the line of June brides."

His soft answer had the effect of relieving Amy of any sensible reply she might have made. Schooling her features into a mask of composure, she gave him a bright smile as he rose to stand beside her.

"Well, I certainly have a nice selection to choose from. What did you have in mind?"

"Amy." The change in his voice startled her. A fire was in his eyes, and his almost aggressive stance caused her to take a hasty step in retreat. Confused, she frowned at him.

"Yes?"

At her withdrawal, his face changed dramatically. He shoved his hands into his pockets and gave her a rather lopsided smile. Her eyes were focused on the tick in his cheek.

"Nothing. Never mind. Could you suggest something?"

"I think not, Michael," she answered gently. "This seems rather more personal than the others. I think *you* should choose."

She preceded him through the door and watched as he stalked like an angry tiger among the display shelves.

Periodically, his eyes would meet hers, and she was surprised at the frustration she saw. What on earth had she said or done to cause such a reaction? If he was peeved at her for not helping to choose a gift for his girlfriend, well, that was just too bad.

She waited while he roamed the store, finally choosing a gold cross necklace from her small supply of jewelry. Although she hadn't much in the way of trinkets, what she had was of the finest quality. The necklace had been one of her most recent additions to her shop.

The brilliant gold cross sparkled with reflected sunlight when he laid it on the counter. Amy lifted it to check the price, though she knew the price of every item in her shop by heart. Still, it was something to do to keep from looking into those disturbing dark eyes.

"That's perfect," she told him softly, carefully folding the necklace into a small piece of tissue paper.

He smiled then. "Yeah. Just like she is."

Amy struggled to keep the smile on her face. Without saying anything else, she placed the necklace in a small paper bag and handed it to Michael. He, in turn, gave her a roll of bills.

"Keep the change," he told her, wrapping his hand firmly around hers. She opened her mouth to protest, but he placed a finger over her lips. "Don't."

He turned and left the store so quickly, she couldn't have said anything if she had tried. More puzzled than ever, she went to the window and watched him walk down the street, as had become her habit, until he was well out of sight.

Sighing, she began to straighten her already pristine shelves. Time ticked slowly by until she was ready to bring her Father's Day table back inside and get ready to leave. Today was Tuesday, and on Tuesdays she closed the shop early so she could spend time at the local animal shelter.

Resources were at a minimum at the shelter since the city didn't give it a high priority when it came to tax money. Being an animal lover, Amy volunteered her services each Tuesday and Saturday. Saturday was her favorite day since the shelter held its open house, inviting anyone to come and browse and perhaps give a lonely animal a home. The only problem Amy had was she wanted to take all the rejected animals home with her. Knowing that was impossible, since her apartment manager didn't allow pets, she spent as much time with them as possible, trying to make them feel loved.

She grinned, remembering the last time Michael had gone with her, before the night she was sick. Amy showed him dog after dog and cat after cat. He knew exactly what she was trying to do, and helplessly he had succumbed to her silent pleading.

He left that evening with a small mongrel pup that had only a few more days to live before it would have been put to sleep. Michael had been her last hope, since most of her friends had already surrendered in the past to her entreaties for help.

The smile slid from her face. The way Michael was behaving lately, she seriously doubted whether there would be any more such trips together. That was a pity, because Michael was such fun to be with. She knew she had no hopes of a romantic involvement with him, but she still enjoyed his friendship. In the short time she had known him, he had done more to help bring her out of her shell of isolation than anyone else ever had. Even her best friend Glenda hadn't been able to do what Michael had done.

Sometimes when he looked at her, she thought he might be interested in her with more than a fond regard, but then he would pull away again and put some distance between them. Like now. She was beginning to believe it was his unique way of teasing, those looks and bantering remarks that made her feel so special. But she knew she shouldn't take him too seriously. How embarrassing for Michael if girls thought he was in love with them just because he was friendly with them.

Since she was unused to the ways of men, she was left more muddled than she cared to be. Consequently, she felt stilted lately when she spoke with Michael about anything. Anything, that is, except the Lord. When they discussed the Scriptures together, Michael forgot to be reticent, and Amy forgot to be shy. With Michael's encouragement, she had begun to delve into the Scriptures, not just on the surface but deeply. Amy's shelves were now filled with concordances, books on Bible geography, Bible handbooks, biblical history, and a wealth of other information. The more she learned, the more excited she became.

She locked the door to her shop and turned to find Michael standing behind her. Jumping back, she placed a hand over her heart.

"Michael," she breathed, "you scared me half to

death." How a man so large could be so quiet, she had no idea. He was always taking her unawares.

"I thought you might like some company at the shelter today." His voice was almost uncertain when he asked, "Do you mind?"

Amy pretended to be searching for something in her purse. When she had schooled her features into a polite mask, she lifted her eyes.

"No, I don't mind at all."

His lips twisted wryly. "Just, please, don't finagle me into taking home another animal. Okay?"

Relieved to see the laughter in his eyes, she smiled. "Oh, I don't know. You have a dog. Wouldn't a cat make your family complete?"

"I'm allergic to cats," he told her.

Surprised, she studied his face. "Are you really?"

"No." He took her by the arm and led her toward the car park at the end of the street. "But if I don't have something to protect me from those soulful eyes, I'm doomed."

Amy grinned. Thinking of the white Persian cat and the amber tabby at the shelter, she asked him hopefully, "Which soulful eyes? The brown or the blue?"

He chanced a quick look at her face. "The green."

Realizing he was talking about her own eyes, Amy stumbled and would have fallen if he hadn't been holding her arm. There he was, at it again! Not knowing what to think, she remained silent.

He helped her into his car, reached across, and buckled her seatbelt. With his face close to hers, he smiled slightly at her confused expression. While he went around the car, she kept her gaze firmly fixed on the green maple trees in the park to her right. All of her good intentions to stay out of Michael's way had been thrown out the window. Somewhere along the line, she had lost control of this whole situation.

For the first few miles Michael concentrated on his driving, one part of his mind trying to decide what to do about his developing relationship with Amy.

After realizing his feelings for her were growing, he had decided to back off and give her some room. By nature, he was passionate in everything he did, and he guessed that would include romance.

There were times he thought that he really frightened Amy. Like today.

He glanced sideways and noticed her attention focused on the green scenery. If he were a betting man, he would wager she wasn't even seeing what she was looking at.

"Penny for your thoughts," he coaxed.

He sucked in a sharp breath when she turned his way. She reminded him of the puppy she had cajoled him into taking home.

"Michael," she began hesitantly, "I really value our friendship."

His heart stopped for an instant, then thundered on. What was she trying to say?

"As do I."

She turned and looked to the road ahead of them. "You seem to be. . .angry with me lately."

He sighed heavily. "Not angry, Amy, and certainly

not with you. I just have a lot on my mind."

She would have said more, but he wheeled into the parking lot of the animal shelter, and after that, they had no more opportunities for conversation. Amy's attention quickly turned to the task at hand.

Michael watched as the woman he had come to love surfaced from her self-imposed shell; he saw a woman who was gentle, loving, and kind. A woman whose laughter made his heart do double time.

His gaze softened as he watched her tumble about with first one animal, then another. She had a cuddle or a pat for each animal at the shelter, and they knew she loved them. If only he could be as certain of her feelings for himself.

Chapter 7

Amy closed and locked the shop door behind her. She would be late if she didn't hurry, but she had promised Michael she would bring his gift to the Fourth of July picnic. Since her shop wasn't open on the Fourth, she had to make a special trip to accommodate him.

She smiled slightly as she hurried down the street to the park, glad that she and Michael had managed to regain their friendly footing. Last Friday, they had stayed after devotion time at church and talked for a long time.

She was beginning to think she understood him a little better, and as a result, she promised him her friendship while making it perfectly clear she desired nothing else from him. Of course, that wasn't entirely the truth.

Instead of the effect she had expected, however, her words had seemed to make him angry. He had stared at her so long without saying anything, it seemed as though he had turned to stone. Finally, he heaved a great sigh, brushed his hands back through his hair, and

dropped them to his sides. All he had said was, "Okay."
Just that one word, but then, what had she expected?

Now she was hurrying to meet him at the park.
They were singing a duet of "The Star Spangled Banner"
in a program the town council had put together.
Standing beside her during church when the congrega-
tion sang hymns, he had often complimented her on
her voice—and somehow that had led to her agreeing
to sing with him today. Her insides twisted into knots
just thinking about it. She knew her friends were aware
of her painful shyness, but that didn't make it any easier for her to deal with it. Sometimes, she wondered
how she managed to run the shop.

The money her father had left her in his will had
enabled her to rent her small shop and start her own
business. At first, dealing with people on a regular basis
had been hard for her, but eventually, she had made
friends of her regular customers. Still, handling people
one-on-one was much different from doing so in a
group, and it was a far cry from standing up in front of
a crowd and singing. Sighing, she wondered for the hundredth time how had she ever allowed Michael to talk
her into this.

He met her by the grandstand, taking the bear she had
brought from her hands. The little creature was dressed in
red, white, and blue, and was holding a flag. Michael
smiled as he examined it, nodding with satisfaction.

"Why a bear, Michael?" she asked him now.

His eyes twinkled down into hers. "Because I can't
bear to be apart from someone I love."

Amy rolled her eyes. "Oh, Michael. That's awful!"

Grinning, he took her by the arm and led her to where others from their singles' group were waiting. "Maybe," he agreed. "But since I'm not getting any help from a certain young lady, I don't have much choice. Besides, I thought it was a cute idea."

Amy sat beside Michael and watched while Cynthia Walker began to hand out the food from the basket the girls had prepared earlier. The girls had provided the food while the guys had brought the drinks and place settings. All in all, it worked out well.

Amy watched to see if Michael paid attention to any one girl, but she had to admit that he didn't, although he got encouragement enough from the females present. She chastised herself for such a catty thought.

She watched him now, his brown eyes lit with laughter. Even dressed casually, he looked immaculate, not a strand of his raven black hair out of place. Her look passed slowly over him where he reclined, and she could see why some of the other men envied his physique.

He turned and caught her glance, holding it for several long moments. The breath caught in her throat as she tried to read what was in his eyes. Suddenly, he smiled and turned away.

That smile made her uncomfortable. If she had to describe it in one word, that word would be "satisfied." What had he read in her eyes that would cause such a reaction?

After helping the girls clean up, Michael came and took Amy by the hand. Lifting her to her feet, he told her, "Come on, songbird. It's almost time."

Her lowering brows were the only sign that she was

upset with him. He grinned.

"You'll do fine," he reassured her. "You have a beautiful voice."

Tugging her forward, he refused to relinquish her hand. It was as though he knew she needed this one visible sign of support. They were almost to the bandstand when she balked. She jerked her sweaty hand from his.

"I. . .I can't do this, Michael."

He lifted his hands, hesitating slightly before settling them on her shoulders. "Look at me," he commanded.

Involuntarily, she lifted her eyes to his.

"Amy, you can do this. Look around you. Most of these people are your friends, people who love you."

Her gaze flickered around the small park before coming back to his face. Why was he so insistent? Why did it matter to him whether she crawled out of her shell or not? For a moment she was tempted to tell him to leave her alone; but searching his face, she knew he was only trying to help her overcome her shyness.

Nodding, she allowed him to take her hand and lead her on to the bandstand. She almost panicked when she looked out and saw the crowd of people, but Michael's slight squeeze of her hand helped her to rein in her near hysteria. She couldn't think of another person in the world who could have gotten her to do this.

Although her voice wobbled at first, she soon forgot the crowd as she was caught up in the powerful words of the country's most patriotic song. She had been taught the story concerning Francis Scott Key's penning of the words, and ever since, whenever she sang the song, she could see in her mind the air filled with explosions over

Fort McHenry and the flag bravely flying, torn and tattered. The song never failed to move her.

As the last stanza came to an end, silence permeated the park grounds. Opening her eyes, Amy found Michael staring down at her, such pride glowing from his eyes that it almost started her tears flowing.

The silence seemed to last for an eternity, though in truth it was but mere seconds. Suddenly, everyone came to their feet, their thunderous applause and loud cheers sending the color flying to Amy's pale cheeks.

After that, things were a blur. She was separated from Michael when the crowd surged forward to congratulate them. Amy was surprised by everyone's vehement praise. They patted her on the back and told her how beautifully she sang. Others told her they had taken the national anthem for granted, but that she had made them remember their own love for their country with the beauty and purity of her rich voice.

Michael made his way through the crowd to her side. Again taking her hand, he led her back to where the others from their group were waiting. Congratulations were made all over again.

Cynthia looked at Amy with respect. "I didn't know you could sing like that!"

Blushing profusely, Amy told the whole group, "Come on guys. I wasn't singing a solo."

Their astounded looks fastened on Michael.

"She doesn't know!" Debra sputtered. "She really doesn't know."

The whole group started laughing.

"Amy," Cynthia laughed, ignoring Michael's flailing

hands. "Michael stopped singing after the first verse."

Shocked, Amy stood gaping at him. She should have been angry, but seeing Michael looking so at a loss was worth the embarrassment. He had the nerve to talk to her about soulful eyes when his own brown orbs stared at her like a wounded animal.

He turned his palms outward, shrugging his shoulders. "I told you that you had a beautiful voice."

Their eyes were locked together in a battle of wills. "Michael. . ." Amy stopped, not knowing what else to say. "Michael. . .so help me. . ."

A woman from the church interrupted Amy. "Oh, Amy. We never guessed that you had such a beautiful voice. I was wondering if you would be willing to sing at my Imogene's wedding."

Amy could only stare, her mouth parted in surprise. Taking a deep breath, she turned back to Michael in vexation, only to find him walking away from her across the park.

༒

Children were playing dodge ball in the grassy area of the park. Michael ducked among them, grinning when they tried to tag him with the ball. He easily side-stepped their attempts.

He leaned against his car and watched while Amy tried to fend off Imogene's mother. Crossing his arms over his chest, he grinned. Whether she liked it or not, Amy was the center of attention. He wasn't sure whether the color in her face was from the warm sunshine or embarrassment. Maybe a little of both, he decided.

It surprised him that she wasn't angry. He still didn't quite understand what had made him do such a thing. He knew how painfully shy she was, yet for that brief moment, she had allowed him to thrust her into the public eye. Her trust humbled him, but left him feeling as though he had betrayed her.

Little by little, his shy violet was opening to the world around her. And little by little, she was finding the world wasn't such a bad place after all. Everywhere, there were people who loved her.

He watched her now crossing the park, her eyes centered on him. Usually, her face was an open book to him, but now it seemed veiled. Hidden. It made him uncomfortable.

She stood before him, her earnest eyes beseeching him. "Why did you do it, Michael?"

A man could drown in those eyes, he thought, *but they still demand an answer.*

" 'Fear of man will prove to be a snare, but whoever trusts in the Lord is kept safe,' " he quoted softly.

He could see that she understood. They had talked often of her timidity around people and how it had affected her service to the Lord. She had no problems dealing with people when hiding behind a counter or when she was among animals, and she could even handle people on the other end of a telephone. But whenever she had to step outside her secure little world she faltered.

For that reason he had decided to try and help her climb from the hole she had dug herself into. The more they studied the Bible together, the more agitated Amy became over her growing desire to reach the world with God's Word. In their singles' group she had prayed for the ability to overcome her fears, and Michael wanted to help her. *Needed* to help her. Because until she was willing to tread among this world, she would never be ready to step into his.

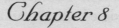

Chapter 8

Amy hid a grin as she watched Michael stalk the displays in her store. What on earth would he find for the month of August for his girl? Since back to school was the usual theme, apple paraphernalia layered the shelves and display cases. She couldn't wait to hear what analogy Michael would come up with this time.

She frowned in puzzlement. After the Fourth of July picnic, he had become unusually attentive. Even now Amy felt uncomfortable thinking about his actions of the last few weeks. He would sit by her during each devotion time at church, helping her find her place in the Bible. After church he always made sure she got home safely. His nearness, his very presence made her nervous. She was so afraid she would betray her feelings in some slight way, but she knew he was only trying to be a good friend. She really wished he wouldn't. Even the other singles were beginning to notice and make comments. Michael remained unperturbed, but perhaps he just hadn't noticed their comments. Maybe she should talk to him.

Now as she watched him, she felt a sense of despair. Her feelings for Michael ran deep, but surely God must have someone else He intended for her who would return her love. She wrinkled her nose. Even thinking of someone other than Michael made her feel like she was committing adultery in her heart. Foolish, yes, but one couldn't control one's feelings. She had tried, but she just couldn't.

He finally made a selection and brought it to her. When he laid the book on the counter, Amy was curious to see its title. She leaned forward eagerly, pretending to take notice of the price tag.

"*Apples from God,*" she quoted aloud, lifting her eyes to his. She waited for an explanation.

"Sayings from the Bible." He answered her unspoken question. He then laid an apple bookmark next to it, the gold reflecting the warm sunlight streaming in through the shop windows.

There was something almost hypnotic in the intensity of his brown eyes as they stared into hers. "She's the apple of my eye, you know," he told her softly.

Her eyes flickered and then dropped to the counter. Taking the book, she began wrapping it. How could Michael look at her that way when obviously he cared about another woman? Was she again reading more into his look than he intended? Probably. Either that, or she was engaging in purely wishful thinking. She bit her lip to keep from saying anything as she slid the package across the counter toward him.

Amy smiled. "You know, Michael, I'm looking forward to seeing what you come up with next month."

He grinned. "That's why I only do a gift a month. It takes me that long to think of something."

She focused on the cleft in his chin. "Maybe you should just tell her how you feel outright."

"Maybe I will," he told her huskily. "But the time isn't yet right, I think. She's still a little uncertain of me."

Amy could well understand why. "After eight months? Surely not," she demurred.

"She needs to believe in herself more," Michael told her.

Now *there* was something Amy could empathize with! All her life she had hidden from other people. Although she wasn't ugly, she certainly wasn't pretty. And with the way she dressed, men rarely gave her a second glance. Only Michael had taken the time to see beyond her contrived walls—but she knew he wasn't interested in her as a woman.

"Maybe she just needs to know that *you* believe in her," she countered.

"Give me time, Amy," he commanded, his voice like soft velvet. "Give me time."

Since knowing Michael, Amy had certainly begun to believe in herself more. If anyone could reassure this girl, he would be the one to do it. He had that funny way of looking at a person that made her feel she was the most important person in the world. Did he make this other girl feel the same? Deciding that she really didn't want to know, Amy changed the subject.

"Are you going to the Harvest Festival?"

"Sure am," he told her. "How about you?"

She lifted an eyebrow and told him sardonically,

"As long as I don't have to sing."

He chuckled. "You'll never forgive me for that one, will you?"

She leaned across the counter and batted her eyelashes coquettishly. "Paybacks are terror. Your time is coming."

The smile faltered on his face. For an instant, he seemed at a loss for words. Finally, after taking a deep breath, he argued, "Whatever happened to turn the other cheek?"

Amy knew what she would like to do to his cheek. Coloring hotly at such thoughts, she began stuffing money into the cash register. What had gotten into her lately? First, batting her lashes at him, now having such thoughts. This relationship was doing things to her that she never thought possible.

"I promise not to hurt you too badly," she joked.

"You have absolutely no idea just how much you could hurt me," he told her softly.

She glanced at him sharply, her look arrested by the sheer male vitality he exuded. He was one of the few men she knew who was equally at home in a business suit as in jeans and a T-shirt.

His shirt with the Lord's Gym logo on it made her wonder if he did, indeed, work out at a gym. Catching her look, his eyes once again seemed filled with satisfaction. There was a biding-my-time aspect about him that made her apprehensive. She had no idea what he was waiting for, but she wished he wouldn't look at her that way.

Was it possible she had been wrong about him after all? If his girl wasn't close at hand, maybe he was having a little flirtation, thinking that he could have some fun in the meantime. Having realized how shy and introverted she was, did he feel safe trifling with her feelings, believing that she felt nothing but friendship?

She met his direct look, wondering what he would say if she told him just what she really felt for him. One side of his mouth slowly tilted upward.

"Go ahead," he told her gently, almost as if he could read her thoughts. Her eyes widened in surprise.

"Go ahead and what?"

"Go ahead and do your worst," he answered. "Just remember, you have cheeks, too."

Relieved, she chuckled. "Michael Compton, if only there was a way! Nothing embarrasses you."

He grinned in return. "Boy, have I got you fooled." He leaned on the counter until his face was mere inches from hers. "Come with me to the festival?"

"Um. I can't."

Michael watched as Amy fiddled with items on the counter.

"Why not? You said you were going."

"Yes, well. . ." She lifted guilty eyes to his before dropping her gaze to the counter. "I promised Alan Marcus I would go with him."

Michael slowly stood away from the counter. Peeping at him, Amy was surprised at the emotions flitting across his face. Finally, a shutter seemed to come down to conceal his thoughts and feelings.

Knowing she had accepted Alan's invitation to try and make Michael jealous, she felt even guiltier. Alan was a really sweet guy. She was being unkind to use him in such a way. Even now, she didn't know how she had come to accept his invitation. When she had agreed to go with him, she had felt none of the panic that usually beset her when faced with these situations. Realizing it was through Michael's gentle guidance that she had grown to such a point, she felt the guilt increase.

When Michael smiled, she felt her hopes plummet to her toes. He really didn't mind after all. This wasn't what she had hoped for, but at least now she knew for certain.

"I'll see you there, then." Lifting his book from the counter, he gave her another brief smile and exited the store.

The glower on Michael's face caused the waitress to quickly lay his sandwich in front of him and just as hastily depart.

Pushing the plate aside, Michael began drumming his fingers on the table. So fierce was his concentration, he failed to notice the two waitresses huddling together as they discussed his unfriendly countenance.

So, Amy had a date. And with Alan Marcus, of all people! Not that there was anything particularly wrong with Alan. It was just that, if possible, the guy was more timid than Amy. He wasn't what Amy needed at all.

Well, Michael had wanted to help her believe in herself more. Apparently, he had succeeded even more than he had at first supposed. The only problem was, he hadn't done it for Alan Marcus! Instead of worrying about Amy's fear of a relationship, he should have made his own move a little sooner.

He knew she was attracted to him. He had seen it in her eyes. Twice now, he had caught her looking at him with unmistakable admiration. So why would she go out with Alan Marcus? Of course, admiration was not the same as attraction, either. Perhaps she admired his looks, but then was charmed by someone like Alan.

This whole thing was getting on his nerves. Dropping some money on the table, he left the restaurant and his untouched sandwich.

Chapter 9

"Will you wrap it, please?"

The question snapped Amy out of her preoccupation with the couple in the corner. "Wrap it, Mrs. Jennings? Certainly."

As Amy cut gold embossed paper to wrap the box, she stretched her ears almost to breaking point trying to hear the conversation going on between Michael and the woman with him. She was a stranger to this small community, and most probably, Amy decided, she was Michael's *friend*.

Since Mrs. Jennings continued her diatribe about inflationary prices, Amy gave up her attempt at listening to Michael. She focused instead on the little gray-haired lady standing before her, but still, her mind wandered.

The woman with Michael was gorgeous. Platinum blond hair fell elegantly around a model's body. The woman's clothes were tastefully selected from the current fashion. Unconsciously, Amy sighed.

Mistaking the sound, Mrs. Jennings pulled herself to her full height, which still left her several inches shorter than Amy's five-foot-four inches. "So, you agree."

Not willing to admit she hadn't heard a word Mrs. Jennings said, Amy gave her brightest smile. She watched the elderly lady leave the store in a huff. Amy felt ashamed at her overwhelming sense of relief. Although Mrs. Jennings was a frequent customer, the woman's constant complaining always left her feeling guilty and depressed, though she knew it shouldn't. Amy knew her prices weren't exorbitant. When she had opened the store, her aim had been to have a place where people could buy quality goods at affordable prices. She had never desired to become wealthy. Money had never been an issue with her.

"I want you to meet someone," Michael told her. Amy jumped, not realizing he had approached the counter.

The blond crossed gracefully to the counter. Her wide, friendly smile put Amy instantly at ease, and Amy shook the hand that was offered, careful not to damage the long, elegantly polished nails.

"Hi, I'm Alicia. Michael's told me a lot about you. He says he couldn't have a better friend."

Amy flinched at the term. He might have discussed Amy with Alicia, but he certainly hadn't told Amy anything about Alicia. Amy avoided the blue eyes and found her look drawn irresistibly to Michael's face.

He was smiling, but as he studied Amy's white face the smile was quickly replaced by a frown. "Is something wrong?"

Amy brushed a hand down her oversized jumper, wrapping her arms defensively around her waist. "No.

Not at all." She pulled her gaze from his and turned back to the woman. "Are you in town for long?"

Alicia looked from one to the other, her face clearly puzzled. "No," she answered, her perusal once again focusing on Amy. "I was just in the vicinity and thought I'd stop and see my best buddy."

"I see." If anything, Amy's face grew even whiter. Michael's eyes narrowed in speculation before a look of comprehension crossed his features. His face relaxed into a smile.

"Alicia is my sister," he informed Amy.

Amy felt her face go from pale to scarlet, but for the first time, her smile reached her eyes. "Oh! How nice to meet you."

Alicia glanced at her brother. "Michael and I wondered if you could join us for supper this evening. I have to leave again in the morning, so I wanted to spend some time with the two of you."

Seeing no reason for such a request, Amy was about to decline. Surely Alicia would want to spend time alone with Michael.

"By the way," Michael interrupted, his eyes on Amy's features, "I need to purchase this."

He held out the gold leaf pin that had been clutched in his palm.

"It's fall," he suggested, waiting to see if she caught on. She didn't. He grinned. "I really *fell* this time."

Lips twitching, consumed with curiosity, Amy turned to Alicia. "I'd *love* to have supper with you." Maybe, just maybe, Alicia would have the answers Amy was seeking.

The interior of the Italian restaurant was dim with the coming darkness, and the sunset reflected through the large glass windows and turned the parquet floor from gold to amber. Lit candles on every table and red-and-white-checked tablecloths gave the room a cozy atmosphere.

Amy seated herself in the chair Michael held out for her, then watched as he performed the same act for his sister.

Alicia looked around her with genuine pleasure. "Who would have thought there was such a place in this little town? If the decoration is any indication of the food, it must be delicious. How did you find it, Michael? Though I shouldn't be surprised!" She grinned at her brother. "Your bottomless stomach must have brought you here."

"Hey!" He threw her a mock glare. "One should talk." Turning to Amy, he said, "Would you believe this woman could eat me under the table?"

Amy lifted a dubious brow, her glance flicking from one to the other. If Alicia ate anything more than carrot sticks, she would be surprised.

"It's true," Michael argued, clearly noting the doubtful look on Amy's face.

Alicia chuckled. "Actually, he's right. I'm fortunate to have one of those metabolisms that seem to take care of all the extra calories."

Amy felt her envy rise another notch. Trying to suppress her inclination to covet that which wasn't hers, she pasted a smile on her face, trying hard not to let her gaze drop to her own round figure encased in another oversized dress.

"The owner of this place, Mr. Delagado, is a member of the church Michael and I attend." Amy answered Alicia's first question.

Although Alicia accepted the change of conversation readily, Michael glanced suspiciously at Amy. She met his look with wide, innocent eyes and swallowed hard at his slow smile.

She turned back to Alicia. "So, Alicia. Tell me about yourself."

"You mean Michael hasn't told you about me?"

Amy shook her head. "Not a word."

Affronted, Alicia rounded on her brother. "Well, I know where I stand in your eyes, don't I?"

He grinned incorrigibly. "Don't get your feathers all ruffled. The conversation just never developed that far." His gaze softened when it rested on Amy for a brief moment. "Actually, Amy and I haven't gotten quite that personal."

Amy's cheeks colored. That was certainly true, though it was not Michael's fault. Every time he had tried to turn the conversation to more personal things, Amy had hastily changed the subject. She wasn't exactly sure why she was so reluctant to share her life with him. And although she was dying to know more about Michael's girl, she was also averse to hearing something that might prove her suspicions correct.

Besides, her feelings for Michael had grown all out of proportion, and she was afraid to get any closer than she already was. At times she was tempted to just ask

Michael outright about this mystery girl, but she truly was afraid to hear the truth. If Michael was in love with her, Amy wouldn't feel justified in spending so much time alone with Michael, whether they were studying the Bible or not, and she just wasn't ready to give up that time with him. She seemed destined for pain whichever way she turned.

Alicia looked from one to the other. She opened her mouth to say something, but at a warning frown from her brother, she subsided, then apparently substituted a different question for the one she originally intended to ask.

"So, Amy, I love your shop. How long have you owned it?"

Amy lifted her water glass and took a quick sip before answering. "About six years now."

"It's really charming," Alicia complimented. "But you seem so young to have owned a shop of your own that long."

Smiling wryly, Amy told her, "I'm not so young, really. I'm twenty-eight. My father left me the money when he died. That was eight years ago." Her voice softened; the pain of that separation, though dulled by time, was still with her.

"I'm sorry," Alicia told Amy, reaching out to cover Amy's hand where it lay on the table. "Michael and I just lost our parents a few years ago. They were killed by a drunk driver as they were coming home from church."

Amy glanced from one to the other, her melancholy forgotten in the face of this unexpected news. Michael's eyes were dark, their normal glow missing. He smiled faintly. "So you see, we have one more thing in common."

Amy shook her head. "Not really. I still have my mother. If it wasn't for her, I would be completely alone."

Michael opened his mouth to say something, but he was interrupted when Alicia placed her hand over his. "And Michael has me."

The waiter brought their food, relieving them of the awkwardness that seemed to have settled over the table. Amy inhaled the robust aroma of her chicken Parmesan, her eyes twinkling at Alicia's obvious appreciation of the hearty serving of spaghetti she had received.

"I've died and gone to heaven," Alicia breathed happily.

Michael shook his head. "And she'll eat it all, too" he told Amy, chuckling.

Conversation was minimal while they ate, but Amy managed to insert a question or two about Michael and Alicia's past. When she asked Alicia if she were married, the woman started off on a tangent of hers and Michael's dating habits. Amy grew frustrated when Michael would continually interrupt his sister's stories.

Some time later, Amy sat back replete, half of her food still on her plate. Although she wasn't a picky eater, Mr. Delagado's servings were beyond her. Not so with Alicia. Michael had been right. Not a morsel remained on Alicia's plate. Amy was stunned by the amount of food the young woman had eaten. Apparently, she had told the truth when she spoke of a higher metabolism. Amy was surprised at the sudden surge of jealousy that washed through her.

Distressed at her thoughts, Amy concentrated on

folding her napkin to avoid looking at her companions. Ever since Michael had come into her life, she had spent an inordinate amount of time worrying about her looks. Before, she had been content with her life. Now, thoughts of weight and clothes consumed her. If anyone had told her ten months ago that she had such a weakness, she would have laughed. She had always considered herself above such ridiculous thoughts.

She peeped at Michael and found him watching her, frowning. Something in his dark gaze she couldn't fathom, as though he were trying to tell her some message. She had the feeling that if his sister hadn't been sitting there, he would have said something.

❦

Michael dropped his keys on the breakfast counter that separated his kitchen from the dining room.

"I like her, Michael," Alicia told him, crossing to the living room and seating herself in the wing chair next to the fireplace.

Michael followed her, collapsing on the sofa across from her. He studied his sister knowingly. "But?"

Alicia's direct look unsettled him. "But face it, brother, she's hardly your type."

Michael tried to control the rush of anger that raced through him. "Just exactly what do you consider my type?"

Tilting her head to the side, Alicia asked him wryly, "Do I need to elaborate?"

Images of past women paraded through his mind, all beautiful and alluring. Blonds, brunettes, redheads, too many to count. Embarrassed by the memories, he shook his head. He was not proud of his past, but Jesus had helped him to overcome the guilt. "No. You don't need to remind me."

Alicia got up and crossed to his side, seating herself on the sofa next to him. She patted his knee. "That was in the past. This is now, but I still don't see what attracted you to her. True, she's friendly and sweet. She even has a wonderful sense of humor. But Michael, she has absolutely no dress sense."

Michael snorted. "Not every woman lives her life to buy clothes, you know. Some women have brains."

At his sister's hurt look, Michael was appalled. He took her hand, kneading it gently. "I'm sorry, Alicia. I didn't mean that. It's just that when I think of how embarrassed Amy was tonight, how she became a shadow of her normal self, I get so angry. All night she compared herself to you; and in her eyes, she came up short."

Instead of staying offended, Alicia thought about what he said. That was one of the things Michael loved about his sister. It was also one reason why he often failed to curb his tongue; he knew she wouldn't stay angry. She always considered whatever anyone told her, and then accepted or disregarded it.

She winced. "You mean because she's overweight? Like when I wolfed down a whole plate of food and knew I didn't have to worry over my figure?"

"Yeah, like that. Among other things."

Alicia lifted her eyebrows, her lips tucked together. "Sorry. I can see what you mean. But, Michael, the woman needs to take charge of her life. She doesn't have to be that way."

Michael sighed, rolling his eyes. His sister still didn't get it.

"Alicia, I like her just the way she is. I don't want her to feel like she has to change. I want her to know she can be liked for just who she is."

Alicia studied him curiously. "I think you mean *loved*," she told him and looked into his eyes. He didn't bother to deny it, because he knew it was true.

"Does she know?"

He sighed heavily, rubbing a hand behind his neck. "I don't know. I didn't know it myself until lately."

"And how about Amy? Does she feel anything for you?"

Michael's intent eyes met hers. "You tell me. There was a time that I thought so. . .but now I'm not so sure. She told me she only wants to be friends. Besides, she dated Alan Marcus."

Alicia leaned forward, grasping his hands where they lay cupped between his knees. "Maybe she thinks friendship is all you have to offer. I don't know who this Alan Marcus is, but I know Amy loves you, Michael. I could see it in her eyes."

His fingers twined with hers, and he smiled. "I hope you're right. But I don't want to scare her away. Maybe I just need to give her some breathing space." Never having come across a woman like Amy in his life, he wasn't sure about anything where she was concerned.

Chapter 10

Adding the small scarecrow to the already loaded shelf, Amy wrinkled her nose playfully. Since she didn't favor celebrating Halloween, she limited her contribution to the season with pumpkins, fall colors, and these little stuffed people. Well, not *people* exactly.

The shelf next to this one displayed the holiday she preferred for this month. Small replicas of the *Niña, Pinta,* and *Santa Maria* nestled among blue and green tinsel, which represented the water of the Atlantic Ocean. There were Italian flags, pasta kits, and other Italian gifts from which to choose.

She was curious to see what gift Michael would think of for this month. His girl was part Irish. Did she have Italian blood, too? Or would he choose Halloween? Maybe a witch? Chastising herself for these uncharitable thoughts, she grinned nevertheless. If she wasn't careful, *she* would be the perfect representation of that unholy being.

The dinner with Alicia had been unhelpful, to say the least. Any time she started to talk about Michael's previous girlfriends, he would cleverly change the subject. Amy came away from that dinner more curious than ever.

It didn't help that Alicia's beauty had left her feeling dowdy and dumpy. Several days went by before Amy could talk herself out of her feelings of self-pity. Only by reading her Bible had she been able to overcome her depression. A verse from Romans, one Michael had pointed out to her, came back to her each time she felt depressed: *"And you also are among those who are called to belong to Christ Jesus."* She was a child of the King—but it had taken Michael to open her eyes to that fact.

Something had been different about Michael after that night. She couldn't quite put her finger on it, but it was there nonetheless. She had seen much less of him than usual, for one thing. He told her he had needed to work overtime, but she had wondered.

Her feelings for Michael grew every day, and lately she found herself struggling to hide them from him. She wouldn't embarrass him for the world. He had been a wonderful friend, often taking her places when he had the occasion, showing her things she hadn't taken the opportunity to see before. She missed that now.

The door jangled and Michael walked in.

"No one here today, huh?" he asked, glancing around the store.

"Nope. You're the first."

He held out a hand to her. "Come help me choose a gift."

She started to answer negatively when she noticed the pleading in his dark brown eyes. Sighing, she took the offered hand and allowed him to lead her around the store.

"How about this?" he asked hesitantly.

She frowned at the golden bracelet. "Well, I'm waiting to hear *this* explanation."

"It's a charm bracelet, isn't it?" he asserted.

"Yes?" Still puzzled, Amy took the bracelet and examined the little golden discs dangling from it. Each contained one of the Ten Commandments. She caught his look, and felt her heart thump when his lips drew up into a heart-stopping smile. "Because she's a Christian?" she asked faintly.

"That, too. But the real reason is because she's one of the most *charming* women I have ever met."

Amy thought that if she were a candle, she would melt. "Michael, that is *so* sweet."

His hand came up and cupped her chin, lifting her face to his. "Tell me what you have learned about her so far," he commanded softly.

His touch sent fingers of awareness coursing through her body. She could barely concentrate when he was so disturbingly close. Taking control of her emotions, she moved away from his touch and thought back over the gifts he had chosen. "Well, let's see. She's a Christian."

He nodded. "Go on."

"She's Irish, at least part. She likes flowers and, it would seem, jewelry. She's charming, but not quite sure of you. And I believe you once said she was perfect."

He grinned and his eyes sparkled. "Add very bright to that list."

Amy's narrowed gaze questioned the remark.

"But not always," he continued mysteriously. He handed Amy the money for the gift, squeezing her fingers slightly when she returned his change. Leaning forward, he slid his hand behind her neck, pulling her toward him. Her flustered gaze met his, and he smiled that slow, heart-stopping smile. Before she could think, his lips closed warmly over hers. When he released her, he had the same contented look that she had noticed about him before.

He opened the door and glanced back. "She's learning fast, though."

Chapter 11

Amy stared into the mirrored wall that lined the back portion of her shop. What she saw was less than reassuring. Her looks were nothing spectacular, but add to that she was slightly overweight, and now she had dark circles under her eyes from sleepless nights. She couldn't imagine how she could inspire Michael's romantic interest.

So intent was she on her perusal, she missed the jingling of the bells on the door. She also missed Michael moving behind her from the opposite side of the store.

He placed his hands on her shoulders, and she jumped, embarrassed to be caught staring at herself in the mirror. When she would have turned around, he held her in place.

"What do you see?" he questioned, his soft voice gently stirring the hair next to her ear.

She shivered slightly, meeting his eyes in the glass. "I see an overweight, rather plain girl."

Anger sparked in his eyes and was quickly veiled. He kept her facing the glass. "Shall I tell you what *I* see?"

She wanted to shout *no*, but she found her head nodding instead.

He squeezed her shoulders slightly. "I see a woman who loves God. A woman who is slowly coming out of her forced shell of solitude. Someone who is both loving and giving, who needs to help others. Not just me, but so many others."

She knew he was referring to the fact that she helped at the crisis center in Albington, a few miles away, besides her volunteer work at the hospital and the local animal shelter. Michael had gone with her to all three places on several occasions.

"I also see," he continued, "a woman who is unselfish with both her time and money."

Not only did she volunteer her time at the shelter, but often her financial resources as well. She hadn't realized he knew that about her, though.

"I see a woman who is beautiful, both inside and out. Someone kind enough to befriend a man who had no one."

Amy flinched. She must never, ever forget that he saw her as a faithful friend. The fact he had kissed her meant nothing to him, she was sure. People were always kissing one another. Just because his kiss had left her trembling with longing didn't mean he felt the same. He was watching her carefully, and she felt her face color hotly in response. She pulled out of his hold, moving away from him.

"Are you here for your November gift?"

At first she thought he wasn't going to answer; then he heaved an enormous sigh. "Patience has never been one of my virtues, and mine is growing steadily thinner," he told her.

Amy's eyebrows flew upward. "What?"

Sighing again, he turned away. "Never mind. I'm just rambling."

She eyed him warily. "Well, just about any gift can show thankfulness," she ventured.

Nodding, he began studying the shelves. "Tell me what *you* like."

Amy rolled her eyes. *Not again!* "I don't know, Michael. *You* choose."

He touched a small ornament that swung gently from its display stand. The diminutive angel held a scroll that read, "I always thank my God as I remember you. Philemon 1:4."

Michael's eyes took on a decided glow as he handed the ornament to her. "This. An angel for an angel."

Amy was growing tired of this paragon of virtue. It had been almost a year, and she still didn't know who this girl was. Glenda had told her that Cynthia Walker was wasting her time flirting with Michael because he was already taken. When she had asked how Glenda could be so certain, Glenda had smiled slyly and told her it was in his attitude.

That had hurt. She had known all along that Michael had a girl, but Glenda had confirmed it. Everyone knew that Glenda had an uncanny insight into people's personalities. If Glenda said Michael was taken, then Amy was fairly certain he was.

For a time Amy had been hopeful that Michael cared for her, that he might give up this unknown woman. He had been so solicitous of her welfare, her heart had opened to him like a budding flower. But then she started noticing how much he did for others, and not just women. He helped Debra by working on her car and saving her money she could not afford to spend. Then he had helped Cynthia Walker by offering her a job at Comlink. Although Cynthia said she rarely saw Michael, she tried to make the most of the opportunities afforded her.

Why hadn't she bothered to notice these things before? Had he offered these women the same kind of comfort he had offered her? Like that kiss, maybe? The thought left her feeling sick.

"Are you finally sure of this girl now?" she forced herself to ask.

For a brief instant, his gaze focused on her lips. "Oh, yeah. I think it's about time to let her know."

She watched him leave the shop, confusion uppermost in her mind. Shaking her head, she jumped when the door opened and Michael peeked his head back inside.

"By the way, your halo needs a little polishing."

❦

Michael grinned as he headed across the street to the post office. If that had not been a big enough clue, then maybe his Amy wasn't as intelligent as he thought.

The kiss had assured him of her feelings. No woman could kiss with such warmth unless she had some kind of interest in the man she was kissing. If he hadn't been so afraid of frightening her, he might have tried to repeat the experience. A month was a mighty long time to keep his hands off the woman he loved.

He had shaken her, he knew that. She had come so far, yet she still had a ways to go. That didn't bother him, because although his patience was growing thin, he would wait an eternity if he had to. A woman like Amy was well worth the wait.

Chapter 12

T he snow drifted down outside the shop window. Peaceful. Silent. However, Amy, nose pressed against the pane, felt anything but. It was past time to close the store, but Michael had called her asking if she could remain a little longer. Since it was Christmas Eve, and he had yet to purchase his December gift, she assumed that was his purpose.

She slid her hand down the soft folds of the green velvet dress she had purchased for this special day. Her flaming hair was curled becomingly into a French knot. Amy had finally decided the time had come to stop hiding from the world. From now on, she would be a different person. A daughter of the King. And if that was the case, then she should dress as though she were proud of herself. And honestly, she was. She had Michael to thank for that.

She was supposed to spend tonight with her mother. This was a tradition they had shared for the duration of Amy's life, and she wouldn't think of missing it. She glanced at her watch once again, wondering what was keeping Michael.

Moments later, she saw him coming down the street, head bowed against the drifting flakes. For the past several weeks she had been in a mood of turmoil, lost between the hope that Michael cared and the certainty that he couldn't. Surely his words to her about a halo weren't meant to be construed that *she* was the angel he was referring to.

She fluctuated daily between hope and denial. The denial was uppermost in her mind right now, since it had been three weeks since she had last seen him. He had been called back to Houston for some big corporate meeting shortly after purchasing his last gift.

When he entered the store, she noticed he was carrying a large box. He laid the box on the counter before coming to stand beside her at the window. His eyes roved her body from the top of her shining hair to the bottom of her new green pumps.

"You look beautiful," he said, the shine in his eyes doing strange things to her insides. For a long moment, neither of them spoke.

"I wanted to give you your Christmas present." His hand reached out to brush a stray tendril of hair behind her ear.

Amy swallowed hard. She lifted uncertain eyes to his. "I thought maybe you wanted to purchase your gift for December."

There was a soft glow in his eyes as he solemnly shook his head. "No. I bought my gift for December elsewhere."

Unaccountably hurt, Amy moved past him to the counter. She fingered the bright red ribbon on the package he had laid there. "You want me to open it now?"

He nodded, waiting for her to comply. He was so still that she felt even more uncomfortable.

"I don't have your gift here," she told him nervously as she undid the wrappings.

"That's okay." He smiled mysteriously. "Maybe you do."

Mystified, she was about to ask what he meant, but the exposed lid of the box arrested her attention. Gently pulling back the flaps, Amy looked inside. Her breath caught in a soft gasp. Her eyes flew to Michael's, a frown creasing her forehead. "I don't understand."

"I think you do," he told her so softly that she barely heard him.

Michael began pulling the items from the box, one at a time. First the candle, then the CD of Christian music. The Irish mug followed, Michael's eyes gleaming as his look caught the telltale blush on Amy's cheeks. The porcelain bunny was next, then on and on. All the gifts Michael had purchased over the last year for his unknown girl.

"For *you*, Amy. They were all for you." He wrapped his arms around her, waiting for her reaction. Conflicting emotions scattered her thoughts. Finally, his words penetrated her mind and reached her consciousness. She uttered one word. "Why?"

He smiled wryly. "When I first came here, I noticed you right away. You seemed to be everywhere, helping everyone. You intrigued me. I wanted to get to know you, but your friends warned me that you were extremely shy. I thought since you were always helping others, you might do the same for me. But then you thought there was another girl, and by then it was too late to say different. I thought I would just watch—and wait."

She shook her head doubtfully. Unable to take in what he had said, she returned to his earlier words. "You said you bought another gift somewhere else?"

He pulled a black velvet case from his pocket and flipped the latch to reveal a sparkling emerald surrounded by tiny diamonds. "This," he answered. "The color of your eyes. Will you marry me, Amy? I had hoped you loved me, too. Do you?"

The love shining in his eyes eliminated all her doubts. Amy threw her arms around his neck. "Oh yes, Michael. I do."

He smiled that heart-stopping smile, settling the ring on her finger. "It's about time. My angel, my Irish lass. I love you." His lips came down on hers.

Laying her head against his shoulder, she sighed. "Why didn't you tell me sooner?"

He lifted her chin to look into her eyes. "My darling, I wanted you to believe in yourself. I wanted you to be proud of yourself. Not because of me, but because you are who you are. I needed to give you that time. I needed to give us both time to get to know each other so that there would be no doubts in our relationship."

She stared deep into the depths of his eyes, reassured by the message she read there. "I love you, Michael."

When he kissed her again, Amy showed no restraint.

Michael responded to her kisses with a warmth that left her with no doubt he found her attractive.

Amy reluctantly pulled away from him. "Oh my goodness," she breathed shakily. "My mother is expecting me."

His grin reached all the way to his sparkling eyes. "Then by all means. Let's go meet with my future mother-in-law."

Amy thought her heart would burst from happiness. She threw her arms around his neck, and as things turned out, they didn't leave the shop for some time. When they did, the opened box was forgotten on the counter. After all, who needed objects to represent love when they had the real thing?

DARLENE MINDRUP

Darlene is a full-time homemaker and home-school teacher. A "radical feminist" turned "radical Christian," she lives in Arizona with her husband and two children. Darlene has written several novels for Barbour Publishing's **Heartsong Presents** line. She has a talent for bringing ancient settings like the early Church in the Roman Empire and Medieval times to life with clarity. Darlene believes "romance is for everyone, not just the young and beautiful."

A Letter to Our Readers

Dear Readers:

In order that we might better contribute to your reading enjoyment, we would appreciate your taking a few minutes to respond to the following questions. When completed, please return to the following: Fiction Editor, Barbour Publishing, Inc., P.O. Box 719, Uhrichsville, OH 44683.

1. Did you enjoy reading *Gift of Love?*
   □ Very much. I would like to see more books like this.
   □ Moderately—I would have enjoyed it more if _____
   _____
   _____

2. What influenced your decision to purchase this book?
   (Check those that apply.)
   □ Cover   □ Back cover copy   □ Title   □ Price
   □ Friends   □ Publicity   □ Other

3. Which story was your favorite?
   □ *Practically Christmas*   □ *The Best Christmas Gift*
   □ *A Most Unwelcome Gift*   □ *The Gift Shoppe*

4. Please check your age range:
   □ Under 18   □ 18–24   □ 25–34
   □ 35–45   □ 46–55   □ Over 55

5. How many hours per week do you read? _____

Name _____

Occupation _____

Address _____

City _____ State _____ Zip _____

*H*EARTSONG ♥ PRESENTS

Love Stories Are Rated G!

That's for godly, gratifying, and of course, great! If you love a thrilling love story, but don't appreciate the sordidness of some popular paperback romances, **Heartsong Presents** is for you. In fact, **Heartsong Presents** is the only inspirational romance book club, the only one featuring love stories where Christian faith is the primary ingredient in a marriage relationship.

Sign up today to receive your first set of four, never-before-published Christian romances. Send no money now; you will receive a bill with the first shipment. You may cancel at any time without obligation, and if you aren't completely satisfied with any selection, you may return the books for an immediate refund!

Imagine. . .four new romances every four weeks—two historical, two contemporary—with men and women like you who long to meet the one God has chosen as the love of their lives. . .all for the low price of $9.97 postpaid.

To join, simply complete the coupon below and mail to the address provided. **Heartsong Presents** romances are rated G for another reason: They'll arrive Godspeed!

YES! Sign me up for Hearts♥ng!

NEW MEMBERSHIPS WILL BE SHIPPED IMMEDIATELY!
Send no money now. We'll bill you only $9.97 postpaid with your first shipment of four books. Or for faster action, call toll free 1-800-847-8270.

NAME _____

ADDRESS _____

CITY _____ STATE_____ ZIP_____

MAIL TO: HEARTSONG PRESENTS, P.O. Box 719, Uhrichsville, Ohio 44683